Sean Hayden

Book One of the Demonkin Series

Untold
Press

www.untoldpress.com

Origins

Published by Untold Press LLC
114 NE Estia Lane
Port St Lucie, FL 34983

ISBN: 978-0692287293

PRODUCED IN THE UNITED STATES OF AMERICA

10 9 8 7 6 5 4 3 2 1

Dedication

Natus es tu quidem es
You're born, you live, you die

You're born into a family
Raised by a family
Loved by a family
You leave that family
You get a job, go to school, find a career
You make a family of your own
Sometimes it doesn't work out
Sometimes you get a second chance
Sometimes
Sometimes things get so bad you need to be saved
Sometimes you need a friend
Sometimes you need saving
Sometimes you need an angel
Sometimes an angel finds you

This book is for her. My Angel
The one who saved me and gave me my second chance

Prologue

Mary Elizabeth Thorn sighed as she layered the final stroke of her thirteenth coat of blood paint. The smell assaulted her nose and made her stomach turn. The combination of milk, lime, and blood became almost too much for her to bear. If she had chosen to summon a creature of light, the milk and lime would have sufficed, but in order to summon a demon, blood had to be spilt. The tome she had spent most of her savings on had been very specific.

She checked the lines of the pentagram painted on the marble tile she laid herself in the center of the room. A smile formed on her lips. They lay perfectly straight with no overlapping of the perfect circle enclosing it. Next came the runes. This task made the others pale in comparison. The runes couldn't be painted on; they had to be cut from the paint itself. She grimaced at the pain in her knees as she rose from the cold floor beneath her and strode to the large bench against the wall of her workroom.

The tome rested in its familiar place of honor at the very center of her altar and worktable. She remembered building it many years ago. Each copper nail driven with love, each board cut perfectly by hand without power tools, the blood, sweat, and tears that completed the dark recipe. Mary Elizabeth had chosen to follow the tenants of earth magery, but had succumbed to the promise of power only a summoner could deliver.

She gingerly picked up the silver carving tool and went to the northern point of the star, knelt down and began her grueling task. Hours passed as she carved the intricate runes into the face of the blood paint without scoring the marble. Only that level of precision could contain the demon, a perfect plane of marble below and the power of the runes around to encase the evil within.

The tome, written in ages past, bore only one flaw. When it had been penned, tiles of marble hadn't even been a fleeting thought in the minds of early masons. The tome called for a slab of marble to contain the spell.

Asmodeus sat on his throne and listened to the call. It had been many years since he had heard its ilk. While it had not been meant for him, he heard it nonetheless. Asmodeus had fought many wars, answered countless challengers to be Lord of this Realm, and as such obtained the power to answer any summons meant for his minions. He laughed at the feebleness of the call, plucked it from the air, and held it in his mighty claw. He contemplated tossing it away, and then thought better. It had been eons since he had been allowed to cause havoc upon the mortal plane. Boredom overcame good sense, and he traveled down the line of the summons.

He appeared in a blast of fire and smoke and looked

around at his surroundings. Smells of blood, milk, lime, and spices assaulted his demonic senses. He lowered his gaze and noticed the small human woman staring at his greatness with fear and respect. He stood motionless and assessed the woman. She bore the marks of beauty as far as humans went, but the lack of horns and wings he found disappointing. He snorted as she stood and watched her walk to the edge of the circle.

"I have summoned you, vile beast, to do my bidding. What say you?" He could hear the fear in her voice as it filled her words with a perfume more enticing than the blood-infused paint she had drawn her pentagram with.

Asmodeus glanced down at the circle cast thirteen times and found no flaw. An emotion akin to panic flashed through his mind. Never before had he seen its equal, and if he found himself truly trapped, he might be forced to answer the whims of the pitiful creature before him. Then he noticed the marble beneath him.

He looked up at the human and smiled. Lifting his taloned foot up to the level of his knee, he brought its mass down in one fell swoop. He laughed when he felt the marble shatter. He laughed harder when he saw the face of the human summoner. He felt the fear of his new toy.

Chapter 1

I felt the power flow from the tiny circuit board in my alarm clock to the tiny speaker less than an inch away before I heard the annoying *bwa bwa bwa* reach my sensitive ears. I hadn't slept at all today, and yes, I mean day.

My name is Ashlyn Thorn, and I am a freak. I don't mean a "card carrying circus performing" freak; I mean a "nothing quite as unusual as me" freak. I am a nocturnal, blood drinking girl of seventeen, and I know what you're thinking; vampire. I used to think so too, but I'm not. I was born this way. I know what you're thinking now, and no, my father wasn't a vampire. I investigated that possibility as well. Vampires have been legal in these here United States for over forty years, and they all have one thing in common. They're infertile. Every last subspecies of *homo cruentus* from *dementis*, to *informis*, to *plurimus*, to *dominus* reproduce asexually through their bite. There has even been talk of reclassification of vampires from the genus of homo all the way back to the class of mammalia. However, the "they were born human" side of the argument seems to be winning, so *homo cruentus* is the legal classification.

None of that changes the fact I have no idea what the hell I am. I have lived with my Aunt Margaret since the day my mother gave birth to me. I have met several of her closest friends, the ones she can trust with my secret, and none of them have blood that even remotely appeals to my senses. So for the past seventeen years I have been feeding off her every other night. Nothing boosts your self-esteem like being a parasitic niece.

I even look like a vampire. I have pale skin that only makes my red hair look brighter, and fangs. Yes, I have bitten my tongue and it hurts. Everyone asks. The only difference between my fangs and a normal vampire's is mine have a slight backwards curvature, whereas all subspecies of vampire have straight fangs. How could I possibly know all this? Well, I fully matured at the ripe old age of seven, and I haven't aged a day since then which puts another tick mark in the column labeled freak. My aunt also thought it would be wise if I didn't leave the house where I might be seen, so ten years stuck in the same location with nothing but television and a computer probably would have given me the equivalent of a doctorate degree in supernatural biology. Lucky me.

It's not really Aunt Maggie's fault. I asked her about my mother. She told me they had never really been close, and she had lost all contact with her about a year before her death. She seems really sad whenever I bring it up, so I try to keep my questions to a minimum. She and my mother were identical twin sisters. My aunt went into medicine and my mother went into magic. One night my aunt received a phone call from the San Diego police department, and they told her of an accident involving my mother. She hopped on the next flight from Chicago and flew out there only to find my mother in the hospital, pregnant and brain dead. They explained it as a magical ritual gone awry, and even though they couldn't detect an embryonic heartbeat, the sonogram showed fetal movement. My aunt flew my mother back to Chicago and set her up in a hospital bed in her guest bedroom. I emerged three months later. Mom didn't survive. I'm kind of surprised my aunt doesn't hate me, but she has been wonderful my whole life. I have the killer bedroom with a flat screen TV, stereo, video games, and all the little gadgets to drive my friends insane with envy. If I had any.

All right, back to the freak list. All vampiric subspecies abhor sunlight. Most burn when exposed. The weaker Nosferatu, or *homo cruentus informis*, actually burst into flame. Common vampires, or *homo cruentus plurimus*, burn out from within and leave nothing but ash. *Homo cruentus dominus*, or master vampires, as they prefer to be called, merely smoke and get a really bad burn. But if fully exposed for too long they would die a horrible death as all the moisture from their bodies evaporated. Me on the other hand, I simply get really sunburned. It hurts the hell out of my eyes, though. My pupils are slit like a cat's, and I can see fine in complete darkness. My hearing and sense of smell would rival a hunting dog. The only other differences I have noted between me and vampires are my claws. All vampires have stronger than normal fingernails and hair. They often let their fingernails grow longer either because they think it adds to their vampire otherworldliness, or because they make useful weapons. Mine however, are more like predator claws. The kind of claws you would find on a hunting cat or eagle. Mine don't retract like a cat's, though I wish they did. They're kind of dangerous. Especially when I first wake up and try to rub my eyes.

I reached over and switched the alarm clock to the off position and got out of bed, noticing it read 7:00 p.m. The sun would be down completely in a few minutes, and my senses told me my aunt wasn't there, leaving me alone in our small house in the suburbs of Chicago. My aunt, being a doctor, keeps some unusual hours, so I wasn't surprised to find myself alone. Knowing I was alone didn't change the nagging feeling I had in my gut. The same feeling had kept sleep from me most of the whole day.

I went about my usual shower and wake up routine and found myself back in my room in front of the television. Eight o'clock programming on a Monday always brightened my day. I had used my DVR to record my favorite shows, and I always preferred to watch them recorded. I hate very few things in this world more than commercials. When you can't use a lot of products, advertising them to your face is a little insulting. So when fast-forwarding through the commercials, I almost missed the breaking news story about the fatal accident on the Kennedy Expressway.

My finger hit the play button, and the picture jumped back to before the newsflash. I watched through the last few seconds of a car dealership add with my heart in my throat. The newsflash came back on, and I saw the helicopter footage of the expressway. Traffic had backed itself all the way into downtown Chicago, but the crumpled mass of twisted metal lodged underneath the semi in front of it occupied my entire field of vision. It, at one time, had been a blue Volvo just like my aunt's car. The image appeared too distorted for me to tell if the car belonged to her or not, but the sinking feeling I had plummeted even further into the abyss.

Grabbing the phone from my nightstand, I dialed her cell. It didn't even ring, just went straight to voicemail. I didn't leave a message, and just stared at the television. I had no idea what to do. My mind raced in fifteen directions, from catching a bus to Northwestern Hospital to running the twenty miles to the scene of the accident. Cursing my inability to do anything, the tears started falling. For a moment, they stopped and I briefly hoped it wasn't her, but it didn't last long. I don't know how I knew, but I did. The car belonged to my Aunt Maggie, and she didn't survive. I had to face the fact I would have to live life alone.

The recorded programming aired an hour ago, so the accident had to be in the final stages of cleanup, with traffic rerouted to move around the last remnants. Most likely, the police had identified her body and were probably looking to notify her next of kin. I had the honor of being her only kin. The only problem is I don't exist. No birth records, no social security number, no driver's license, absolutely no legal documentation on file anywhere. I wouldn't inherit the house or anything in it. I found myself waist deep in crap. Not only had I lost my aunt, but also my home, sanctuary, and only means of sustenance.

Lost in my own thoughts, I wandered the halls of the house. From kitchen, to living room, to my aunt's bedroom, I roamed. I found myself sitting on my aunt's bed and staring at her four cream-colored walls and familiar furniture. I had to leave, but I didn't want to go. For seventeen years, this place had not only been my home, it had been my world. Sometimes I would wander around our little neighborhood in the very early hours of the morning. I had always been careful never to be seen or heard by anyone in the surrounding homes. Superior senses had made it almost easy, but other than those little forays, I had never been anywhere. Not the mall, not the movies, nowhere, and now I had to find my place somewhere in the rest of the world.

I stood and made my way to my aunt's dresser and fingered the top to her mahogany jewelry box. She kept everything of fiscal and sentimental value locked it its many doors and cubbies. She had given me a key on my tenth birthday. "Just in case," she had said. I didn't know what she meant until this very moment. I ran to my room, grabbed the key from my little chest on the nightstand, and made it back into my aunt's room in under a minute. Little time remained. If the Chicago Police Department had one trait that made them shine, it was their efficiency. I expected officers at the front door at any time to check for relatives. I had to be gone before they arrived.

Fumbling with the lock, I lifted the top of the case and rifled through the mishmash of jewelry and trinkets but found nothing specifically meant for me. When I opened the first drawer, my breathing stopped. The necklace my mother had always worn lay there with a tiny envelope with my name on it. I left the necklace in its place and gingerly picked out the envelope. I tore off the outer edge and dumped the contents into my palm. A heavy key and an identification card with my picture on it perched precariously on my shaking palm. The identification card bore the seal of the State of Illinois and had my likeness on it, but had Margaret Thorn on it. How my aunt had gotten the identification card forged, I couldn't even begin to imagine. It just wasn't something doctors did from what I had garnered watching television. I cast a last glance in my envelope and spied an address scrawled in my aunt's hardly legible writing on a post-it note. I put two and two together and figured the key must have been for her safety deposit box, and the address would lead me to her bank. I had a place to start, and a problem to solve. While I could actually go out in the sunlight, the experience would be quite painful.

I stuffed the key and I.D. card into my front pocket and removed my mother's necklace from the box. It was the only keepsake of a mother I never knew and an aunt I would never see again. It was time to go, so I ran to my room, stuffed my clothes into the one backpack I owned, and left through the front door into the night.

Chapter 2

It had been three days since I left my home. On my first day, I had armored myself against the sun and gone to the bank where I retrieved the contents of my aunt's safety deposit box. She knew she wouldn't be able to leave me her savings or her house, but she had left me ten thousand in cash as a start for my new life. I wept when I saw the contents, I would trade it in a heartbeat to have her back.

Using my fortune, I checked into a nearby motel. In Chicago, even the cheapest of nightly accommodations had rooms specifically designed for use by vampires. I could have checked into a regular room and just drawn the shades, but even the tiniest rays of light would have bothered my eyes while I slept. There was one other reason. I looked like a vampire and had many similar traits as vampires, and yet had no answers as to why. I had a brilliant notion to pretend to be a vampire, so I might as well start playing the part.

The first night I spent in my room flipping through the meager channels of my motel TV. The second night I rolled around on the bed, writhing against the hunger in my stomach. Now, it gnawed at my insides a thousand times worse than yesterday. Almost five days had passed since the last time I fed. I had no idea what to do. When I checked into the hotel, I had used all my senses to notice the people around me, and not one appealed to my appetite. I'm kind of a picky eater, I know, but I don't think my taste buds were calling the shots. Something special about my aunt's blood made it nutritional to me. I had no idea what it could be. Maybe it could be something in her DNA? Maybe a mineral most people lack? Neither she nor I had come up with any answers. If I didn't find a suitable match soon, I would most likely shut down and go comatose. I might even die.

I wasn't going to find a solution to my problem lying in bed, so I got up and headed to the bathroom to clean up. I tossed my clothes in the laundry bag, turned on the shower, and looked at myself in the mirror. My red hair was a frazzled mess, and my eyes sank into their depths, sporting dark rings under them. My ribs were visible beneath my skin, and I didn't look healthy. I closed my eyes and made my way into the shower.

I turned the knob for cold water and it still burned my skin, warming me from within as I stood under the gentle spray. It felt good for a moment, but the hunger wouldn't let me enjoy anything until it was sated. I climbed out and dried off. I threw my hair back into its usual ponytail and dressed quickly.

I slipped into some panties, but skipped the bra. I'm a small A-cup anyway. Lifting and separating wasn't an option. Still shivering, I pulled a warm shirt over my bare torso and slid into my jeans. Leaving the light on in my room, I left and rode the elevator down, then waltzed through the lobby into the cool night.

Things got scary after that.

I don't remember anything after the sliding glass doors closed behind me. I must have wandered through the downtown area of Arlington and climbed aboard the train, because when I started thinking again, I was magically transported into the heart of downtown Chicago. Bars and clubs lined the street. Cars honked from both directions waking me from my trance. I leapt from the middle of the street onto the crowded sidewalk, hearing a couple of muffled "fucking vampires" as the crowd around me parted to give me a wide berth.

When I sat in my room, bored at home, sometimes I would walk through my neighborhood in the predawn hours. Sometimes I would run, and sometimes I would leap through the air. I had never really tested my abilities, but as I stood from the crouch I had landed in, I gasped in amazement. I knew the strength I possessed, and that I was fast, but that shocked the hell out of me. I looked around at the ring of faces staring at me with both fear and awe. Smiling, I shrugged and started walking up the street until I hit Milwaukee Ave. I looked around at the surrounding neon and regularly illuminated marquees. *Now what?* At that moment, the hunger struck *again.*

I smelled blood and the promise of quelling my hunger. It smelled just like my aunt only a thousand times more potent. Like the difference between a hamburger patty and filet mignon. I had once told my aunt she smelled like spice. One Thanksgiving she made a turkey, potatoes, and even baked a pumpkin pie. Of course, I couldn't share the bounty with her, but to me she smelled like cinnamon, cloves, nutmeg, and everything good all mixed together. She laughed and told me her perfume smelled like lilacs, not Thanksgiving dinner. I tested her perfume, and even stopped to smell some lilacs once, but to me she smelled of spices. Now I smelled it again, but the vastness of it reminded me of what an apothecary would smell like. A thousand different varieties assaulted my senses. I didn't just smell them. I could see them and taste them, hear them and touch them. I felt their essence curl around my body like a lover I had never met before, and I became drunk with their intoxicating aroma.

When I had been a year or two old, I watched cartoons. I remember a specific one about an adorable mouse and a cat of questionable virtue, but I would always laugh when they smelled something delicious. The smell itself would curl a finger at them, beckoning them to follow. Sometimes the smell would pick them up and carry them along. I felt just like the cat standing there on the cold, wet sidewalk.

The smell pulled me to a set of double doors with tinted glass. Normally at night, you can see through tinted windows if there is enough light inside. Not this tint. It looked as if someone had taken a giant tub of black ink and used it as paint on the inside of the windows. I looked around and saw no illuminated sign welcoming patrons, just a simple gold embossed lettering on the door labeled, "Fangloria's." Personally, I didn't care if the place bore a skull and crossbones sign labeling the establishment, "Condemned," I needed to get in there.

I pulled on the door handle and it opened easily. The spice smell became strong enough to make my mouth water. I stepped inside and found myself in a brick hallway divided lengthwise by a red velvet-covered rope. People, and I do mean of the human variety, were corralled within its confines, waiting to gain access inside. A mountainous man of African descent stood behind the entrance to the velvet waiting pen. His attire ran black from head to toe, making him look like an immovable onyx mountain. The Fangloria's logo embroidered on his chest in scarlet was the only splash of color.

"Identification," he grumbled in a voice three octaves lower than bass.

"Um, I don't have one," I said meekly to the man-mountain.

He sniffed the air and hissed. I swear to gods, he hissed, so I hissed back. I didn't plan to, it just came naturally, leaving me with the strangest feeling. The hiss-fest only lasted for a moment before he stopped. He bowed and made a sweeping gesture to his right, ushering me past the cordoned-off area and down the length of the hallway. As I walked past him, I caught his scent. He reeked of cinnamon and vanilla, and he smelled good enough to eat. *Oh, shit.*

I stared at him wide-eyed as I walked past, and my entire body began vibrating with the urge to pounce and sink my fangs into him, but attacking him probably wouldn't be a good idea. I may be strong, but a six foot eight mountain of vampire would probably mop the floor with my red head. The question of why he smelled tasty made its way across my addled brain. *My aunt certainly wasn't a vampire, so what could the connection be?* The hall turned to the right, pulling me from my thoughts. The velvet ropes followed, and about six feet down, the line of people ended at another bouncer. This one topped the last by at least three inches. Where did these people shop for employees?

There wasn't anything stopping me from entering the club, nor did the second bouncer even glance my way–and in case you wondered, he smelled like nutmeg. I walked into a smoke filled room with a bar encompassing the entire length of the back wall. Booths and couches lined the remaining walls, with a dance floor taking up the rest of the space. I would normally expect techno or trance music to be pumping into a club with a mile-long waiting list, but they piped classical music in through speakers from around the room at a tolerable level. Thank gods. Nothing tweaked my sensitive eardrums more than loud music. I gasped in surprise to see people dancing intricate waltzes and other similar bygone dances. I stifled a yawn. The sound levels were tolerable, but the music sucked various parts of donkey anatomy.

I found myself at a loss. I couldn't wander up to the bar and order a Slippery Nipple, nor did I have a dance partner. I wanted food of the two-legged variety and I wanted it now. It was all I could think about. I couldn't even smell the cigar and cigarette smoke anymore. Spices invaded my sense of smell from every direction. I had hit the proverbial jackpot; I just couldn't collect my prize.

I looked around to see if I could find an empty couch or booth, but no such luck. Even the bar had patrons stacked three people deep, so I settled for standing by one of the columns surrounding the dance floor.

After getting a good look at the occupants of Fangloria's, I felt a little underdressed. Most wore elaborate evening gowns, and even the guys dressed in a minimum of slacks and button-down shirts. I had to be the only person in sight wearing anything of the denim persuasion. Even my long sleeved T-shirt screamed, "I don't have a stick shoved up my ass!" I probably looked like I had hitchhiked my way here from a rock concert.

I heard a tentative, "Madam?" I turned around. A youngish man stood behind me with one hand clasped over his wrist. His entire body screamed nerd, but the myriad of bite marks on his neck caught my eye. I fed from my aunt on a regular basis, but always from her wrist. Every time I finished from her, the wound I made would close before my eyes and leave nothing behind. I read master vampires held similar powers, something to do with enzymes in the saliva, which sped the healing process at an almost magical rate. People were even talking about trying to reproduce this enzyme for use in medicinal applications. So far, they had little success.

I considered ignoring the little man, but my aunt had raised me never to be rude. I turned toward him and gave a tentative sniff. He smelled of spice, but unfortunately, it belonged to the cheap aftershave variety.

"Can I help you?" I tried for polite, but I sounded bitchy even to me.

"Could I offer you something to drink?"

For a moment, I thought he was joking, but the look in his eyes spoke volumes. I felt hunger, but not for him.

"Thank you, but no. I'm looking for someone." The lie slipped easily from my lips. He looked crestfallen, but he wasn't pushy. He smiled and escaped back into the crowd.

Thanks to a PBS special, I knew a vampire's bite could be pleasurable to humans, but my mind couldn't fathom why humans would willingly offer themselves to vampires they didn't even know. My aunt fed me regularly, but I never saw pleasure on her face while it happened. The absence of pleasure alone let me know she did what she did out of love, and not some addiction to pleasure or pain. The thought of people *wanting* to be somebody's dinner for five minutes of shivers not only grossed me out, but made me want to slap the crap out of them.

My thoughts drifted to the smell of spices all around me, and the hunger roared through my mind. I had to eat! I could barely control my body. Lethargy crept into my limbs and the music turned to sludge in my ears. Making my way to the bar, I frantically searched for something. I knew what I wanted, and if no one offered it to me, I would take it.

My vision became blurry. I spun in place looking for the closest source of palatable blood, finding him at the bar a mere five feet away. He stood about six feet tall and he was *hot*. He conversed with a demure blond human dressed to the hilt in a black cocktail dress. I could see both hunger for blood and something else in his eyes, and I'm sure she could see it, too.

I remember taking a step toward him and not much after that. I vaguely recall launching myself at him, and I definitely remembered my teeth piercing the flesh of his neck and the first spurt of his lifeblood striking my tongue. Images of steel hands pulling against me, trying to haul me away from the handsome stranger whose blood tasted so sweet, and the shouts of anger and outrage at what I had done, flittered away to nothing.

Chapter 3

I came to sitting in a high-backed leather chair in a nondescript office, I didn't know if I remained at the club or had been moved somewhere else. Regret for what I had done and fear of the consequences sent shivers through me. I wasn't just sitting, I had been bound hand and foot with not one, not two, but three sets of handcuffs. I must have kicked some serious bouncer ass to be trussed up like a velociraptor. The hunger in my belly told me they had finally succeeded before I finished my damn meal.

Looking around the room, I was happy I was alone. Waking up with somebody staring at me would have been a little unnerving. I thought of the handsome vampire I had attacked with a pang of guilt. Briefly, I hoped he was okay. I don't think you can kill a vampire by ripping out his throat, but for every interesting fact I did know about vampires, there are probably a million no one had documented yet. If you want to talk about secretive sects, vampires outrank most supernatural species by several hundred thousand degrees.

I glanced down at the sets of handcuffs encircling my wrists and gave a tentative tug. They weren't standard police-issue cuffs either. I could tell because instead of being a bright chrome color, they had a grey matte finish. I wondered what they were made of. Even though they were cool to the touch, metal would have been colder. I pulled my wrists apart to see if they would give, but the material refused. I had heard the expression "up the creek" before, but now I could actually pinpoint the location on a map.

Footsteps echoed in the hall, and I glanced up just as the door swung open. An angry-looking woman stopped just inside and stared at me with hatred in her eyes. I gasped a little at her beauty. She stood about five foot seven and probably weighed a little more than my hundred pounds. Her hair, the color of spun gold, weaved intricately above her beautiful face. Green eyes flashed at me and her lips pursed in an angry line. Her skirt and jacket fitted against the lines of her body with grace.

"Give me one goddamn reason why I shouldn't turn you over to the fucking police." She stood with one hand on her slim waist and one foot tapping on the hardwood floor.

"I'm sorry ma'am. I wouldn't blame you if you did. I haven't eaten in almost a week, and I don't know what came over me." I looked down as I said it and tried to seem as meek as humanly–or inhumanly–possible. I didn't even lift my head when I heard her close the door and walk behind the mahogany desk in front of me to sit.

"Who are you, and more importantly, what the hell are you? I know you're a vamp, at least a master, but how did you get so fucking strong? I have seen hunger do strange things, but it took ten of us to pull you off Charles. Those handcuffs you are wearing are carbon nanofiber cuffs. I couldn't break through one of them, and yet you broke through not one set, but two. I didn't think even three sets would hold you, so again, what the fuck is going on?"

"I don't know. I swear!" Tears welled up and my voice cracked, and they weren't faked. Fear flowed through my veins like ice, hunger burned me from the inside, and loneliness threatened to push me from my unstable perch on the precipice of the abyss that was my sanity. "I have always been like this. I don't remember ever not being a vampire, and I don't know how I got like this. Please, just kill me or call the fucking cops. I can't do this anymore!"

Bringing my cuffed hands to my face, I hid behind them and cried. I wasn't expecting anything from the female vampire, and she didn't disappoint. She just sat behind the desk and left me to my despair. I don't know how long I went on, but it took quite a while, or at least it felt that way. Hysterics eased to wracking sobs, to sniffles, and then finally to quiet lip quivers. When they finally subsided, my mysterious captor stood and pushed her chair back.

"What is your name?" Her tone sounded five hundred degrees softer than before.

"Ashlyn," I answered.

"Ashlyn, if I take those off are you going to attack me?"

The timbre of her voice made me pause. I heard her ask, but the words kept repeating themselves over and over and over. I could feel them trying to insinuate themselves into my brain, trying to force me to answer truthfully. I wouldn't have lied anyway, but I felt the compulsion almost forcing the truth from my lips. Knowing I could have lied, I didn't.

"I don't know. I'm still hungry."

If I judged the look on my new friend's face correctly, I

surprised her. She closed her eyes for a moment. A soft knock echoed on the door before it opened to the large man mountain from the front door, who pushed his bulk through its inadequate frame.

"Yes, mistress?"

"Anan, come in and close the door," She said and waited for him to comply. "I need you to bare your wrist for our famished guest. Do so now."

I had to give the guy credit. Her voice left no room for argument, but I probably would have told her what she could go do with herself. Anan however, removed the watch from his left arm and lowered his wrist to my mouth. It looked like an entire leg of lamb splayed out in front of me. I raised my eyes and locked gazes with the woman behind the desk as I bit down. I fought the instinct to grab his arm, which would have been damn near impossible anyway because of my spiffy restraints.

The blood hit my tongue, and I felt ecstasy consume me. I had lived on the blood of my kin for over seventeen years. It had nourished me, kept me alive, and kept me sane. I never enjoyed it. This however felt like liquid fire pouring itself through every nerve of my body. The puzzle of what made my aunt's blood nourishing became clear. It was power. My aunt told me my mother had been an earth mage of considerable ability. The vampire I feasted on was no slouch either. My aunt must have had the aptitude to use magic, just not the desire. I was a fool not to have pieced it together earlier.

I drank deeply, and he made no motion to stop me even as I felt his legs start to quiver. His power began to ebb, and neither I, nor the hunger inside me, felt the desire to stop. Then his blood became even sweeter. I could taste his fear. I like to consider myself a good person. I have never harmed animal, vegetable, nor mineral in the scant two decades of my existence. Tasting his fear made me a little sick to my stomach. Hooray for morals.

I let him go and made sure to be careful extracting my curved fangs so as not to rip his flesh anymore than necessary. I don't know if I expected a modicum of gratefulness from him for my delicate work or what, but I did feel a little hurt when he grabbed his wrist and fled to the far side of the office. I let it go and rolled the power and taste around on my tongue. It was exquisite. I stretched like a cat and felt the hunger slumber finally as contentment washed over me.

I couldn't contain myself. I looked down at my bonds and snapped the three sets of cuffs without even straining. If I had thought about it beforehand, I probably wouldn't have done it. I looked again at my captor. She closed her eyes, and a moment later, a group of large vampires in the Fangloria's regalia came surging into the room. A fraction of a second later and bouncers surrounded me.

"Whoa!" I wasn't going to do anything; I just wanted to free my hands. I held my hands up in the classic "freeze" posture and multiple hands grabbed my wrists and arms.

"Stop," she said. Again, she used her double voice. It whispered to me, compelling me to do what she said. I'm not going to lie; I wish I had her ability. It would be pretty handy in a bank.

"I'm not doing anything, the cuffs started to chafe," I told her. Doubt washed across her face and something else. Maybe fear, but I doubted it. "Can you please undo my feet? I promise to leave and never come back."

She motioned her private army to release me. I rubbed my wrists and settled my hands into my lap.

"Ashlyn, first you have to answer some questions for me." She used a compulsion again to prohibit me from lying. "How old are you? What house do you claim as your heritage? Who is your master?" The questions kept repeating themselves over and over in my mind. I wanted to lie, and I knew I could, but what would be the point? The truth would probably be more believable than any lie I could concoct.

"I'm seventeen. I don't know what you mean by 'what house,' and I have no master. Now you know my name, could you please tell me who you are?" She seem to ponder both my answers and my question.

"Gloria is my name, child. I am the proprietor of the establishment you chose to wreak such havoc upon. How dare you come in to my house, attack one of my customers, and create problems for me? Tell me child, what am I supposed to do with you now? Call the authorities and tell them you attacked one of my guests and let them figure out what to do with you? Vampires in jail don't last too long. Should I kill you myself? I can tell you are going to be nothing but a huge inconvenience if you don't outright get me killed. Or should I turn you over to the Master of Chicago and let him deal with you?"

I didn't think she really expected an answer so I kept my mouth shut. Gloria stared at me as she drummed her fingers on the desk, leaving small nail-shaped imprints in the hardwood. I wish I could set her at ease. I wouldn't be a problem, and I had no desire to cause her trouble, but she didn't strike me as the trusting sort.

"Can I just leave?" I tried not to sound too hopeful.

"I sincerely doubt it would do any good. You could probably take out the strongest of the servants I own. I wouldn't put money against me fighting you, and don't think I have ever uttered those words before. I thought your hunger gave you the strength to snap the V-cuffs, so I fed you. Yet you snapped three sets of them without batting an eyelash. No, Ashlyn, of unknown origin and power, I think I shall introduce you to Cicero and let him decide your fate. If I let you go, and he finds out, I wouldn't even begin to ponder my fate. If I kill you outright, he may be pleased or he may not. Either way it is not a chance I'm willing to take."

She stood and gave a "watch her" motion to my guards and left the room. I considered making a break for it, but I didn't want to call Vegas to see what kind of odds they would give me against ten large vampires. I did the only thing I could think of. I waited. Thank gods I didn't have to do it for long.

Gloria came back into the office and sat at her desk. She removed a piece of stationary from one of the desk drawers and wrote something down on it. She then handed it to one of the larger vampires and stood.

"Make sure she gets there, Demitri. Take two others and don't disappoint me."

"Yes, mistress," he said as he bowed and motioned to my two closest guards.

"Ashlyn, it would be best for you to go without resistance. Should you even manage to escape, Cicero will hunt you down and destroy you. Trust me," her tone not quite masking the worry in her voice.

I didn't respond, merely nodded. Standing, I filed out of the room, sandwiched between Demitri and the two others. I had a date to meet the vampire, Cicero. Again, fear washed through me like a wave.

Chapter 4

We pulled up to another vampire club a few miles away after an uneventful ride in a non-descript cargo van. Didn't these people believe in offices? They could have spiffy names like the vampire offices of Dewey, Bitem, and Howe. The van pulled into an employee parking lot in the rear of the building, and my escorts ushered me to the back door. Demitri knocked three times, and the door opened. I gasped at the more impressive muscle standing before me; they stood taller than the bouncers I had seen at Fangloria's.

The vampire wore what looked like a 1920's gangster-approved pinstripe suit and hat. I thought it might be a personal attire choice until I saw the two behind him wearing similar outfits. Either I had entered a themed club, or I really stood before prohibition-era vampires.

"Demitri," one of the goons said, and nodded to my delivery boy.

I hoped to catch his response to see if he had Russian ancestry as his name suggested, but he just nodded and handed me over to gangster boy.

"Is this her?" Demitri nodded. "Don't look like much. You two, bring her to the boss." Goons Two and Three ushered me down the hall and up three flights of stairs to a solid oak door. I fought down the urge to laugh at the "private" sign–how cliché. There we waited for Goon One to catch up and knock.

I heard the muffled "come in," and Gooney opened the door. The elaborateness of the office shocked me. It comprised the entire floor of the building. Dark cherry wood paneling covered every wall complete with matching crown molding and baseboard trim. The floors even matched and gave the room a dark Elizabethan façade. A bar that could have been in any 1920's speakeasy lined one wall. Brass rails gleamed from natural gas wall sconces encircling the room and casting shadows across everything. Several leather couches ran the length of the opposite wall.

My eyes fixed immediately to the monstrous cherry wood desk facing the door. A complete matching bookcase lined the wall behind it and rose from floor to ceiling. An ornate brass gilded leather chair sat behind the desk. Cicero gazed at me through lidded eyes.

The goons prodded me forward, and I walked the length of the room, stopping several feet away from the desk. Cicero's eyes gave me a once over from head to toe. He seemed almost surprised by my appearance. If I had known I would be meeting vampire muckity-mucks, I would have dressed nicer. Well, maybe not. I don't own any nice clothes, but I would have worn jeans with fewer holes in them.

"You are Ashlyn?" His voice shocked me. I think deep down I expected a James Cagney voice. The eloquent timbre of his tone enthralled me instantly. This was a man you didn't lie to, not just because you didn't want to, but mostly because you feared getting caught.

"Yes, sir," I replied meekly. At least I didn't whimper like I wanted to.

"You are the girl who broke three sets of V-cuffs and rocked the very foundations of Gloria's little world. Here before me stands a tiny thing, and the mighty Gloria trembles?"

Cynicism saturated his voice. He wasn't afraid. I would have smelled it on him. Of every vampire I had met tonight, his scent set my nerves afire. He smelled of fine vanilla and cocoa. I rolled his scent across my tongue like a fine Belgian chocolate. I have always wanted to try Belgian chocolate. Damn my whole inability to digest human food.

"Apparently I am, sir. I apologized for my actions at Mistress Gloria's establishment, and I asked her to let me leave, but she feared what you would do." Wow, I could be eloquent when I was scared shitless. I had made myself seem weak and Gloria paranoid in one sentence.

"Frederick, snap her neck for me," he whispered. My mouth fell open in disbelief. *I spoke eloquently gods damn it!* Gooney swung his fist at me from behind, so I ducked. I spun to face him at waist level and watched him as if he moved in slow motion. His arm descended in a sweeping arc, and I raised my left arm to intercept. I didn't know the limits of my own strength, but I hoped it would be enough. As soon as my hand met the joint of his arm, his swing stopped. Surprise registered on his face, right until I smashed it with the heel of right hand. He didn't drop to the floor until he completed an arc through the air. I was stunned when he landed six feet away from me.

Goons Two and Three witnessed Frederick's fate, and

they turned to complete his orders. Time curiously slowed as they made their first steps. The slow motion effect also allowed me to see the silver stakes as they broke through two different windows and continue their trail straight into the backs of my assailants. The whole incident occurred without the sound of breaking glass and the wet thud you would expect from the tiny missiles impacting and penetrating through flesh. They had almost made it to me when the sounds finally came and the shock of the impacts registered on their faces. The snarling rage morphed into disbelief and then a blank stare as they dropped to the floor.

I turned to Cicero to see if he decided to attack me too, but he ran from his desk and launched himself through the remaining unbroken window into the Chicago night. His office sat four stories up, but I doubt it mattered much to him. His feet disappeared from view just as the solid wood door burst from its hinges. A group of armed and armored men in black vests with the yellow letters FBI stenciled across their chests and backs poured into the office and pointed their unusually-shaped weapons at everyone and everything.

If I had been born a smart little non-human, I would have followed Cicero into the night and extricated myself from what I had no doubt would be a royal mess. However, I had little experience with FBI crime raids. I just stood there rooted to my spot and raised my hands into the air like I was told to by a man with a matte black helmet and tactical mask that covered everything down to his lips. I didn't, however, notice he also had told me to get down on my knees and put my hands on top of my head. My brain became addled, and I uttered the mantra,

"Shit, shit, shit, shit." My lack of cooperation earned me a leg sweep from "get down" boy. I didn't see his movement until his leg made contact with mine. Let's just say mine won. The bones in his leg cracked as the force of the sweep halted immediately. I looked down at his prone form and started to apologize, but then became the center of a dog pile led by several other agents. This time I didn't win. I probably could have flung them off me, but I didn't fight back. I even let them bring my hands behind my back and cuff them together.

They left me on the floor as they cuffed Frederick and the two goons with silver stakes in their hearts. Their precautions seemed a little redundant, as the two vampires were obviously quite dead. They didn't feel like master vamps in my head, and to any other subspecies, silver through the heart is fatal. Maybe the guys with the guns weren't taking any chances.

When the dust settled and all of the blood drinkers–including me–had been nestled snugly in our V-cuffs, the men started their radio communications. Yes, the room was completely secure, and no, Cicero escaped, and they had four prisoners for transport. They raised me to my feet as they brought in stretchers for Cicero's men and led us out through the same stairwell and door I had come in, out into the back parking lot. I guess I never would find out the name of the club they dragged me into. My very first time to the city proper and I had no time for sightseeing.

My new FBI friends unceremoniously dumped me in the back of a large armored transport vehicle and shut the door behind me. I guess the goons had travel arrangements with an ambulance or the coroner wagon. The mental image of that made me giggle a little. At least I could still sit.

The trip lasted around twenty minutes and judging by the downward angle of the vehicle, we probably had pulled into an underground parking lot of some sort. The truck rolled to a stop and the rumble of the engine died only to be replaced by the *tick, tick* sound of cooling metal. I expected the doors to open right away, but disappointment reigned supreme yet once again. Apparently, I got to stay in the vehicle while they arranged my accommodations. I had just considered the feasibility of breaking my restraints and kicking out the door when it opened.

My gaze met the muzzle of one of those unusual weapons I assumed shot the five-inch long silver stakes. I didn't want to be on the receiving end of one of those like the vampires from the club, so I waited for instructions.

They led me through a door from the garage into the building and down a linoleum-floored hallway to a service elevator. Apparently, prisoners don't get the front door and stainless steel and glass elevator ride. The fact I had become a prisoner kind of irked me. It irked me a lot. I hadn't done anything except defend myself from vampire henchmen, and now here I sat in FBI custody. I guess shit happens for real sometimes. At least I could take satisfaction that when they ran my prints they would come up with a big, "Huh?"

The elevator whined as it lifted us up three floors to our destination. They led me down another carpeted hallway and into a room with a two chairs, a table, and yes, you guessed it, a mirror running one length of one wall. I'm sure it wasn't so I could fix my makeup. Not that I wore any. I guess some television clichés often had basis in reality. My guard plopped me down on the cool metal chair and restrained me using actual manacles attached to the chair. They consisted of the same material as the V-cuffs, so I assumed they designed the room specifically for interrogating vampires. Two of my guards backed off to the wall behind me, their spike-shooting weapons lowered and aimed at my back. The rest filed out of the room and left me to sit in silence again.

Minutes later, a short balding man with wire rimmed glasses came in and took my prints. I guess the FBI was eager to find out whom they had in custody and why they had found me in the Master of Chicago's office. He seemed to be a pleasant little man. He wore a white lab coat and used a colorless inkpad, so I wasn't sitting there with black fingers waiting for my interrogator. He finished his work quickly and exited the room, and a sigh of relief escaped from one of my guards. I guess he thought I planned on eating the little lab tech or something.

"You can relax guys; I don't eat humans," I couldn't resist calling over my shoulder.

"Quiet, miss, you're in a lot of trouble," one of them responded.

I wasted my breath telling them I had done nothing wrong, and I had been the victim here, but they didn't respond. Here I thought I had been honest and told them something they probably hadn't heard a thousand times before. I can't believe they didn't believe me. Everyone's such a cynic these days.

I sat in silence until another FBI agent strode through the door with a file folder. He sat his six foot two frame on the little chair across from me, placed the folder on the table, and crossed his legs. He stared at me for what felt like a full minute before starting his questions.

"Name?"

"No thanks, I already have one."

"Name?" Apparently, he wasn't a jokester.

I sighed and gave him my first name. I thought about giving him my last, but I decided it would be best to drop it. My last name had been given to me in a different life, and I didn't want to tie anything back to the memory of my aunt. She couldn't get in trouble anymore for what she did, but she didn't deserve to have her memory tarnished. Raising the illegitimate monster of your dead sister might raise a few eyebrows.

"What's your last name, Ashlyn?" He must have been a little psychic.

"I have no last name, sir, just Ashlyn."

"I am waiting on your prints to come back. I had the tech put a rush on it so I should have the results back in an hour. He's running them through Homeland, Interpol, VLAD, and the IDOLV. Are the results going to come back with anything I should know about? You aren't wanted for anything, are you?"

"Nothing is going to come back, sir." I must have smiled a little at my own joke because his face hardened a little.

"Explain," he said sternly.

Damn he had a knack for this. It probably gave him the leeway to be in here by himself. He played good cop and bad cop, so either he was very good at his job, or had multiple personality disorder. Maybe I should just try a little honesty. It hadn't worked very well with the vampires I had met tonight, but this guy seemed entirely human.

"Nothing is coming back, sir. I don't exist according to anyone's records. I have no birth record, no death certificate, nothing. That's what I mean by nothing. This is the first time I have ever been in custody. I don't even have a driver's license!"

"This is going to be an interesting conversation, miss. Do you know why you are here?"

"I'm sure you have heard this like a zillion times, but I didn't do anything." I started and then thought about it. If honesty was my goal, maybe I should stick with it. "All right, my hunger drove me to attack a vampire in a bar, but I hadn't eaten in a week and he smelled good. I got busted by the owner of the bar and freaked her out a little because of my strength and the fact that I had no "master" or whatever it's called, so she sent me by force to go see the head vampire honcho, Cicero. He had told his hired help to snap my neck when you guys showed up and put metal stakes in their chest cavities. So to answer your question, detective, no, I have no idea why I'm here." I breathed, but my body didn't do it to get oxygen to my brain. I breathed to talk and to appear alive, so I had never been "breathless." After spilling my guts to the FBI agent, I understood the expression.

"Special Agent Stone, Miss Ashlyn. Not detective. Sorry I forgot to introduce myself, but it's not every day you find a vampire who looks like a teenager, hits like a Mack truck, and breaks the legs of FBI Agents."

Now I was a little pissed off. I tried to keep the anger from my voice, but it didn't work so well. "Excuse me, Mr. Special Agent, but I didn't break his leg. I felt a little stunned by what happened with not only the vampires, but your agents, as well. I didn't hear him tell me to get on the floor, so he kicked me! I didn't break his leg, he did, and just for your information, I am not a fucking vampire!"

When I saw his head snap in the direction of the mirrored wall, I realized I had carried my honesty probably a little too far. I considered backpedalling or even adding a feeble, "Who does bad things," to the end of my last sentence, but I figured it wouldn't fly.

I heard a "What exactly do you mean?" come from a little speaker in his ear, an electronic link with the people in the little room on the other side of the mirror. So I answered facing the mirror.

"It means I came out of the womb like this, you son of a bitch, seventeen years ago. Vampires aren't born the last time I checked my facts on the internet; they're made. Vampires drink the blood of humans; I can't! Vampire's don't have claws, and guess what? I do! Vampires don't have pupils like a cat, but can you guess who does? *Me!* I don't know what I am exactly, but I can promise you one thing: I am not a vampire."

"Do you have a heartbeat?" This time, the voice came from a loudspeaker in the room behind the mirror directly. I guess they had given up on the illusion Special Agent Stone was in charge.

"Sometimes yes, sometimes no," I answered.

"Do you drink blood?"

"Yes, but it can't be plain old human blood. It has to be someone who has power. Like someone who uses magic, or vampire blood."

"Do you have to breathe?"

"No."

"Are you nocturnal?"

"Yes."

"Are you sunlight intolerant?"

"Sunburn extraordinarily fast, yes. Do I turn into a cinder? No."

"But you're not a vampire, correct?" Doubt laced his voice, even as it came through the speaker. I just wasn't sure if he thought I was lying to him or to myself.

"From every bit of information I have garnered from the internet on every subspecies of vampire known to man, there are many similarities and dissimilarities between myself and vampires. The greatest of them being vampires are created and not born because they are sterile, sir." Uh, oh, there goes the eloquence again. I just hoped it didn't get me in trouble, even though I impressed myself. If I ever went to school to get my degree, I may actually make my doctorate thesis on the differences between myself and vampires.

I heard the tiny voice in Special Agent Stone's ear, telling him to leave the room. I didn't know if things were moving in a positive direction, but at least the session of twenty questions had come to a halt. Hopefully they wouldn't drum up some charge to hold me with, and I could get out of here soon. Dawn was coming and tired didn't begin to describe how I felt.

"I will return shortly, Miss Ashlyn, do you require anything while I'm gone?"

"Could you let me out of these damn cuffs? They're starting to chafe."

"Regretfully no, they are a standard protection for our benefit, not yours. We have lost too many agents to vampires during interviews. They don't like to cooperate very much with the Federal Bureau of Investigation. Sorry."

After he left, I decided against playing the "I'm not a vampire" card once again. Obviously, he didn't believe me either. I felt the sun come up in my mind's eye. Daylight had come again. I stifled a yawn and tried to make myself comfortable in the chair. At least I had the benefit of being in a windowless room. The sun would have me crying in a few minutes, but the temperature and brightness of the room had been set at a comfortable level.

I waited over an hour for someone to return, and it wasn't Stone. A gray haired gentleman of upper years entered and closed the door behind him. He wore a crisp black suit with a maroon tie. From the way he held himself, I could tell he was somebody important. I wondered if his voice would match the one I heard over the loudspeaker earlier. Watching him as he watched me while he sat down across the tiny table, I noticed his lack of file folder, and wondered if Stone had anything in the one he brought earlier. Probably just some doodles of robots shooting down jet fighters.

Mr. Cool nodded to the two guards still standing behind me, and to my surprise, they departed. Now he and I were the sole occupants of the tiny room. Either he held every confidence in himself, or he thought I probably wouldn't be a threat. I could be if I wanted to, but I didn't want the entire FBI hunting me down every minute of every day.

"Miss Ashlyn, thank you for not hiding the truth of your

lack of fingerprints, documents, or past. All the channels returned a ‘person not registered’ answer. To tell you the truth, I have never seen such a thing. You remained hidden quite well for the past seventeen years. How did you manage to pull off such a miracle?" His was the same voice as earlier so I felt a little more comfortable talking with him.

"My aunt hid me, sir. Don't ask me her name. She died in a car accident recently so she can't be of any use to you. If you want, I'll write down the story of my birth and life for your records. I guess I don't have to hide anymore."

"I would greatly appreciate you doing so. Let me introduce myself. I am Special Agent in Charge of the Chicago branch of the FBI. My name is Clifford Reese. I would shake your hand, but I wouldn't want you to needlessly snap another set of perfectly good V-cuffs." He smirked.

"How did you…" I started to ask, but he held up his hand. He stood and walked around the table, producing a key from his jacket pocket. He not only unlocked the ones binding me to the chair, but also the ones binding my hands and feet. I rubbed my raw wrists. Whatever the cuffs were, the material wasn't dull.

"We have had a busy past hour, Miss Ashlyn. We dispatched a team to Fangloria's and apprehended Gloria herself for kidnapping. Unfortunately, she is in some serious trouble. Kidnapping is a horrible offence in and of itself, but throw in the facts you are minor and she is a vampire…it does not bode well for her future. Let's just say she is being very cooperative. I would like a separate statement about the incidents at her place of business, if you don't mind."

What a shrewd man Clifford Reese seemed to be. I thought I might find a pang of guilt over the fate of Gloria, but she decided to fuck me first. Cicero had planned to kill me, so she got what she deserved in my book.

"Am I free to go?"

"Not yet, I'm afraid. You're not going to be charged for the attack at the bar, nor for resisting arrest, which is good news. And yes, I know it's not your fault the agent broke his leg. However, there are still some matters to clear up. I need some more information on Cicero." He paused and rubbed his eyes. I could tell I wasn't the only one who was tired. "I know you weren't in his office for very long, but we have several outstanding warrants on the current Master of the City, and an attempted murder charge and kidnapping of a minor would greatly help. I even think Gloria may aid in his capture to save her ass. Would you mind giving a statement on the incident as well?"

All I could do is shrug. I may not "die" when the sun came up like a vampire, but my body still didn't like it. I stifled a yawn, and thankfully, Clifford Reese noticed.

"We have overnight accommodations that are free during the day at this facility. Would you like to rest for a while before giving your statements?

I nodded in gratitude. He motioned me to the door. I made a graceful "after you" motion with my hands, and he led me through the door and past the two agents assigned as "guards." As we walked down the hall, they fell into step behind us. He may have trusted me more than before, but it obviously went only so far.

We climbed aboard the shiny stainless steel elevator and descended two floors, ending up right above the parking garage. We passed a small kitchen, the standard office kind without a stove; just a fridge, coffee maker, microwave, and toaster oven. Next to that were two large bathrooms. One was marked agents and the other marked agentesses. Apparently, someone in the office had a sense of humor. We entered another hall with a bunch of nondescript doors running the entire length before stopping at the last one on the right.

I glanced inside and found a small cot with what looked like a standard military-issue pillow and blanket folded at the foot of it. A small nightstand and table lamp lay right next to it. It looked Spartan and cozy at the same time.

"Enjoy your rest, Miss Ashlyn. Just let one of your guards know when you are awake. I will be waiting for you."

He turned and spun on his heel. I didn't even look at my guards, just walked into the tiny room, shut the door, and lay down on the most comfortable thing I had ever slept on. I didn't snuggle or make myself a nest. I just put the pillow and blanket at the head of the bed, kicked my tennis shoes off, and went to sleep. I didn't even dream.

Chapter 5

I awoke mid-afternoon. I could feel the sun making its descent into the west, but I knew it wasn't even remotely dark out. I rose, straightening out my rumpled clothes before slipping on my tennis shoes. One of the benefits I enjoyed with my unique physiology is I produced no body odor. I guess when you are designed to be a predator, walking around stinking to high heaven wouldn't be too helpful.

I shuffled over to the door and thought about just opening it. It probably wasn't a good idea to start the day full of holes, so I knocked to alert my guards of my presence. They must have heard me in the room because as soon as I knocked, the door swung open.

I saw two new faces, so the agents assigned to me must have been relieved at some point during the morning. The one who opened the door actually smiled at me. I wondered if he was responsible for the bathroom labels down the hall. He seemed like he had a sense of humor. I gave him a goofy smile back, and they both turned to lead the way through the maze of hallways. We made it to the elevator without encountering another soul, but while we waited for the doors to open, another agent walked up to share our ride.

She stood taller than me by about two inches so I guessed

she was around five foot eight, at least if she wasn't wearing two inch heels. She was beautiful, and I felt shabby standing next to her. She wore a plain white blouse under a gray skirt and jacket. Between the heels and the skirt, I figured she didn't see much field work. She seemed pretty interested in my second guard though. She kept glancing at him to see if he made eye contact, but to his credit he didn't. I wondered if they had a little history between them.

"Another Hacker?"

"She's wanted for industrial espionage," the funny guard answered, saving guard two from having to talk to the pretty agent.

"Nice. Pretty soon these kids are going to take over. I hope they don't screw with my paycheck," she replied.

Funny Guard pressed the button for the sixth floor. *Must be the executive offices*. I hoped our hitchhiker would press a button for a sooner floor but it looked like she would be sharing our ride for the duration. Gratefully, she made the minimally acceptable amount of small talk. She exited ahead of us and drifted off to the left while we made our way to the right.

We wound through the cubicle farms and hallways to the rear of the building. Apparently being the Special Agent in Charge of the Chicago Office warranted a corner office made mostly of glass. Agent Funny Man rapped his knuckles and ushered me into Agent Reese's domain. I walked in and glanced back to see my new friends take up their usual posts at the door. Number two actually reached into the office and pulled the door closed behind me.

Reese gestured to one of the chairs situated in front of his large gray desk, and I complied, giving him a small smile as I sat. He finished signing whatever documents he had been working on and placed them in a clearly labeled "out" box on the corner of the desk. Finally, he pulled out another folder with my name on it.

He set it down in front of him, folding his aged hands across the top with a smile. I wanted to say, "Thank you," but his smile made me a little wary. The phrase about the cat and canary popped unwillingly into my head.

"Glad to see you a little rested, Miss Ashlyn," he began.

Personally, I had grown quite tired of the Miss.

"Agent Reese, you have been more than kind to me since you brought me in. Would you please call me Ashlyn, or even just Ash? The “Miss" makes me feel like I'm still in trouble, and I'm not, am I?"

"No, Ash, you're not. All charges have been officially dropped in lieu of your cooperation with the Bureau. Would you like to begin? I can get the forms for you now, or I could have the statement recorded, whichever you prefer. Though written forms will allow us to continue our conversation while you work."

"Writing would be fine with me, Agent Reese. Trust me when I say I'm not in any hurry to go anywhere. I probably am safer here right now than on the streets with a certain Master of Chicago still on the loose anyway. Any luck finding him?"

He laughed. "No, Ashlyn, finding any vampire's daytime hiding place is difficult, finding the Master of Chicago's would be impossible. We had to wait until he was awake to try to capture him. Most cities in the country have Masters of the City who are law-abiding citizens, or at least they haven't gotten caught yet. A lot of them have achieved almost a Hollywood star status. They have paparazzi following them and pose for pictures and sign autographs. It's kind of funny actually, but not Chicago. We have a bona fide gangster for the Master of the City. He's a hell of a lot older than prohibition era Chicago, but during that time he flourished, and so he became stuck in it. How'd we get so lucky?"

As I sat through his little rhetoric on Chicago's vampiric history, Reese walked over to a gunmetal-gray filing cabinet and opened the top drawer. It must have been well oiled because it stood almost four feet wide and yet he pulled the massive drawer open easily. He reached into one of the hanging file folders and pulled out several forms, before returning to his seat at the desk. He handed me one form after filling in his pertinent information and asked me to write my statement about the events at Fangloria's. The events unfolded in my mind. I set about the task of putting them down on paper when he handed me a second sheet and told me to do the same for the events at Cicero's. *This could take a while*.

"I'm setting up a tape recorder so you can tell me your story about how you came to be. It will save you some writing, and I'll admit I'm more than a little curious," he said reassuringly.

"No problem. I can multitask," I responded.

So it went for the better part of three hours. I told him of my early years living with my aunt, but never giving her name. He seemed to respect my privacy and didn't try to pry it out of me while I focused on writing my statements. I told of how I had fully matured by the time I reached the ripe old age of seven and how I spent my nights wandering through the neighborhood. My voice cracked when I explained how I fed every other night off my aunt who could have been a witch but chose modern medicine. I sounded a little depressed when I got to the how lonely it felt never venturing out into the real world and spending most of my time with books, computers, and television part. When I told him about watching the newscast of my aunt's fatal car crash, the tears started falling. I had never grieved for the only human I had ever loved, and I couldn't hold back the tears anymore, writing with watery eyes.

A drawer opened, and a hand waved in front of my face, holding a tissue. I didn't look up, just took it, dried my eyes, and kept writing while telling my brief tale. Lady luck finally smiled down on me. The rest of the story he already knew, and I had finished with my second and final statement. I pushed the documents forward and refused to make eye contact with the only person who had ever seen me cry. Not even my aunt had had to deal with childish tears. When you are as tough as the toughest vampire, it naturally became hard to skin a knee or get a boo-boo. Even on those rare occasions when I had caused enough damage to pierce my skin, why cry when the damage healed before my eyes. Sometimes it was cool being a freak.

Agent Reese hit the stop button on the digital recorder and placed it in the main drawer directly in front of him. "I'll save your story to a thumb drive and place it in your file. We will be the only agency with a record of you, and I promise you as long as you stay out of trouble, I will keep it with us and not pass it around for general knowledge."

I nodded thanks to my new benefactor and watched him stand up and walk back over to his filing cabinet. He placed my statements in the second drawer and reached up to the small surround sound system perched atop the cabinet. I have never been a fan of opera, but apparently he liked it because a screeching aria permeated the room as he sat back down.

"Pardon the music, Ash, but I wanted to talk to you about your plans. The only drawback to having a glass office is soundproofing. They gave me double paned glass, but even someone hard of hearing could eavesdrop if they wanted to. I have found opera, with its greater fluctuations, pretty much fills the gaps. I just wish I could stand listening to the shit."

"I feel the same way. If I understand television correctly, most girls my age listen to pop music, but if there is one thing I hate more than opera, it's pop…and rap…and country. Okay, maybe all I like is rock and alternative, but hey, whatever."

He smiled at me again, and I found it a little less predatory and a lot more conspiratorial. He shifted in his seat and folded his hands. "What are your plans now? Are you going to go back to your hotel until your money runs out? Are you going to get a job and buy a small house in the suburbs? Maybe you could find a nice vampire to go work for at one of their fancy clubs? Have you thought about the future at all?"

He had me. I had been planning to lie low for quite a while. I hadn't even begun to tap into the ten thousand cash my aunt had left me. It would hole me up in my cheap hotel for quite some time. My greatest concern would be finding a stable food source. I couldn't exactly run around the city feeding off every vampire I met. Maybe my fairy godmother would poof up a magic boyfriend I could munch on every night.

"Agent Reese, my future is a very dark vision in my mind. I have some cash hoarded that would keep me comfortable in a hotel for a bit. My problem is food. I fed off one vampire, and you see the trouble I got into. Either I pay for some kind of blood prostitute or I'm going to be knocking a lot of vamps over the head to get what I need. When my hunger gets too strong, it takes over."

"Come work for us," he said without even a pause. "Be a Federal Agent. Your salary would cover all your living expenses, and we'll figure out a way to keep you fed. I have already called the Deputy Director and told him about you, and he agrees you pose quite an opportunity."

His eyes sparkled with excitement. My chin was on the floor. Sure, I may be a freak, but why would he possibly want me as an agent for the FBI? I had no high school diploma or a college degree. Hell, I didn't even know how to drive a car! "Why?"

"When things get out of control in the vampire community, it's our responsibility to police it. It's up to us to take into custody or remove the source of the problem. We are comprised of humans, mages, and a large number of wereanimals such as wolves and lions, but there is not one vampire on the payroll. We have a lot of tools to help us deal with the problem, but most of the time we get our asses handed to us. You could even up the playing field immensely."

"Why don't you hire actual vampires?" I had a feeling I already knew the answer.

"Because, Ash, whenever a vampire is created, he is bound to the will of his maker. You can't have someone at your back with double loyalties. We found that out the hard way. Back in the early fifties, we wanted a vampire on the payroll. We forced a common vampire in custody to turn a volunteer agent. He did it, and then had the agent release him from our custody. Agents caught both of them trying to escape. The master ended up dead, and when he died, we lost our agent. He just died for no apparent reason. With you, we won't have that problem. You have no master but yourself. Frankly, we need you. Vampires don't trust human authorities, and we don't trust them. We know for a fact, every vampire you have met thinks you are a vampire. Help us please?" He leaned forward and I half expected him to beg.

I thought about all he said, and I wanted to say yes. I would finally have a purpose. I had some nagging doubts I just couldn't shake, though. What if they expected me to do things I thought wrong? Being forced to do something I didn't want to truly bothered me. What if I ended up working for someone who would just use me? The list kept getting bigger the more I thought about it. Then I thought of the good I could do. I saw myself saving innocent people, maybe even rescuing people from certain death. The wave of doubts ebbed.

"Agent Reese, what guarantee would I have, if things don't work out, that I wouldn't be stuck working for the FBI for the rest of my life?"

"Agents are allowed to quit at any time, Ashlyn. We are an employer, not slave owners. You do understand there is a lot of training involved as well. I don't want you to think I am going to hand you a badge and magically make you a field agent. We're talking school and combat training, weapons training. I could go on and on about all the things you would have to learn. You need to understand what coming to work for us would mean, and pardon the expression; I don't want to blow smoke up your ass. It will be a lot of hard work."

"I understand. If I say yes, what would happen next?"

"You would head to Virginia, Quantico to be exact. The FBI Academy is there. Is this a yes, Ashlyn?"

"I think so, Agent Reese, just some nagging doubts. Does the Academy have night courses?" I meant it as a joke, but I really had concerns.

"Yes, some of our supes prefer to train at night."

"What's a supe?"

"Supe is slang for supernatural entities, our classification of agents with extraordinary physical manifestations. They include, but are not limited to, wereanimals, any of the classifications of the fey, mages, etc, etc. You'll probably meet some people at Quantico who'll make you feel a little more ordinary. Twenty-five years ago, when I trained there, I had instructors you wouldn't believe. So, Miss Ashlyn Nolastname, do we have a deal?" He rose and extended his hand, and I timidly took it. I had sealed the deal. I just hope I hadn't sealed my fate.

Reese shut off the music and made his way to the door. He motioned for me to remain seated and left. I slunk down in my chair and kept muttering to myself, "Ash, you're an idiot." I found myself in mid-babble when Reese came in with one of my guards. At least he brought Mr. Senseofhumor.

"Ashlyn this is Agent Michaels. Normally we would just put you on a plane to Virginia, but we're going to arrange special transport for you. He will make sure you get there okay. Just to be clear, I'm not doing this because I don't trust you. I'm doing this because I know how new you are to the real world. So far your education has been from computers and television, and I'm sure they left out how a few things really work, especially airports."

"Agent Michaels, pleasure to meet you." I shook his hand and got another one of his smiles.

"Ashlyn is going to be joining the Bureau. I want you to escort her back to her hotel where she can collect her things and then double-time it back here to catch a flight to Quantico. I'll have your itinerary and everything else when you return." Reese spoke with the calm collectedness I had grown accustomed to.

"Come on, kid, let's go get your things," Michaels said to me. I didn't care for the "kid," but at least he didn't ruffle my hair. I would have had to hurt him.

We left Reese's office and made our way down to the parking garage. As we exited the elevator, Michaels pulled a key ring from his jacket pocket and pushed a button on a key fob A telltale *honk* came from my right, and I looked up to see the yellow running lights blink merrily announcing our transportation, a big black Suburban complete with tinted windows.

Michaels made for the driver's side and climbed in, so I did the same on the passenger's side. My vehicle experience so far had consisted of the back of a cargo van, so I found this to be much nicer. The size of the thing shocked me. I could easily have curled up into a ball on the floorboards and still have room.

"You like music?" Michaels broke the silence first.

"Some," I replied and watched him punch a few buttons on the stereo. Led Zeppelin wasn't too bad. I could live with Robert Plant.

"So, I hope you know what you're getting into. You always want to be an FBI agent when you grew up?"

"I'll let you know if I ever grow up," I replied jokingly. I assumed he knew I wasn't a normal human, but his quizzical look made me think twice. If I had to spend time with Agent Michaels, I might as well fill him in. "You do know I'm not normal right?"

"You look normal to me."

I held out my hand and showed him my talons. I usually spend my entire day with my fists clenched, so they weren't noticeable. I have never been around people, so it had to be a self-conscious way of hiding what I considered a deformity. "Not normal," I told him.

He looked at my hands and then at my face. He had shaken my hand earlier in Reese's office and not noticed them. I didn't want to scare him, but I didn't want secrets from anyone anymore, so I showed him my teeth. To his credit, he didn't drive off the road and crash.

"You're a supe? Cool," he said, making an appreciative

gesture by frowning and nodding. "You spend too much time in your wereform? I had heard some parts can get stuck."

"No. I'm not a wereanimal. I'm kind of like a vampire, but a little different. I have no idea exactly what I am," I answered honestly.

"Are you strong like a vampire? You don't look dead to me."

"Yes, I am strong, very strong and very fast. Vampires aren't dead, you know. They don't have a heartbeat per se, but it still pumps the blood throughout their system in a fluid motion rather than a spasm. Mine's the same way. See, I have no pulse," I said, and held out my wrist to him.

He took one hand off the steering wheel and placed his index and middle fingers on my wrist. "Creepy," he said, but with a smile. "So you have fangs, and super strength, super speed, and no pulse. Why don't you think you're a vamp?"

"I have never been human."

"Oh, this I got to hear. Do tell, lady friend," he said with a smile. I figured we had about forty-five minutes until we got to the motel, so for the second time in one day, I told my story from start to finish, just an abbreviated version. I might as well get used to telling, because I had a feeling once I reached the training facility in Virginia, I would be telling it quite often.

By the time we reached the motel, I finished my tale. He didn't stop me to ask questions, and I paused only to give him directions. He said nothing until we pulled into the parking lot. Finally, he placed his hand on my arm and gave me a warm smile.

"I'm glad we found you. Welcome to the FBI. Now all

you have to do is make it through the academy. Come on, let's go get your stuff, and since you're so strong you can carry the heavy crap. You might be vampiric, but you're still a girl, so I'm expecting at least twelve suitcases."

I laughed and led the way to my room. I saw the shock on his face when I packed all my clothes into one backpack, and then his shock turned to disbelief when I emptied the room safe of all my cash. I placed my small fortune into the backpack, and in minutes, I was ready to go.

I palmed my fake identification card and stuffed it into my front jeans pocket when he wasn't looking. I gave up my old life, and I had to destroy the last link. I would have to burn it later when I could do it with a modicum of privacy. Maybe I should have a little ceremony.

We made our way to the SUV and drove back to the Chicago office. The dashboard clock read nine o'clock, and the parking garage seemed deserted except for Reese standing there waiting for us to park. He walked up to my window as I rolled it down.

"Here's everything you need. Transport has been arranged. You leave from O'Hare in a little more than an hour. I wanted to make sure you got to Virginia well before sunrise. They are expecting you there. Good luck, Miss Ashlyn. I have included all my contact information in the packet, so if you ever need to contact me, you can." He shook my hand and stepped away from the vehicle.

"Thank you, Agent Reese, for everything. I'll call when I can."

Michaels backed out of the spot and headed for the

airport. I pulled the travel itinerary from the packet and handed it to him. I glanced through the rest of it and found a temporary letter of appointment, copies of my statements about the incidents in the city, a hard copy of the verbal statement of my life, a business card bearing the name Clifford Reese, and a sealed envelope with Special Agent in Charge Vincent Morello written in blue ink across it. It piqued my curiosity, but I didn't open it.

Michaels glanced at the itinerary. The traffic thickened closer to the airport. Fortunately, it kept moving at a good pace, so we had no trouble getting to the airport on time. When we pulled onto the off ramp, Michaels didn't follow the directions to the terminal like I expected. Instead, we followed the signs to the private hangar areas. *I guess I'm not flying commercial.*

We wound our way along the frontage road and pulled up to a nondescript hangar. Its white corrugated metal walls supported a standard rounded roof just like every hangar I had ever seen on TV. The front doors lay open and I saw a small jet parked inside. Michaels pulled right inside and parked the Suburban off to the left.

We then stepped out onto the hanger floor. The smell of jet fuel permeated the air, turning my stomach. Michaels started walking toward a man in blue slacks and a white shirt with blue and yellow stripes on the shoulders. I would have bet money the guy was the captain.

"Agent Michaels?" Michaels nodded. "Climb aboard and we'll prepare for takeoff." He turned to me. “Miss, welcome aboard."

I followed Michaels up the stairs built into the door of the plane and gave a little gasp. Commercial airliners had always looked so cramped and uncomfortable whenever I had seen them in the movies. This looked like an RV with wings. Comfortable-looking leather swivel chairs dotted the aircraft as well as a table and booth setup. A pretty woman waited inside, dressed in a blouse and shirt combination that matched the captain. She was busy stowing some gear in the overhead bins and making last minute preparations for takeoff.

When we entered the plane, she walked over and introduced herself as Tiffany, giving the “if you need anything" spiel. Yuck. I didn't care for Tiffany right away. Michaels mumbled a thank you and sat down in one of the swivel chairs. He fastened his seatbelt and gripped the armrests like he wanted to bend them around his waist for added restraint. I didn't know what to expect since I had never been in an airplane, but I wasn't going let his skittishness rub off on me.

I stuffed my backpack in the overhead above us and took the chair next to him. I fumbled with the seatbelts for a few moments and then finally heard the satisfying little click, which told me I had succeeded in mastering the art of airplane safety. We sat in silence for a few, and I heard the whine of the engines as they fired up. Without warning, we lurched forward out of the hangar bay and as we turned, I glimpsed a small yellow vehicle towing the front of the plane. After a few minutes of being towed by the curious little tow truck, the plane stopped and the sound from the engines increased.

We taxied for several minutes before the captain came over the loudspeaker announcing our takeoff. A thrill rushed through me as the engines whined out to maximum power. The jet shuddered as it picked up speed. I looked out the window as the front of the plane lifted into the air and watched the ground as it pulled away. The ride was exciting, exhilarating, scary, and a thousand other emotions all rolled into one. I loved it. We leveled out and the features of the ground became almost even too small for my eyes to make out. I could barely see the cars on the miniature roads and the trees planted in the yards of the miniature houses. I bounced in my seat like a little girl who ate an entire pack of Pixie Sticks.

I looked over at my travel partner and his eyes were closed. He might have been nervous about flying, but not enough to keep him from dozing off. Tiffany came by and asked if I needed anything to drink. I thought about asking for blood and flashing fangs, but I probably couldn't drink the blood anyway. Besides, I didn't want to spend the next hour with a hysterical flight attendant. I just shook my head and did my best impersonation of Michaels.

Chapter 6

I must have done a better job impersonating Michaels than I imagined. When I woke up the tires had literally hit the tarmac. My first airplane ride and I slept through it. Missing most of the flight frustrated me a little. Michaels had already awoken and gingerly sipped on a Coke. It looked really good, and I found myself wishing I could have one, but alas, the whole "I need magic blood" thing put another damper on my lifestyle.

The airplane taxied over to the area by the terminal. I hadn't even glanced at the itinerary so I had no idea where we landed. It didn't pull in directly to the terminal either, just off to the side and stopped. The engines wound down and shut off. I had a feeling the captain had been instructed to wait for Michaels.

The captain came back to the passenger area and opened the door at the forward area of the compartment. It swung down on hinges and the stairs opened to the tarmac. Michaels unfastened his seatbelt and stood. I let him move out of the way. I did the same and retrieved my bag from the overhead.

Chicago's weather had been a little cool, but Virginia's dipped into the realm of chilly. A brisk autumn breeze swirled around the plane and over my arms. I found it refreshing after the pumped-in oxygen of the hour-long flight. I followed my companion down the stars where two new agents waited in front of another one of those FBI-issue black Suburbans. I watched warily as the two agents greeted Michaels with handshakes before one of them opened the rear door for us.

I climbed in and slid across the back seat to the other side so Michaels wouldn't have to walk around. The seat shifted as he got in next to me and did his seatbelt. I didn't bother with mine. When you can snap handcuffs like peanut brittle, putting on a seatbelt is about as reassuring as tying yarn around your waist before getting on a roller coaster.

The two agents climbed in the front and the driver started the car. They strapped themselves in, just like Michaels had, so I assumed the FBI had made it mandatory for their agents to wear them. I still didn't fasten mine. I'm such a rebel. The agent behind the wheel shoved the car in drive, and we sped away out into the cold Virginia night.

Thanks to the handy signage surrounding the airport, I learned we had landed at Dulles International Airport. I finally relaxed and began to enjoy the nighttime scenery and the silence of the ride. I reached the second chapter of my life and I wanted to relish in the final few paragraphs of my first. How nice it would have been if we had driven from Chicago instead of flying. Too soon, I found our SUV pulling up to the Quantico Marine Base. Who knew how long it would be before I could leave again.

We drove through wooded areas until we reached the

academy. Another checkpoint and we entered the belly of the beast, so to speak. Once the car rolled to a stop and the agent driving put it in park, I grabbed my bag and followed all three agents into the main facility. We passed through the reception area and into the bowels of what had to be offices set aside for administration purposes. We wound our way around the halls of education at its finest and stopped in front of a door with a placard engraved with the name, Vincent Morello. The same name on the envelope given to me by Agent Reese.

One of the new agents knocked on the door and entered. I followed behind everyone and found a large man with graying spiked hair sitting behind a desk very similar to Reese's. He looked up and nodded to the two agents who delivered Michaels and me from the airport. They turned and departed, leaving us alone with Morello.

"Agent Michaels I assume?" He rose and offered his hand to my friend, who accepted heartily.

"Here she is, sir, as promised."

"Thank you, Michaels. Tell Reese he owes me lunch next time I see him," he said jovially.

"I will, sir, and take care of her. She's a little 'special,' if you know what I mean." Michaels turned to me and smiled.

I knew what he meant. He even did the stupid little quotation marks with his fingers when he said "special." I expected a firm handshake before he left, but he surprised me with a hug. The whole experience surprised me, but I liked it. Compared to mine, his body burned like a furnace and I enjoyed the warmth.

"Take care of yourself, little girl. I expect to see you again soon, and listen to Morello. He's good people."

"I will," I said as I squeezed a little harder to remind him I wasn't so fragile. He grunted, and I thought I might have heard a rib or two give a little creak.

Michaels left after a nod to Morello and headed back out to Chicago, which left me alone with the head of the FBI academy. I sat down and pulled my backpack onto my lap from the floor next to my chair.

"I have something for you from Agent Reese, sir," I said to the bear of a man behind the desk.

"I know. I just got off the phone with him. I let him know you arrived safely. He filled me in on your special dietary needs. I'm at a loss as to what to do there, but I'm sure our medical people will come up with something." He stared at me for a moment before he began tapping his fingers. "I've got to be candid with you, Ashlyn. I wasn't too keen on the idea of having a vampire recruit, but after seeing how much of a shine an old hard ass like Reese took to you, it set my mind at ease. Just please don't make the mistake of thinking your time here is going to be a breeze. It's just plain hard work."

I nodded to him as I handed over the sealed envelope. "I won't, sir."

He placed the envelope in his desk and locked the drawer. He then came around and motioned me to follow. I zipped up my belongings and followed him through the door down a different hallway to a rear exit. We went back into the night and over to another building marked clearly as the base hospital. The scents of alcohol, antiseptics, and other unpleasant odors permeated my nostrils. He led until we reached an unmarked door. He knocked, and without waiting for a response, entered. "Doctor Gibbs, here is the recruit I called you about earlier. Do you have time to get her processed before daylight?"

"Yes, sir, I can! You must be Ashlyn. I'm Doctor Gibbs." He held out his hand, but unlike most people, he didn't miss the small talons protruding from my fingers. He shook it anyway, but while he did so, he had his hand turned so he could study my fingers. "Extraordinary," he muttered.

"Yes, but they're a pain in the ass when I rub my face," I said. I'm sure he hadn't meant for me to hear his mutter, so he looked up with an apologetic look on his face. I laughed.

"No harm, doc."

"You can leave her with me, Agent Morello. I'll have her physical done shortly and get her registered at the dorms. If you'll follow me, Ashlyn?" He turned toward the door in his office.

"Good luck, Ashlyn. I'll be keeping an eye on you." Morello shook my hand before leaving me all alone...with the doctor. Who was about to enroll me in agent school. My stomach flip flopped and I fought the urge to puke.

Chapter 7

Sitting in a paper gown on a cold ass–pun intended–examination table was *not* how I wanted to start my career as an FBI agent. It wasn't horrific, except my butt cheeks kept sticking to the paper. Then the questions began. I told my story once again to the middle-aged doctor who smelled slightly of peppermint. I wasn't sure if it meant his blood was palatable to me or if he had a fondness of breath mints, but I tried to ignore it. If he had power, it wasn't much. The whole time I talked and answered his questions, he poked and prodded and measured and touched. It went quite well until he tried to take a blood sample. He just couldn't get the needle to pierce my skin. I gently grabbed the hollow syringe and pushed it through my skin until it filled, and then handed it back to him.

I had seen my blood before, but never in such quantities. I couldn't smell it because it pumped directly into an airtight little capsule, but the sight of it made me hungry. I might have even growled a little, because Dr. Gibbs gave me a startled glance.

"How long has it been since you last fed?"

"Two nights ago," I answered

"How often do you usually feed?"

"I need to eat every other night."

"Morello told me of your diet requirements. Have you ever fed off a lycanthrope?"

I knew from watching television some people used the term to describe weres, but I hadn't met one yet. I shook my head, and he left the room after letting me know he would be right back. I waited on the cold table until he returned with a clear thick plastic bag with red liquid in it.

"Sometimes the lycanthropic recruits get hurt badly enough they need a transfusion before they can heal themselves. Human blood works all right, but lycanthrope is better, so we keep some in stock. Try this," he said, and handed me the bag.

It had a little blue plastic stopper on the bottom of it that I assumed was for piercing with an I.V. needle. I pulled the plug and sniffed the liquid. It didn't smell of the sweeter spices like cinnamon or vanilla, but rather the earthier spices like thyme and oregano. It smelled heavenly.

I squeezed the liquid into my mouth and the sensation dazzled my senses. I couldn't help but think if something tasted this good cold and from a plastic bag, a live lycanthrope would be pure winner-winner-chicken-dinner. Yummy didn't begin to describe the fiery liquid in my hand.

The exam continued while I sipped merrily from my lycanthrope juice pouch. The doc asked me if I would mind consenting to a MRI. I had a feeling it would be more for his benefit than mine, but I grew up watching television shows about emergency rooms and hospital dramas, so I kind of wanted to see the end result. Maybe I would learn a little more about myself. "No problem," I said, and followed him to the imaging room.

We entered a linoleum room with only one feature, a hollow metal tube with what looked like a cold table protruding from the end. The doctor asked me to get up on the table and he left through another door on the opposite wall. I walked over, climbed up, lay back, and the whole table slid into the tube. I heard him come over the intercom, telling me to relax. The machine began to hum and the magnetic fields danced over my skin. It tickled a little bit. I knew humans didn't feel a thing, so I made another tick mark in my mental "freak" journal. The list kept getting longer and longer.

Before I knew it, the MRI ended. The machine stopped its incessant humming and the door to the room opened. Slowly, the table I had been lying on slid from the machine, and I stared at ceiling tiles again. Doctor Gibbs smiled down at me and lent a hand to sit up. I didn't need it, but felt touched by his thoughtfulness, so I accepted.

"It will take a few days to complete the examination of all the data. I'll schedule a follow up and go over the results with you. I'm sure you're probably even more curious than I am. Come on, Ashlyn; let's get you set up in processing. They have all your information already, so you should be in your bunk shortly."

We made our way back to the exam room so I could change into my clothes and collect my things. Once I dressed, I met the doctor in his office, and he led me down the sterile hallways to a door labeled "New Agent Processing." He opened the door and let me pass through first. *Here we go...*

The front office looked just like I expected. Light tan

walls, plenty of filing cabinets, and a counter running the length of the wall. A bored looking, middle-aged woman sat behind the counter with a mountain of paperwork in front of her. She had to have heard the door open as we walked in, but she paid us no mind, merely kept on doing whatever occupied her.

We stood there for several minutes, and I saw an amused look on the good doctor's face. He briefly made eye contact before rolling his. Apparently, he had been in this situation before. I stifled a laugh and continued my wait. I was about to cough to politely announce our arrival when she finally spoke.

"Ashlyn with no last name?" Her voice came out as a raspy croak. It sounded like someone poured glass and gravel in a concrete mixer.

"Yes, ma'am."

"I have everything ready for you."

She began pulling papers from the pile in a specific order and stacking them face down neatly atop each other. When she finished, she flipped the whole pile over and smoothed the bottom edge against the countertop. She handed me the entire pile, a large number of cellophane tabs sticking out of the left side.

"Go through the papers and sign by the tabs. While you're signing your life away, I'm going to wrestle up someone to take you over to provisioning and get you to the dorms."

"Thank you, ma'am," I replied, and began reading through the stack. I grabbed the pen with the little beaded chain attaching it to the counter and began the long process of signing on the proverbial dotted line. Most of the paperwork contained the standard "do you agree" and “I hereby promise" type documents. Unfortunately, several copies of each filled the stack. I guess the old "fill these out in triplicate" rule still applied to the US government. I expected to get a hand cramp by the time I reached the middle of the pile, but didn't.

I did get a nice surprise though. A social security card slipped out from in between the stack. *How the hell had they arranged it so quickly?* I stared at the little card and its shades of blue and a wave of sentimentality washed over me. I pulled the card from its tiny paperclip and set it aside. I looked up and saw the doctor had sat down on one of two chairs I hadn't noticed were there. He stared up at the acoustic ceiling tiles lost in thought. The good doctor piqued my interest. I thought about asking him if he needed to get back to work, but I appreciated his company. I'm sure if he had more pressing issues to attend to, he would leave.

I returned my attention to my task. I resumed filling out forms I had never heard of, such as an I-9 and other various forms with alphanumeric titles. I found two other interesting things as well, one of them being a State of Virginia Identification Card. I signed the acceptance form and set the card on top of my Social Security card. I remembered the fake ID in my pocket and glanced around for a pair of scissors. A shining metal-handled pair sat in the desk organizer on Ester's side of the desk. I reached over to grab them and pulled the card from my pocket. My hands became a blur as I snipped the card piece by piece into a small pile of plastic bits. I doubted the doctor even noticed what I held in my hand before I destroyed it.

I swept the pile into my palm and looked around for a garbage can. Nothing. I guess recruits weren't allowed to create trash on this side of the counter. I stuffed them I my front jeans pocket. On the way to the dorm, I'd just scatter them on the grass.

Just as I finished, Ester walked back with a youngish man in blue sweatpants and a white FBI T-shirt.

Gorgeous.

He stood about five ten or eleven, and if I had to guess he weighed about a hundred and ninety pounds. Muscular arms extended from the slightly tight cuffs of his shirt, with beautifully dark skin. He looked like he had spent a fair amount of time at the beach. Most of his hair gleamed natural chestnut, but the outermost layers were streaked from the sun. Most surfer dudes you see on television have a stereotypical "dumb and stoned" look on their faces. When he looked at me, intelligence shined behind his eyes. While I ogled, I caught his smell.

For a moment, I was *very* glad the doctor had fed me. If he hadn't, I might have jumped over the counter and tore a hole in his neck…or other places. He smelled delicious. Several different spices layered his blood, but I couldn't name a single one of them. I had to curl my fingers into a fist to stop myself from making him dessert.

"Are you all done, dearie?" Ester's voice snapped me out of my reverie.

"Yes I am, ma'am. Here you go," I said as I handed her back the pile.

While she flipped through the pages one by one, checking

my work, my gaze drifted back to the hunk of Manwich behind her. His focus lay on the pile of papers before Ester. I had no way to tell if he was a fellow recruit or an instructor. Personally, I hoped for the former. If he held recruit status, I could daydream about him being my roommate. I doubted it, but a girl can dream if she wants, right?

"Thanks for staying with her, Doctor. We'll get her settled from here," Ester said.

The doctor stood and nodded to me, giving another brief smile. "Good luck, Ashlyn. I'll have someone contact you about the follow up to your exam. Have a good day, Ester. You too, Agent Walker." He then left through the glass doors.

So, he was Agent Walker? Hunky had a name–unfortunately, with the word "agent" in front of it. I guess I wouldn't be bunking with him. Damn it.

"Excellent. Everything is complete. If you would follow Agent Walker, he'll help you secure your personal effects and get you suited up for your stay. Good luck," Ester said to me without offering a handshake.

I looked up at Agent Walker and he pointed at the door to my right. I walked over to it, and an electric buzzing noise came from the latch as I pulled the door open.

Agent Walker led me down the hall to another large windowless steel door. When he opened it, sunlight poured from the exterior of the building into the hallway. I gave a little scream and closed my eyes. I instinctively jumped back about ten feet, putting my body well outside the range of the sunlit square. I blinked rapidly, screeching, "Shut the door!" Tears poured freely from my eyes, preventing me from seeing anything.

The door slammed close as Agent Walker's hands encircled my upper arms. "Are you okay? What happened?"

I still couldn't see, but I managed to blurt out, "The fucking sun!"

"Are you all right? What are you, a vampire?"

"Yes!" Time stopped for a moment with the realization of what I had said pierced my heart. I had spent seventeen years denying what I truly was and in a moment of panic, I subconsciously came to the realization of my true heritage. I may be a little different than a Nosferatu, a common vampire, or a master vampire, but aren't they different from each other as well?

His hands released their grip after my little revelation.

"I'm sorry, but it caught me by surprise. My eyes are very sensitive, and now I have a headache. Damn, usually I can feel the sun, but it must have breached the horizon while I was getting my MRI."

"I'm sorry, too. Nobody told me about you. I thought vampires burst into flames when you got exposed to sunlight?"

"I'm a little different. Trust me."

"How am I supposed to get you to the dorms?"

"Just get me a blanket, I'll be okay."

"Wait here, " he said, and stood from his crouched position. His footsteps grew faint as he retraced our previous path, hopefully to retrieve a blanket.

Moments later, two sets of running footsteps raced down the hall. I opened my eyes and looked behind me to see the blurry forms of Agent Walker and Doctor Gibbs with his hands around a dark gray blanket.

"Ashlyn, are you okay? I'm sorry. I didn't realize the sun had come up! Is there anything I can do?"

"I'm fine. I just want to go to sleep. Can you guys guide me? I won't be able to open my eyes." I tried not to sound too pathetic.

They lifted me to my feet, and Doctor Gibbs handed me the blanket. I unfolded the scratchy wool blanket and threw it over my shoulders, walking over to the door and pulling the cover over my head. I wore jeans and tennis shoes so I didn't have to worry about getting sunburned there. Closing my eyes, I gave my guides a muffled, "I'm ready." The door opened and warmth washed over the blanket. I closed my eyes even tighter because I could feel the sunlight bouncing from the floor below me and up into the confines of my shroud.

Verbal directions came from Agent Walker. He told me when to step down and up, walk forward, turn left until we reached another door. Someone opened it and instructed me to move forward. I kept walking, the door creaking shut behind me. The change in temperature told me I had moved out of the sunlight, but I wasn't taking any chances by removing my blanket without verbal direction to do so. The guys pulled me along until we reached another set of stairs leading up. I hoped we had almost reached our destination. Holding on to my backpack and the blanket had gotten more difficult every moment.

"Stop here for a second. There's a window at the end of the hall. I'm going to switch your room. I had you in a dorm room on the other side of the hall. Unfortunately, it is the side facing out. The ones on your right don't have windows. I need to go get a key to let you in. Doc, stay with her, would you."

Sleep overwhelmed me a little, so I slunk down the wall to sit on the floor.

"You doing okay?"

"I'm fine, just exhausted," I told him.

I sat there in my little wool cocoon for about ten minutes until Agent Walker returned. He ran down the hall, his feet thumping quickly on the linoleum floor.

"Here you go, Ash. I'm unlocking the door." The sound of the key entering the lock clicked right before the swish of a doorknob turning.

I let them guide me into my room. A light switch flipped and the door closed behind me.

"Is it okay if I take this blanket off now?"

"Go ahead. It's safe. Welcome to your new dorm for the next seventeen weeks," Agent Walker said.

I lifted the blanket from my head and looked around the room. Cream-painted concrete blocks formed the four walls. It had been designed for two people to share, but apparently, I was lucky enough to be the sole occupant for now. The room itself had symmetry. If someone held a mirror down the center of the room, it would look exactly the same The closet and a part-desk, part-bed combination sat on one side, with the matching setup on the other, just facing the opposite way. Hopefully I wouldn't end up with a roommate.

"There's a bathroom down the hall. It's a community shower, so you'll need to share, and there's a commissary down on the first floor if you need to buy toiletries or snacks. The dining hall is the next building over. I'll come by a little after sunset and check on you. Classes won't start till tomorrow so don't worry about it. In the meantime, I'll have maintenance spray paint the window in the hall black in case you need to use the lavatory facilities. There's a padlock in the desk if you want to lock the closet. Get some rest and I'll see you tonight," Agent Walker said and sighed.

"Good night, Ashlyn," Doctor Gibbs said, and laughed at his own joke.

The two of them left, the door closing behind them. I set my backpack in the closet and stripped out of my clothes. I tossed them in a pile by the desk, opened the top drawer, and found the little combination lock. I followed the directions on how to open the thing and memorized the combination. After putting it through the locking rings and snapping it shut, I secured my cash and clothes away for the day. Exhaustion crept back into my limbs. I stumbled over to the bed and lay down on top of the blue coverlet. I yawned and thought about putting on a T-shirt in case someone came in. *Eek, a naked vampire!* I laughed, my brain finally shutting down as I fell asleep, never making it to the closet for my T-shirt.

Chapter 8

Incessant knocking finally woke me. I glanced at a small digital clock next to the bed–7:05.

I dragged my exhausted carcass from my bed and headed to the door. I caught my reflection in the full-length mirror mounted on the door before opening it, and thank gods I had. I looked at a reflection of a naked me. My fuzzy brain told me I had put clothes on last night, but obviously, I had been dreaming.

"Hold on a second!"

I opened the closet after fumbling with the annoying little combination lock, and fished out some clean jeans and a T-shirt, the last of my clean clothing. I needed to do some laundry if I didn't want to start recycling dirty clothes. I fumbled with the jeans and finally succeeded in pulling them on over my hips. The T-shirt presented a much easier task. Once on, I walked to the door.

Agent Walker stood in the hall, waiting. His arms were crossed, his hands gripping his extraordinarily taut biceps. He had on sweats and an FBI T-shirt again, but I could tell he wore a different set than he had on last night. The shirt seemed a little tighter to start with, and the pants he wore last night had a hole about the size of a match head right above his right knee. His attention seemed focused on something down the hall when I opened the door, but then he turned his torso to face me.

"Good evening, Ashlyn. Are you ready to go?

"Sure, give me a minute. Come on in."

I held the door for him as he crossed the threshold. He sat down on the desk chair and crossed his legs while I put on a clean pair of socks and my tennis shoes. I locked up my closet, ready to go.

"Do you need to use the lavatory?"

I shook my head. One of the greatest advantages of being me is that I didn't need potty breaks and I woke up without morning dragon breath. I rarely even showered, unless I had been playing in the dirt. My body had no scent or sweat glands so it just wasn't necessary. Although, I will admit, I did like the feel of standing under the water.

"Where are we headed?"

"Since classes don't start till tomorrow, we're going to get your standard issue FBI training clothes and essentials. We need to hurry, though. A lot of the offices stay open all the time, such as processing and medical, but some don't. Provisioning is one of them."

"Let's go, I'm ready."

The provisioning department lay nestled on the bottom floor of a building I hadn't been to before. There we met a middle-aged man in green camouflage. Hat, jacket, and pants in olive greens and browns from top to bottom shouted military.

"Staff Sergeant, I have another recruit for you," Agent Walker said to the man in green.

"This little thing is your new agent in training? The FBI sure picks 'em before they're ripe. You sure you don't want to let her grow a little first?"

"Nah, they're harder to train when they're ripe. Too set in their ways like most marines I know."

The banter between the two continued for several minutes. The marine insulting the FBI, the FBI making fun of the intelligence quotient of the marines, and then they switched to insulting each other's maternal lineage. I found it all quite fascinating until the testosterone levels became a too high in the room. I coughed just a little to "clear my throat," and they both turned their attention to me. I smiled apologetically at each of them, but my ploy worked.

The staff sergeant turned behind him and started looking through cubbies of sweats and shirts. He found my size and plopped down five T-shirts in cellophane packaging and five pairs of folded sweat pants. He returned to the cubbies and grabbed what looked like two sweatshirts and added them to my pile. A bag of tube socks went on top of my growing stack as well as a pair of running shoes. The shoes being the only item he asked what size I preferred. He did a double take when I told him a size eight. My foot is actually a six, but if I didn't want my claws poking through the front of my shoe, I'd need an eight.

After he deposited the shoes, he pulled a black nylon shoulder holster from a storage locker. I could identify it only from watching late night episodes of NYPD Blue. I did have a problem though, I'd never witnessed someone put one on in the television show. It wasn't wrapped or boxed, so I had a feeling I would have to give it back after training. While I stared at the contraption, the Staff Sergeant disappeared around a corner. I heard a large metal door swing open and then close again with a large bang. The gunnery sergeant came back into the room with a box in his hands.

Placing the box on the counter with the rest of my gear, he pulled a sheet of paper off the top of his desk area and set it and a pen in front of me. He told me to sign for the weapon and placed the sheet of paper in a file folder on his desk. Moving to another storage closet on the back room of the hall and opening it, he pulled out a pair of safety glasses with yellow lenses still in their blister pack, and a water bottle with belt and clip. Again the items made their way to my growing pile. I grabbed the water bottle and handed it back to him. He placed the item back on my pile and turned away before I could hand it back to him again.

He made his way back to the desk and grabbed a different form. Placing it on the counter, he began checking boxes next to items. When he finished he turned the sheet around and told me to sign that one as well. I complied and thought about trying to give him back the water bottle I would never use, but just gave up on it. It'd find a home in my closet.

"You're done, miss, you have it all," he said as he pulled a plastic bag from underneath the counter, sliding it over to me. "Thanks for shopping at FBI mart. Flip the closed sign on your way out would you, Walker?"

"Come on, Ashlyn. Let's get all this stuff back to your room. Is there anything else you need? We could stop by the campus store," Walker said.

"Actually I do need a few things. Let me take this to my room first and grab some cash. Wait right here." I walked around the corner and vamped it up. I shot back to the dorm in a few seconds and then had the door open and the items stowed away in a few more. I wanted to blend in as much as possible so I stripped my clothes and threw on the tee and sweatpants combo and changed my shoes and socks. I grabbed a handful of twenty- dollar bills, stuffed them in a pocket with my room key, and stood in front of Walker in less than a minute.

"Ready?" I know I had acted a little childish showing off for the hunky agent.

He gave me a double take and looked around to see if anybody else saw my little stunt. Satisfied no one else was around, he just shook his head at me.

"Ashlyn, your class is going to be mostly made up of supes, and it's fine for you to be more than human during training on the obstacle course or hand to hand combat, but not around the campus. We consider what you did showboating for the norms, and they don't like seeing it, okay?"

My heart sunk about six inches lower in my chest. I wanted to impress Walker, not end up the recipient of a lecture. I knew he wasn't normal; I could smell it on him. "Okay. What kind of supe are you, anyway?"

Shock skidded across his face. "I'm a werewolf. How did you know?"

"I can smell it on you. It's what makes me different from

other vampires. I can't feed off 'normal' humans. I can only drink from supes. If it's someone I can feed from, I catch a scent from them." I watched his face for any signs of revulsion, but I found only sympathy.

"You don't like being a vampire, do you? I can hear it in your voice. How long have you been one? How long did it take you to get used to it?"

"I don't know. I've always been a vampire. I have never been human," I replied. Telling people I was a vampire kept getting easier every time I did it. Confusion colored Agent Walker's face, so during our walk to the campus store I told him my story. I really needed to get a digital tape recorder, and then just hit "play" and let my story run in the background. I could even add some sad music and kind of make it like my theme song. I could play it whenever I walked into a room!

We reached the store long before I finished with my story, so we waited outside for the remainder of it. I decided I liked Walker, even after his little lecture earlier. I had hopes for a "Gosh you've had a rough life, if there's ever anything I can do for you." But all he said was, "Wow."

"Thanks," I said with just a modicum of sarcasm.

I turned and entered the store. He came in behind me, saying he had to pick up a few things, too. The store carried mostly snack items for humans. The sort of items you would find in a drug store. Medicines and a thousand other items lined the shelves. The only thing that ended up in my hand was a toothbrush. I did like to brush my teeth. Wouldn't want to give somebody a neck infection.

I grabbed a pink toothbrush with hard bristles–I hate the

soft ones–and a tube of minty whitening toothpaste. The last thing I needed was yellow fangs. I went in search of what I really came in for, bras and underwear.

I found them in the rear of the store by the men's boxers and briefs. I wasn't expecting a "Victoria's Secret" but what I did see bordered on the pathetic, sports bras and granny panties. Oh well, it's not like Agent Walker had plans to ask to see them anyway. I grabbed a six-pack of each and stuffed them under my arm. I don't know why I bothered with them. Due to my unique physiology, I don't get my "monthly visitor," so feminine hygiene wasn't an issue for me, nor did I urinate. I probably had no reason, other than modesty, to wear them at all. Maybe I should give them up for Lent. As for bras, I suffered from a hellacious mammary deficiency. I wasn't completely flat, but I would never end up with back issues either. Let's just say I'd never end up with a job as a stripper. If it weren't for my nipples, I wouldn't even wear one.

Purchases in hand, I walked up to the register. I did stop along the way and pick up my one weakness, romance novels. I didn't realize until I set the little book down that the man on the cover art looked just like Agent Walker. I just looked at the title and author.

I placed the remaining items on the counter and looked up at the cashier, a lovely middle-aged woman of African heritage. She looked at my novel selection, smiled, and scanned the rest of my items, shoving them in a plastic bag. She told me how much and I handed her the money. As waited for my change, Walker came up behind me and put his candy bar, soda, and gun magazine down on the counter. When he had his items in hand, we left the store and headed back out into the cool night.

"I've got to get over to processing. Your class is seven recruits shy and the first of them will be here in about an hour. Feel free to explore, but don't leave the fence. Marine's on the base love to catch recruits where they shouldn't be. If you've got nothing to do and don't feel like exploring, you could come with me and help."

"Helping sounds like more fun than sitting in my room. At least I'll get to meet my classmates," I said as we started walking. "By the way, how is this going to work? Am I going to be trained separately from the rest of the class since I can't go out during the day?" Enquiring minds–mostly mine–wanted to know.

"Every month we start three classes. The first two classes are strictly human agents. Each class is separated by about a week with about ten to fifteen recruits. The third class is mostly supes, and there are usually only about five to ten people. Believe it or not, most supes will be working the night hours when they become agents so we prefer to train them at night. You should fit right in," he said and smiled.

We walked on in silence as I pondered the logic of their training schedule. We made it to the admin building without me even noticing, and for the remainder of the night, I helped Walker shuffle recruits from medical to processing and then to their dorm rooms. I ended up with a woman a little older than me who smelled like rosemary as a roommate. She introduced herself as Rose Gates, and she had just finished her degree in criminal justice. Her father, who worked as a Special Agent in

New York, had given her the upper edge when applying for the FBI. She didn't say much as I walked her to our room and I couldn't put my finger on it, but something about her raised my hackles. She was extraordinarily polite, and answered all my attempts at small talk, but something bothered me about the dark-haired beauty. I let it go for the moment and returned to help Walker finish.

The last recruit had a personal escort by marines in a matte green SUV with the initials M.P. stenciled on it with black paint. Out of the van stepped a willowy young man in his early twenties. I thought him cute in a boyish way, but his hair left something to be desired. I'm sure it passed the length set forth by some FBI standard, but it looked like it hadn't been combed or washed in a while. He entered the front door and meandered up to the counter, nervously glancing all around him. He gave his name–Brian Watson–to Agent Walker and then began the routine. I waited while Walker found his name and room assignment, then I took him to medical. I waited outside during his physical, and when he returned, I took him over to the dorms. I wished the newest and last recruit good luck and then headed to my own room for the day. I still had a few hours of night to enjoy, so I pulled my book out of the closet. I had no idea where my roommate could be, nor did I care. I enjoyed the solitude I had grown accustomed to and read.

The sun peeked just below the horizon, and I knew it would rise any moment. I put my book down next to the bed and lazed on my back. I had one leg over the side and let it dangle a few inches from the floor while my thoughts drifted from the events of the day to a certain hunky agent named Walker. How they drifted to the unkempt dirty-haired youth I'll never know, but I dreamt of him while I slept.

Chapter 9

The next night, I woke to Walker pounding on my door. He moved on to the next room, pounding their door as well. On and on he went four or five times and then he began the process again. I looked over and my roomie sat at her desk pecking away at the keys of her sleek little laptop. It made me homesick. My computer at home had been a desktop and way too large to bring with me. I resolved to buy one of the sleek lightweight computers as soon as I finished my training.

I rose from my bed–not coffin–and walked over to my closet. I gave a mumbled "good morning" to Rose, who mumbled something back to me. I wasn't sure if she said, "good evening" or "go fuck yourself," nor did I care. I threw on some shoes and clothes, and grabbed my toothbrush on the way to the community bathrooms.

Five minutes later, I waited outside my bedroom door with Walker and several others. Five recruits stood ready and we had to wait for five more. I leaned against the wall and crossed my arms. Rose was completely dressed and playing with her computer, so the fact we had to wait on her irked me to no end. Our number rose from five to nine over the course of two or three minutes, and only after the ninth came out, did Rose make her entrance.

Walker raised an eyebrow at her and she smirked behind his back. I realized what it was I didn't like about her. She was a bitch. I rolled my eyes and followed the others behind Walker out of the building after he hollered, "We're going to start off with a little run, so follow me."

We ran for an hour, covering gods knew how many miles. Everyone kept up the pace except for willow-boy Brian, who kept falling behind. During those times, we would keep running in a circle about the size of a house with Walker in the lead while Brian caught his breath. I wondered what kind of supe he might be. *Maybe a weresloth.*

We finished the run at about eight thirty. Everybody seemed winded by the time we finished, except me. Let's hear it for not needing oxygen. My familiar hunger raised its ugly head, though. I was going to need a juice pouch from the doctor pretty soon. As everyone stood around panting and stretching after the run, I happened to glance over at Rose. Sweaty and disheveled, she stared at me. She looked pissed off six ways from Sunday, and I couldn't figure out why.

"People, you received water bottles for a reason. I ran you a little extra hard tonight because I didn't see a one of you wearing them," a winded Agent Walker called over everyone's bowed heads. "Get to your rooms and fill them, and I'll see you back here in five. Go!"

Everyone scrambled for their rooms, even Rose. Walker walked over to me and shook his head smiling. I heard him mutter a "show off," but he never lost the smile so I didn't think I had earned myself another lecture. "Please tell me you're a little tired," he said.

"Please don't ask me to lie to you, Agent Walker," I replied, smiling. "I don't have to breathe nor do I sweat, so sorry. The only thing this does is make me hungry."

He paled a little at my last comment, and I wondered if I had shared a little too much, but he swallowed and shook his head in understanding. The others started returning one by one, and shockingly, Rose made her way back last. She had obviously dried her face, changed her shirt, and brushed her hair, but the water bottle sat in its sling on her side.

"Ladies and gentlemen, we will be doing this every day so get used to it. Brian, I suggest you quit smoking, and don't tell me you don't because I can smell it on you. Now if you will all follow me, we will be heading to a classroom for weapons safety." He ignored the groans from the rest of the recruits.

So it went for the remainder of the night. We learned proper shooting techniques, weapons care and cleaning, and the basics. We also learned when to use deadly force–you can't shoot someone for running a red light, damn it. After weapons safety, we had administration classes on the chain of command, proper procedures and so on. By the time they released us to head back to our rooms, I felt exhausted and starved. Sun up wouldn't be for another four hours, but I decided to just take a shower and relax. I could hold out on eating until tomorrow.

Chapter 10

The second day Agent Walker roused us in the same fashion, pounding on our doors repeatedly. Again, Rose exited into the hallway last, and everyone had their water bottles. We exercised for an hour before being led to a large gymnasium. A new instructor stood in the middle of the large room. Mats covered most of the floor, the standard blue ones seen in most gymnastic competitions.

We filed in behind Walker and he motioned us to stand along one side of the makeshift arena. He introduced us to Darenthalis, weapons master and combat trainer. It took me a minute to catch my breath–figuratively–from his beauty. Most men you would use the word handsome to describe, but not him. I realized he wasn't a man, at least not a human male. He had long blond hair down to his waist, and poking out from those golden tresses stood the points of his ears. He belonged to the race known as the fey, an elf, or maybe even one of the Sidhe. He wore a traditional martial arts gi, the kind you find in every karate class, but his resembled black silk and probably cost a small fortune.

"I am Darenthalis, and you will please address me as such. My name is not Daren, nor master, nor sir. I will instruct you in hand-to-hand combat techniques, mundane weapons, and firearms. Many of you are wondering why I will teach you mundane weapons, and the answer is simple. As entities of the non-natural world yourselves, you will be required to enforce your laws on many of those who dwell in this land. I shall teach you to use swords and knives of steel and of silver, but more importantly, I will teach you which one to use against which enemy. I teach you these for the simple reason many things in this world a gun won't kill. That is lesson number one," he said as he walked up and down the line and spoke to each of us in turn.

He asked each of us our names and what made us supernatural. When my turn came, I stated my name and told him "vampire." Surprise crossed his face, matching the mumbled surprise of most of my class. The two recruits standing closest to me sidled away a step or two unconsciously. Darenthalis shocked me by not stepping away. I learned the willowy Brian practiced magic, and Rose was a werewolf. The remainder of the class hailed a mix of werewolves, lions, and bears, and one oriental gentleman claimed to be a weretiger.

He told all of us to sit and watch while he and Agent Walker faced off against each other, and I swear I heard Walker groan before stepping on the mat. Walker crouched while Darethalis stood straight and waited for Walker to make the first move. Walker growled and lunged at the tall elven warrior. Darenthalis held up his hand and a flare of blue light struck Walker in the chest, blasting him back and landing him on the hard floor outside the matted area.

"The second rule of combat, is always expect what you

don't see. All of you would have made the same mistake as Agent Walker. You see a warrior, so you expect to fight with your hands, but remember this, there are many beings out there who would much rather attack you from a distance, and then close in for the kill. I need another volunteer. Perhaps you, young vampire," he said, and pointed at me.

I gulped and stood from my little section by the edge of the mat. I slid off my tennis shoes and stepped onto the mat in only my socks. I had pulled them on loosely to not rip through them with my talons and the ends remained intact.

I stood before Darenthalis. He bowed, so I did the same. I had never in my life taken any self-defense or karate lessons, but I had seen enough on television to know what he expected. I opted for something he wouldn't. I used my vampiric speed to circle around him and push him from behind. I had just made it behind him and turned to make my attack when he spun inhumanly fast and grabbed my wrist. He used my forward momentum against me, spinning me in a somersault. Instinctively, when I landed I jumped high into the air and looked down at my opponent. Anger clouded my vision as I leaned forward in a downward strike. I aimed my fist at his chest as I dove. I saw the same blue glow coming from his hand and the flash of light coming toward me mid-air, along with a smile on his face.

The blue glow struck me dead in the chest while about ten feet away from him. I expected to be blasted back, just like Agent Walker. I expected a lot of things, pain, shock, or even a sizzling sensation, but nothing happened. I didn't even feel it. It felt like my body absorbed it and liked it. His smile changed from superiority to shock, and I struck him full in the chest with my closed fist. I landed on my feet and Darenthalis went flying. He landed just before the outskirts of the mats on the far side of the makeshift arena.

I felt horrible. I hoped I hadn't hurt him and ran to his side. Walker almost beat me to the fallen warrior. Darenthalis looked up at me with fear in his eyes. He must have thought I was attacking him because he swung at me. It must have been the look on my face that halted his swing mid-strike.

"Are you okay?"

"Have you ever fought anyone before?"

"Not until recently. I'm sorry I hit you so hard."

"Stay with me after class. We need to see exactly what your limitations and strengths are. For the rest of the class, please just observe," he said with a grin, and raised himself to his knees and then eventually to his feet.

I turned to find the rest of the class staring at me like I had several extra appendages and heads suddenly sprout from my torso. Blushing, I walked over to a small set of bleachers along one side of the gymnasium. I watched the remainder of the class in silence. Walker took my place as the other recruits paired off for fighting techniques. The others rolled and punched and threw each other across the padded surface. Darenthalis walked around each of them, gave pointers, and pointed out errors. It looked like he was walking with a little limp, and I felt another twinge of guilt.

Soon Walker called an end to the class and lined them up to head to more administration instruction. He motioned me to stay put. Rose glared at me angrily. After everyone had left,

Darenthalis came over to where I sat forlornly on the bleachers. He stared at me for a few moments and then made a motion for me to follow him. We left the gymnasium and walked up the stairs to a loft-like area with weight benches and a small armory. I looked around at the gleaming axes, swords, and nunchucks. The variety of weapons surprised me.

In the back of the room sat a small office. Darenthalis turned the handle of the wood and glass door as I rushed to catch up with him. He held the door open and ushered me in the small room. A silver CD player pumped soft melodious music over its speakers. I found the music eerie and beautiful at the same time, and unlike anything I had ever heard before in my life.

"Sit please," he said, breaking me from the spell of the music.

I did as he asked, sitting in a comfortable chair made of wood. "I'm sorry," I began, but he quickly silenced me by raising his hand.

"You have nothing to be sorry for, child. You simply reminded this old fool to follow his own first two lessons. How is it you had no idea of your own strength, nor have lived in the world of the vampires and never had to fight? Are you recently turned? And what of your master?"

Apparently, no one had clued in Darenthalis about my unique lineage, so I eased back into my chair and told my story for the millionth time. I could see the interest he had for my tale in his beautiful green eyes. I hoped maybe he could provide me with some answers. When I got to the part of my tale when I shared the differences I had noted between me and regular vampire subspecies, he inspected my hand. I slipped my cool-skinned hand into his fiery grip. He turned it from palm down to palm side up and ran his finger along the length of my index talon, testing its strength and sharpness.

The intimacy of the gesture sent a chill down my spine and sent stirrings to other parts of my anatomy I'd rather not mention. I had never before been this close to a male human, let alone elven warrior. I shifted uncomfortably in my seat, and he released my hand. I pulled it back and placed it in my lap as I finished my tale.

He sat thoughtfully for a few moments, and then said, "Tell this tale to no one else. If anyone else should inquire, tell them you are simply a vampire. The more people who know the truth, the more dangerous it could be for you. I will share this wisdom with Agent Walker as well. Come with me back down to the arena. I wish to test you a little further."

I really didn't want to fight Darenthalis again. I felt bad enough for scoring the first hit on him to begin with, but I followed him nonetheless. We faced off against each other on the mat for the second time. He told me just to stand there while he tried to work some more magic against me. The blue light sped from his hand and struck me again in a shower of brilliant sparks. Tiny white missiles flew from his fingertips and struck me with the same result. The same happened with the ball of fire and the lightning he casually lobbed at me as well. Then I stood as he cast a globe of shining opalescence around me, and he told me to walk to him. It didn't even tickle my skin as I walked right through it and heard it pop like a massive bubble.

"I don't believe my eyes," he said.

"What?"

"Over my thousand years of life, on many occasion I have had to fight every type of vampire. Never before has my magic failed me. Either there is something wrong with my magic, or you are just completely impervious to it. There is a young mage recruit in your class. Tomorrow, I will have him try. Only then will we have our answer. Come, now I want to test your speed and strength."

Moving about the arena and lifting heavy objects is how I spent the rest of the night. He ran me through a series of speed, strength, agility, and reflex tests, which surprised me. Not with the test themselves, but at how well I did. I think I surprised Darenthalis as well because after every test he gave me a little nod of approval. By the end of the night, I still hadn't eaten and resolved to go see the doctor before I went back to my dorm room.

"I think you've had enough for tonight. We still have seventeen weeks to train and test your limitations. Are there any other gifts you have I should know about?"

"I've told you everything I know, but if I make any discoveries, I'll tell you right away. Thanks for the lessons Darenthalis. I'll see you tomorrow."

"Thank you for the refresher course as well." He smiled, bowed, and bid me goodnight. I made my way to the medical building for a "juice pouch" before heading back to my room for the rest of the night.

Chapter 11

I woke the next evening before sunset. I hadn't showered the night before and decided it would help wake me up. I glanced around the room and there wasn't any sign of my roommate. Maybe my luck had taken a turn for the better.

I showered quickly, dressed, and waited outside the door with several other recruits for Agent Walker. We didn't have to wait for long. He opened the door to the dorm and saw most of us waiting for him. He smiled and began knocking on the doors of those recruits who weren't ready yet, and they joined the rest of us in the hall. Rose still hadn't made an appearance though, and I found myself hoping she had quit. As soon as the thought crossed my hopeful brain, she came in the door to the dorm. *Damn it.*

"All of you had weapons assigned to you during provisioning. Please bring your side arms and your shoulder holsters. We will be starting tonight's class at the firing range." Everyone returned to their rooms, including me and Rose. I went to retrieve the boxed weapon and holster from my closet. I didn't say anything to my roommate as she got hers; I just went back out into the hall to wait for the others.

When everyone had finished, we followed Walker down the path to a new building. He opened the doors and we filed in one after another. The range itself looked kind of like a bowling alley with a countertop running its length instead of the open pit areas with ball returns. Alleys ran down perpendicularly to the counter top and behind the firing area sat the control booth. A concession stand and bar would have topped the whole thing off.

Darenthalis waited for us as we entered. He told us to take our weapons out of the packaging and to sling them in our shoulder holsters. Most of the recruits had already eagerly unpacked said weapons and just slid them into the holsters. The rest of us fumbled with the boxes and wraps, finally putting them away. Everyone except Rose fumbled with the unfamiliar straps of the shoulder rigs, but she put hers on with practiced ease. Apparently, someone in her family, probably her daddy, had taken her to the range before. *Bitch.*

I'll admit I cheated. Instead of fumbling like a fool, I stood around and watched everyone else as they successfully slipped into the harnesses. After witnessing the live demonstration, I wrapped the rig around myself and clipped it into place, having to adjust the plastic buckles to tighten it enough to where it wouldn't slip. I found the whole contraption pretty damn uncomfortable. On television, most police dramas showed people with the side arm holster attached to their belts. Maybe I should invest a little of my cash into one of those.

Darenthalis directed us to individual little stalls. Someone had stacked clips of live ammunition on the counter in each stall. Safety glasses and earplugs sat right next to those Nerves and anxiety crept through my body. I had never shot a weapon before, nor did I like the idea of starting. Something told me they wouldn't just let me skip this part, though.

We listened to a short safety sermon delivered by Darenthalis, as well as a set of instructions on how to raise our hands when the clip clicked empty. Darenthalis or Agent Walker would come up behind us and monitor our progress on changing out the clips. Seemed like a plan to me. I had no idea what to do, anyway. He demonstrated how the trigger safety worked on the Glock 22 and 23, as we had been issued both as a group depending on our hand size. I didn't even know which one I had until I noticed the 23 etched into the cool matte black weapon.

He barked an order to wait for one of them to help us initially load the gun. Once loaded, we would be given the go ahead to start firing at the paper targets at the midpoint of the range. He then told us to put our safety glasses and earplugs on.

Ten recruits and our two instructors donned earplugs and yellow-lensed safety glasses. My stall sat smack dab in the middle of the range, so I would be one of the last to start. Walker began at the recruit closest to the entrance, and Darenthalis began at the other end. A few moments later, a loud *pap, pap, pap* echoed throughout the room, only slightly dampened by the foam plugs in my ears. The noise continued until I felt a tap at my shoulder. I turned to find Darenthalis behind me.

"Load your weapon, Ashlyn," he hollered over the noise of several discharging firearms. I pushed a button that wasn't a safety since the Glock didn't have one. The empty clip discharged from the bottom of the handgrip into my left hand. I slapped the empty down on the counter and loaded a full clip in its place.

"Very good, begin firing," he hollered once again.

I held the weapon in both hands like I had been shown during weapons safety training and sighted down the barrel. I immediately felt something wrong and I couldn't put my taloned finger on what it was. As a rule, vampires can cease to move. When I say this, I mean it literally. We have no need to take a breath, our hearts don't beat like a normal human's, and we don't even need to blink our eyes. There is no movement we don't consciously control, but for the life of me, I couldn't hold the weapon still. My hands weren't shaking, but the weapon kept drifting to the right or left.

"Darenthalis, I can't do it," I called over my shoulder.

"What do you mean, child?"

"I can't hold the weapon still."

"Impossible, with your abilities, you should be able to carve your initials in the target's chest. What's wrong?"

The weapon felt like acid in my hand, and I wanted to drop it. If I could sweat, I would have. My body started to shake and I wanted to leave the range. I had to do it, though. The FBI required marksmanship for graduating the academy, but I didn't have to like it.

"I'll try again," I said, and fired the weapon.

The first shot went wide of the target by a foot. I could see the bullet as it sped down the range and struck the concrete wall behind the target. I tried to move the gun to the left and fired again with a little better result. The bullet struck the paper target, but not within the figure of the body, just in the white area. *Uh oh.*

"Try again, Ashlyn. You can do this," he called from behind me.

I had an inspiration. I couldn't hold the gun straight enough to shoot where I wanted to go because the gun felt unnatural in my hands. At that moment, I knew I would probably never fire it while working for the FBI, but I had to master it enough to pass the firearms portion of the academy. I let go of the gun with one hand, left it in my right, bringing the gun down to my side. Ignoring Darenthalis' questions behind me, I looked at the target in front of me and focused in on the center of the target's heart and let the sounds of the range fade away until the target became the center of my universe.

With a snap, I brought the gun up with one hand and fired. The entire action only took a fraction of a second, and the bullet speed down the range, striking the target in the left shoulder. I smiled at the improvement and that I had found a solution. I repeated my action and managed to get a group of shots going in the center of the "man's" chest. I could do this, but the strain became too much. My body wanted to be far away from the handgun; like it knew my natural armaments were far superior to the piece of manmade junk in my hand. I felt the urge to leap down the range and shred the paper target with my claws and teeth, but I fought it down. I guess fighting an enemy from a distance wasn't going to be an option.

I pulled the trigger again and the gun clicked empty. I felt relief surge through me, and I prayed my target practice had come to an end. My heart sank when the elven instructor told me to reload.

"Shit," I swore under my breath. I then popped the clip into my hand and slapped it down on the counter to grab a full clip. Without hesitation, I rammed the new clip in my weapon, raised it, and fired. The Glocks weren't automatic weapons, but I made it seem like one. I wanted it to be over and emptied the clip as fast as I could manage. I pulled the trigger in a blur of motion and tried to be careful not to pull the trigger while the semi-automatic weapon expelled the spent casing and chambered another round. I didn't know what would happen, but I knew jamming the weapon would probably be bad.

The thirteen rounds tagged the paper target one right after another and all tore through the targets torso. I hoped my best had been good enough. I wondered if I could excuse myself from target practice and just take the competency exam. I set the weapon down on the counter and spun to find Darenthalis staring at me curiously. I thought he might be angry at my automatic weapons fire, but he just looked at me like he felt sorry for me.

"The gun made you feel uncomfortable didn't it, child?" He removed his protective earplugs.

I nodded and did the same. "I can't explain it… I hated even holding it. Am I good enough to pass the test at least?"

"You'll never be on the SWAT team, but you're good enough to pass the exam, barely. I'm sorry. I've seen vampires shoot weapons before and be more than highly effective. Maybe it's something you can overcome," he said apologetically.

"I don't think so. I'll carry a gun if I have to, but I'm telling you right now, if I ever get into a situation where I need it, I'll probably never even reach for it. I'd have more luck throwing a chair or a car at an enemy."

"I bet you would," he laughed. "Head to the arena, we'll be there for the rest of the night. No administration classes today."

I made my way while the rest of the agents in training continued to unload their weapons.

I entered the gymnasium followed shortly by Darenthalis, and surprisingly enough by Brian, the recruit mage. Darenthalis must have wanted to conclude his little magic experiment before the others arrived. Darenthalis muttered something to Brian and he took his place out on the edge of the blue mat.

"Face off against Brian, if you would, Ashlyn. I want to conclude this test as quickly as possible. Brian, please hit the young lady with whatever you've got."

Brian nodded and turned toward me with an apologetic look. He brought his right hand out to his side and a nimbus of light appeared around the edge of his fingers and palm. Where Darenthalis' light had been blue, Brian's burned white. When his hand resembled a miniature sun, he brought the hand behind his head and flung it at me with all his strength. The ball of light sped toward me with amazing speed and struck me full in the chest. He had tried so hard, and I felt bad for him when it dissipated into nothingness.

"I both hoped and feared this would happen," Darenthalis

spoke solemnly.

"Does this mean magic can't hurt me?"

"Not directly, no. A mage could destroy something around you, and cause harm by doing so, but any spell cast directly at your body seems to be reflected or absorbed. I can see no shield around you, so I think yours is a physiological talent. I can deflect spells, but only if I cast a shield around myself first. Count your blessings, child, for it would seem you have many."

"Thank you, Darenthalis. I will."

The rest of the recruits came in behind Walker, and we trained for hand-to-hand combat again. I ended up paired off with Rose. Didn't Darenthalis just say something about counting my blessings? She seemed a little perturbed, and I couldn't imagine why. Once again, I had done nothing to the dark girl, and yet she still had issues with me.

I let my mind wander as she kept striking at me, trying to find a weakness in my defense. I hadn't even tried to take the offensive. She attacked inhumanly fast, but the speed of a werewolf couldn't compare to that of a vampire. I moved to block her attack and struck too quickly. One of my talons grazed her cheek, causing a bright line of blood to appear from her left ear down to her mouth. I started to apologize until I saw her eyes. They had changed from brown to a glowing yellow, and a snarl of challenge burst from her mouth.

"Rose, I'm sorry," I stammered, but she started moving toward me. "I didn't do it on purpose," I started again, but she wasn't listening.

She jumped, and in midair, her body tore itself to pieces.

Blood and other fluids rained down and a half-wolf, half-human form collided with me. I had a seven and a half foot werewolf on top of me.

Her muzzle stopped inches from my face as she tried to bite my throat. Drool and foamed spittle drizzled down on my face, and while I'm not squeamish, it wasn't pleasant. I held her shaggy head back by the throat with one hand and didn't know what to do with the other. I looked around and saw Agent Walker rushing over to break up the fight, but Darenthalis held him back. Apparently, I got myself into this mess and they had left it up to me to dig my way out.

I did the only thing I could think of. I tucked both legs up to my chest and braced my feet against Rose's belly. I surprised myself when I hurled her off me and into the far wall. She hit with a sickening thud and fell to the floor. I thought the fight was over, so I turned and started walking toward Walker.

Her jaws closed down on my neck before I heard her move. She had me from behind so there was little I could do. I had a five hundred pound werewolf with my neck in her mouth, and the only thing keeping her from biting my head off was the two hands I had gripping her muzzle. I may be a vampire, but I doubted I could live through the separation of my head from my neck. Healing the wounds I already had would probably be a bitch.

I had never really fought anyone in my life. I let my body take over and relied on survival instinct. Her massive strength pulled my feet from the floor, and I dangled from her maw like a torn chew toy. My own blood poured out of the wounds in my neck and soaked my shirt. Instinct took over, and I swung my legs over as my arms wrapped around her head. It finally gave me enough leverage to pull my neck free, but not before severing some serious tendons, arteries, and veins. The blood poured freely now, but I wasn't in danger of being decapitated. I released her head and wrapped my arms around her thick neck, digging my talons in to strengthen my hold. Their purpose became quite clear. Genetics had designed me to eat monsters and had given me the perfect utensils.

My body grew weaker by the moment from the sheer amount of blood flowing from my wounds. The hunger reared itself and I bit down on the side of her neck. Blood flowed thick and hot into my mouth as my wounds began to close by themselves. Strength returned to my hands and legs and I clutched her tighter. I twisted her neck and I stopped myself from breaking her vertebrae. I didn't know if it would kill her, but I'd probably get into a little bit of trouble if I did.

I drank enough to lull her into unconsciousness, and she stopped fighting against me. I released her neck from my powerful jaws and lowered her to the ground. She still breathed, telling me I hadn't gone too far, but I had been damn close. I hadn't wanted to stop feeding, and I did want to break her neck, but I couldn't bring myself to kill her.

Walkers' hands encircled my upper arms as he pulled me away from Rose. I didn't fight him and the battle rage had left me. I found myself cool and calm, like I had observed rather than participated. I had probably just ended my short stint as an FBI agent, but she had attacked me and I defended myself. I felt a little pride that I hadn't killed the stuck up bitch, and a little sorry I hadn't.

"I've called Doctor Gibbs, lie down. I've got to stop the bleeding," he said calmly.

I turned and gave him a "what are you talking about" scowl. I ran my hands over my neck and expected to find a mass of raw meat, but my skin had healed itself fast. It remained slick with blood, but still in one piece. I rotated my head and found no hindering from torn tendons and ligaments. "I'm fine," I told him.

He looked at me and tilted my neck to inspect it closer. He pulled back with a look of surprise on his face and let me go. "Sit down. At least and try to look like you've just been attacked by a werewolf. I'm going to have the doctor check you out anyway."

I sat down on the blood-covered mat and looked over at Rose. Who in the hell would name such a bitch after a beautiful flower? I gasped when I saw she had shifted back into human form and lay prone on her side. Her back faced away from me and I stared at her naked flesh. I blushed a little at the nudity. The wound I had torn on her neck remained, but it wasn't bleeding much. I focused my vision and could see the wound knitting together. It wasn't nearly as fast as I healed, but still impressive.

Doctor Gibbs blew through the door like a whirlwind. He rolled in a stretcher with him and brought a large man in a white shirt and pants, as well. *He must be a nurse or something*. Dr. Gibbs looked at me sitting there, covered in blood, and then at the prone form of my roommate. I could tell he didn't know who to treat first. I made the decision for him and nodded at Rose. He smiled quickly and told the nurse to bring the stretcher.

He examined the wound, placing some gauze and antiseptic over the injury on her neck, and rolled her over onto her back. I watched with little interest as he checked her vitals and began an IV drip in her arm.

"You fought brilliantly, child," Darenthalis said from behind me.

"I fought brilliantly? I almost got killed, and I almost killed her. I don't think brilliantly is the word you're looking for Darenthalis," I retorted with a little snort.

"The only error you made was turning your back on a werewolf. She didn't like you from the start. As you left the firing range, I saw her smile because you failed to be better at her for the first time since you both started your training. This academy is not set up to be a competition between recruits, but she saw it as such. With the exception of firearms, you do seem to have a knack for everything. She sees how fast you are and how strong you are and knows she can't compete."

I sat and digested his observations. I hadn't known, nor had I been paying attention. I wish somebody had told me, and then Walker's little speeches about showing off came back to me. I must have groaned a little because Darenthalis laid a hand on my shoulder even with the blood and all still covering me.

"I must admit, child, I used you a little. She has her flaws, but she has the makings of a great agent. The only remedy for superiority is humility. We could have stopped the fight before it started, and a wiser man wouldn't have paired the two of you together tonight. By all rights, we could expel her from the program, and if you wish it, we will comply, but I think she has learned the hardest lesson of all. No matter how tough you are there is always a chance you will come across someone tougher and stronger than you are," he said and smiled at me. I could tell he hoped I would take the lesson to heart as well. I did.

"Come, child, let's get you cleaned up," he continued, and helped me to my feet. He walked me all the way to the dorm room and asked if I would be all right on my own. He nodded as I said yes and then headed back to the gymnasium to clean the rest of the damage. I stopped at my room to retrieve my toiletries and showered for the second time in one night. I let the water wash away the troubles and the blood until even my nose couldn't smell it on me anymore. I went back to my room and locked the door. I didn't cry, but I wanted to.

Chapter 12

The next few weeks flew by in a blur. Walker moved Rose to a different room once she got out of the infirmary. She didn't protest and neither did I. She never said anything to me after the incident, or I to her. After the fight, she became *very* polite. I don't think she hated me; I just wasn't going to expect a birthday card anytime soon.

The rest of my training I spent sequestered from the remainder of the class. I had no need to continue with practice on the firing range, nor the hand-to-hand exercises. Instead, I worked one on one with Darenthalis learning weapons with names I had never even heard of. I also spent a lot of time learning mundane things like investigative techniques, legal, ethics, interrogation, and forensic science. They helped me overcome another problem, as well. Since I had lived my whole life secluded from the world, I had no high school diploma. They made me take an equivalency exam, which I passed easily. Walker himself gave me my certificate with a smile. It seemed to be a fatherly expression of pride rather than anything else. Damn.

At the end of the third week, I finally heard back from Doctor Gibbs. Walker knocked on my door at sunset and told me to double time it over to medical. I swallowed the lump, which had somehow lodged itself in my throat and left immediately. I wanted to get over there as soon as possible. I looked around the quad and saw no one. I ran so fast if anyone had been there to witness my breaking of the rules, they wouldn't have seen me anyway.

I entered the hallway leading to Gibbs' office and knocked on his open door. He sat at his desk with his nose buried deep in a file folder. Nervousness must have been evident on my face, because he smiled and motioned me to come in. I pulled out one of the chairs in front of his desk and plopped down with a *thud*.

"I've got good news and bad news," he started, and then laughed. I wanted to hit him. "All the results are in, including DNA and the MRI. Guess what. You're a vampire."

It hit me right in the heart. I had subconsciously accepted the fact a few weeks ago, but to hear the doctor say it became something else completely. "I don't understand," I said automatically.

"What don't you understand?"

"How is this possible? Vampires aren't born; they make other vampires through their bite," I said exasperatedly.

"I'll give you a scientific answer. I don't know. What I do know is you share chromosomal traits of *homo cruentus dominus*, but there's more. Some of the data is very confusing, and a lot of what I'm going to share with you is mere speculation, but it is the best I can do. *Homo sapiens* have twenty-three pairs of chromosomes as most people know. Vampires are a little different. I checked three times and Vampires are broken down into several subspecies. We'll go up the food chain," he paused and pulled out some notes. "*Homo cruentus dementus*, or revenants, have the base twenty-three pairs, but this is where they differ. Instead of gaining an extra pair, they gain only one chromosome. It's probably why they are mindless feeding machines and it's still legal to shoot them on sight. Next is *homo cruentus Informis*, or nosferatu. They end up with a complete extra pair of chromosomes giving them forty-eight, or twenty-four pairs," he said and paused to make sure I followed his logic.

I nodded my understanding, and let him continue his genetics lesson. "*Homo cruentus plurimus*, or the common vampire, has twenty-five pairs giving them fifty which is probably what makes them a little harder to kill than a nosferatu. *Homo cruentus dominus* has twenty-seven pairs. Fifty-four chromosomes are a lot of genetic information and is the main reason they are at the top of the food chain. No one can explain the jump from twenty-five to twenty-seven pairs, but most believe there is probably a missing classification along the line somewhere. They died out, Mother Nature goofed, or they are close enough to master vampires no one has genetically coded them. Me, I think it's probably the latter. Then we get to you, Ashlyn. Care to guess how many chromosomes are floating around in your DNA?"

Maybe it's an inferiority complex I had to deal with, but I blurted, "Twenty-six?"

"I'll give you a hint, you're getting colder."

"Twenty-seven?"

"You're getting warmer, but we don't have all night. You, my dear, have the base twenty-three, but there's more! Let's see what else you've won. You share all the genetic markers of the *dementus*, *informis*, *plurimus*, and *dominus*, so you have all twenty-seven of those. It's because of that I know you're definitely a vampire, and still there's more. Since you are different, and if I had to guess, I would have said twenty-eight pairs. I would have gotten a little closer, but still not good enough. You, my dear, have thirty-two chromosomal pairs giving you a total of sixty-four bits of genetic coding."

I didn't know what to say. I sat there and pondered the information he had given me, drawing a complete blank. I was a completely new subspecies of vampire, but still a vampire. Did this mean I get to name my new subspecies? Or did doctor Gibbs since he made the discovery? I decided I didn't really care. "Am I okay?"

"You are better than okay; you're perfect. It's why you don't burst into flame in the sun and probably why you can't feed off regular humans. You, my dear, are a predator of predators. Did you know you're only seven years old, or at least your cells are? You're never going to get old, and unless you come across something much stronger than you, you could live forever."

"Seven, but I was seven when I stopped growing, so I guess it makes a little sense," I pondered aloud. I had been excited when I first entered the office, and the Doctor had provided me with a lot of answers, but for every answer I received, three more got asked. Now the Doctor started squirming in his chair like a little kid.

"Do you want to know what the MRI showed?"

"You tell me. Do I want to know?"

"You definitely do. You have all twenty-three pairs of human chromosomes, so you have a complete set of human organs, but they don't work. Not a big mystery there, the same thing happens to vampires when they are turned. What's different is you have an amazingly dense skeletal structure. Regular vampires don't have this. They are super strong, but if they had one weakness, it would be their bones. Someone could theoretically hit you with a car doing ninety, and it might not break a bone. I couldn't even see bone marrow, just solid bone. When a human is changed, their marrow dies and they can't reproduce red blood cells, scientists believe it's why they have to consume blood. Same thing with you, but instead of wasting the space, your genetic code improvised. It's quite amazing."

"Yeah, it's quite amazing. Thanks, Doc," I said sarcastically. I went to stand but the doctor immediately ushered me back down.

"Wait, there's more! Your brain is different. You know how a standard human brain appears, right?"

I nodded.

"A rat's cortex is very smooth, and then as you move up the cognitive chain the more ridges in the brain are visible. Well most people don't like to admit it, but aquatic mammals like dolphins and whales have even more ridges in their cortex than humans. Most species of the fey who have volunteered for an MRI have even more than them. If I had to compare your brain, I would say it's more fey than human," he ended.

Ever hear the expression, TMI? I had heard it, and now I knew what it meant. I felt dizzy and like I might burst into flame. My brain was overloaded and I needed to get out of the tiny little room. I could tell Gibbs had more to say, so I held up my hand for silence. I am normally pale, but my hand looked positively ghost-like, and I think the Doctor finally noticed it as well.

"Are you okay?"

"No. I'm done. If there is anything else, please keep it to yourself. Speaking of which, are you going to share your findings with anyone?"

"I have to put all the information in your file, but I won't publish. The FBI plans to keep you safe, even if it entails doing it from other agencies, as well as the world at large. I'm sorry, I thought you would have shared my enthusiasm. At least you have some answers."

"And a thousand more questions, Doctor. Thank you

"Are you going to name yourself?"

"Excuse me, doctor?"

"*Homo cruentus* what? If you don't mind, I need to give you a name. Since it's yours, I thought maybe you would like the honor."

I thought about it for a minute and decided to let the Doctor have a little fun. He had done his best by me, and wouldn't be able to publish a paper with the potential to make him famous. "The honor is yours, doctor. Make it cool though," I smiled at him.

"Thanks, Ashlyn. The best of luck to you," he said, and stood to shake my hand.

"Thank You, Doctor," I had a forensic science class to get to. I considered skipping it and just heading back to my room to ponder what I had learned, but some roads lead to madness.

I entered the class, took my seat, and learned what I had to do to keep a crime scene fresh. The instructor introduced himself as Special Agent Williams, and he didn't like me very much. After class, I asked Walker about his apparent hostility toward me and he said Williams' last partner had been killed by a vampire a few years back. I didn't mind him hating me after that. I just kept my mouth shut and paid attention to what the man had to say.

Chapter 13

I colored in the answer bubble with the tiny little label "D" with my number two pencil. I had finished the final question of my final exam in Forensic Science, and after graduation I would be a bona fide diploma carrying, gun toting, badge wearing, bad guy catching, black suit wearing Agent of the FBI. Graduation would be tomorrow, the last Friday of January. Christmas had come and gone as well as the New Year without much fanfare or hullaballoo. All of the recruits had flown home for the holidays except for me. I had elected to stay in the dorms, and spent many of my nights with Darenthalis.

I had expected him to travel to whatever land he came from, but he didn't. I asked him why and he told me time moved differently where he hailed from. He wouldn't be needed back there for another three months before it became time to celebrate Yule. I pretended to understand, and nodded. I appreciated his company anyway.

I gathered my test booklet and raised my hand for the proctor to come and collect my final exam. A woman with both a severe hair and dress style *click-clacked* her heels across the linoleum classroom, taking both my test and little green answer sheet. I let out a sigh, gathered my things, and headed over to the dorms. I opened my door and glanced over to my bed. A box wrapped in beautiful paper sat on the top blanket.

Curiosity got the best of me and I went over to pick it up. I had thought the wrappings to be paper, but as I ran my hand over the beautiful fabric, I knew at once whoever wrapped it used silk. A ribbon wrapped around it, ending in an intricate bow on the top. The silk wrappings were dyed a dark hunter green, the ribbon and bow a luminous shade of silver. I had never seen silver silk in my entire life. In fact, the closest I had ever seen had been a mottled gray that gave the impression of silver. I couldn't resist slipping the ribbon over the corner of the box and removing the beautiful silk wrapping. I had no idea how whoever had wrapped it got the edges to stay together. I couldn't even decently wrap a package with paper and tape.

The box felt heavy and sturdy, but opened easily by sliding the top off the bottom. I gasped when I saw the dark gray silk pantsuit wrapped in a paper-like substance half as thick as tissue. I lifted the beautiful items out of the box and a white silk shirt and black patent leather shoes rested underneath. Inside one of the shoes lay another small box. I opened it to find gold cuff links and a small note on parchment paper.

I read the note and it confirmed my suspicions. Darenthalis.

I finally took my shower and began the arduous task of packing my single backpack. I put on my last clean set of sweatpants and T-shirt and decided to take one more walk around the campus. My tummy started growling at the same moment. I decided on stopping by medical to grab one last juice pouch from the infirmary and say my farewells to Doctor Gibbs.

Snow had started falling when I stepped outside the dorm. I watched the flurries swirl around the buildings and settle down on the frosty ground. At least they had a chance of sticking and not melting away too quickly. Virginia weather often became unpredictable around this time of year. One week hot, the next freezing, but I had always loved snow. Even as a child out in the nights of Chicago, I would always play in the snow.

I made my way over to the medical building and let myself in. I followed the familiar hallway to the good doctor's office and knocked. He sat in his customary position behind his desk and he smiled when he saw me.

"Ashlyn, I'm glad you came by. I feared I wouldn't get to see you again before graduation tomorrow."

"I didn't want to take a chance of you not being there and me not getting to say thank you for everything. Thanks, Doc."

"I'm honored for the opportunity to meet you. Are you hungry?"

"I could eat."

"Wait right here. I'll be back in a moment," he replied jovially and left to get me some dinner. I had eaten two nights ago, and probably could have waited until after the ceremony, but I didn't want to take a chance. My exams had been grueling and I must have expended a multitude of nervous energy for me to be this hungry. He returned with a, "Here you go," and handed me the cool bag of blood. I shook it for good measure and popped the rubber stopper on the bottom.

We continued our conversation while I ate. We talked about where I hoped I would get my first duty assignment, what cities I would be interested in seeing or living in, and how I thought I fared on my exams. Then he surprised me once again.

"I have named your subspecies by the way."

"Okay, what am I? *Homo cruentus painintheassicus* or *homo cruentus psychoticus*, which do you like, doc?"

"Your classification, pending your approval, is *homo cruentus imperator.* Emperor Vampire. I made you an emperor. Hope you don't mind."

I stared at him wide eyed. In fact, I felt them start to moisten and then tear freely. I stood and walked around his desk, bent down, and gave the sweet little man a hug followed by a kiss on the cheek. I couldn't say anything more to him without breaking down and crying, but I managed to croak out a "see you tomorrow," and left. I finished the pouch of blood in the hall, ducked into one of the labs to toss the remains in one of the biohazard bins, and went back to my dorm to have my breakdown. I thought of going to see Walker to brighten my mood, but seeing him would just make me cry, too. I sighed resignedly at how long the night would last.

I woke at sunset and found our grades posted in the hallway of the dorms. We had all been assigned a testing number and were told our scores would be under it. Now no one would know who failed and who passed. I needed at least an eighty-five percent on each of the nine exams I had taken to pass the academy. I searched the column of numbers and found my numerical designation. I took an unnecessary deep breath and ran my finger to the right to see my grades. The breath expelled after I reached the last grade. I had passed! With flying colors, actually. The lowest grade I received had been a ninety-one in interrogation. I could live with a ninety-one. If I had to guess, vampires would probably be pretty effective interrogators naturally.

I had two hours to kill before we had to be at the gymnasium for graduation. I took a long leisurely shower and did my hair. I thought about running down to the store and buying some makeup, but I figured why start now. Instead, I dressed in the beautiful suit from Darenthalis and decided to head to the gymnasium a little early. I really had nothing else to do. This way I could probably say my goodbyes before the place filled up. At least I wouldn't have to worry about my makeup running.

The snow still fell from a cold sky on my way to the gymnasium. I worried about the water from the snow settling and discoloring the silk in my outfit, but I looked down and saw the water beading up on my sleeve. Waterproof silk? I wouldn't have put it past Darenthalis to have magicked the damn thing. It might actually be bulletproof, too.

I reached the double doors and walked inside. The blue mats I thought permanently attached to the floor were removed and a portable stage had been wheeled in and set up, so had extra sets of bleachers. I wondered if they expected a crowd tonight. I settled myself on the lowest row of the closest bleachers and waited, but not for long. Noticing movement, I looked up at the railing separating the second floor from the drop off to the main floor and saw Darenthalis and Walker both standing there and waving me up.

I left my seat and headed up, counting the twenty-two stairs as I had every time I made the climb. I walked over to the elf and the agent and smiled at them both. Walker actually whistled at me so I did a little pirouette, showing off the gorgeous outfit my elven friend had gifted me. "You sure do clean up pretty, vampire," Walker joked.

"Thank you, kind sir, and you may thank the kind sir standing next to you for the beautiful outfit I'm wearing."

Maybe I shouldn't have told him. He turned his head so fast I think I actually heard Walker's neck snap. I looked at Darenthalis to see if I had offended him or gotten him in trouble, but he just smiled at me warmly.

"Has a vampire maiden finally thawed your icy elven heart, Daren?"

"Shut up, you mongrel dog. I simply rewarded a star pupil. I offered her your telephone number instead, but she turned it down, and for good reason! Flea collars are expensive."

I couldn't believe my ears. Daren? How long had these two been working together? I started laughing and couldn't stop. The words "flea collar" kept setting me off again and again.

"Shut up, tick," Walker retorted to me. "It wasn't that funny."

He started me laughing all over again. I would miss these

two, but I had a feeling I would see both of them again, sometime. I held out my hand to shake theirs, but I found myself pulled into two warm hugs instead. I felt like the crème filling in a hunk cookie, and I really liked it. The doors below leading to the outside world swooshed open and closed repeatedly. It sounded like the show would start soon if people had started making their way to the seating area.

"It's time, child. Go take your seat," Darenthalis told me. I hugged the both of them again and walked down the steps to where some of my class had already taken their seats. I slid onto the bleacher next to Brian Watson, our graduating mage. He looked down at me and gave a smile I returned.

The bleachers behind us began to fill up with middle-aged couples and individuals dressed for the occasion. My former roommate walked in and smiled at a gray haired gentleman in his late forties. He wore a black suit and tie over a J.C. Penny button up white dress shirt. This must be her father, Special Agent Gates. I sat there staring at the man wondering if Rose told him about me. I doubted it. She probably wouldn't want her father knowing his precious puppy had been beaten by the bloodsucking undead.

By the time the ten of us had seated ourselves on the bleachers side by side, Special Agent in Charge Morello strode through the front doors carrying manila envelopes and a stack of blue leather–probably pleather–certificate holders. I had already received one for the high school equivalency exam. I assumed these read "academy diploma." He strode purposely toward the dais at the rear of the gymnasium where he joined Darenthalis, Walker, and Dr Gibbs. A single podium occupied the center of the stage, and Morello took his place behind it. He tapped the microphone twice to make sure it had power and to get everyone's attention. The low murmur of voices quieted down and he began our graduation ceremony.

"Members and family of class 010903 welcome and be seated. This is the third graduating class of this year, and by far the most interesting. These members of the supernatural community are now valuable members of the Federal Bureau of Investigation. It is hard to come by such morally superior people in today's world, but these are shining examples of what it takes to be an agent of the FBI. I'm not going to sit here and bore you with speeches about what a difference you can make to save the world from domestic chaos. You already know it, or you wouldn't be here." He paused and let his gaze sweep the attendees. "You have what it takes to make a difference or you wouldn't have passed the exams and expectations of your instructors, who you may now look on as peers. I will congratulate all of you as you come to receive your diplomas, but let me be the first to congratulate you as a group for a job extremely well done. Congratulations to you, one and all."

The audience gathered was small due to the minimal class size we had of less than a dozen, but you wouldn't have been able to tell from the sound of the cheering at the conclusion of Morello's speech. Recruits, parents, relatives, and teachers all screamed with joy. I felt pretty lonely until I saw the beaming faces of my three friends on the stage staring at me.

"I will call your name, and you will please rise and come up to the stage to receive your diploma and your first duty assignment," Morello continued.

Brian Watson had the honor of being the first victim to be called to the stage. I watched his tall gangly form cross the distance to the stairs built into the dais. He entered on the right side and shook everyone's hands before proceeding to Morello to receive his diploma. Minimal clapping coming from behind us, made me guess Watson, like me, had come here without any family.

Morello called Rose's name next, and her father stood and vocalized his approval louder than anyone in the gymnasium. She repeated Brian's journey into agenthood. I found it a little odd, with as much as I despised Rose, I smiled at her graduating. I thought about Darenthalis' words to me, and silently agreed with him; she would make an outstanding agent. I wondered where her first assignment would be. Silently, I prayed for somewhere very, very far away.

The rest of the recruits followed suit and soon nine of us had received our diplomas. I felt a little nervous being the last one, but finally Morello spouted my one name. I walked across the floor to the dais and forced myself to take the steps one at a time.

Gibbs reached out to shake my hand. "Congratulations, Ashlyn," he whispered into my ear as he pumped my hand up and down.

I smiled back at him and rolled my eyes.

Darenthalis' handshake felt a little less enthusiastic but just as sincere. He didn't waste words on congratulations; he just beamed at me. I thought I saw a little pride in the corner of his right eye. *Nah, it couldn't be*. Walker smiled and stuck out his hand after Darenthalis motioned me on. I grasped his meaty paw and felt the warmth come from his grip.

He pumped my hand three times and mouthed a heartfelt, "Good job, kid."

I then faced Morello standing behind his wooden pulpit. He, too, smiled at me. I remembered his words about keeping an eye on me during my training, and wondered if he had. In his left hand he had my diploma and his right he had extended for me to shake. I crossed the remaining three steps and took both.

"I had a feeling this would be easy for you. Congratulations, Ashlyn," he said, but not within range of the microphone. "Wait here for a second." He turned back to the microphone and stared at the crowd.

"I'll like to make a special announcement," he said and my heart sunk into the pit I could have sworn used to be my stomach. "For many years the Federal Bureau of Investigation has been waging a battle against one of the toughest foes we have ever fought. Since vampires gained citizenship in this great country of ours, a few of them have struggled with abiding by our laws. In an effort to combat these few individuals, the FBI has made great strides in technology, which helped us to fight these menaces on a level playing field. Today we have achieved our greatest goal. I would very much like to introduce you to New Agent Ashlyn, the very first vampire to join the ranks of the FBI."

I'll admit it, I expected cricket noises, but something else happened entirely. Everyone, including Rose Gates and her father, gave a standing ovation. It should have made me feel special. Instead, I wanted to die. Morello's hand covered my shoulder. I fought the urge to shrug it off and turn around to slap him.

He leaned in to whisper in my ear. "I'm sorry, Ashlyn, the Deputy Director ordered me to give that speech. Please come to my office after the ceremony. You have a press conference scheduled at the Washington Field Office in two hours."

I should have known. I had been so intent on the FBI keeping my secrets. I didn't even consider them parading me around as their new vampire agent. I looked over at Walker and Darenthalis and saw their faces. They were even more agitated than I felt. Walker sighed resignedly and Darenthalis seemed like he wanted to invite Morello for a sparring match with edged weapons. *Silly Elf.*

Their anger made me feel a little better. When I glanced at Moreno, guilt washed over his face. His guilt made me feel a little better, too. Maybe it wouldn't be so bad, and maybe pigs across America would suddenly sprout avian appendages and take flight. I took my diploma and my packet of orders and returned to my seat. My fellow new agents slid a little farther away from me, all except Brian. I had a feeling not much fazed the willowy mage.

Morello gave his closing speech, and the new agents left to be with their families. I went to my room. I had just finished stuffing the remainder of my items in my backpack when I heard a tentative knock at my door.

"Come in!"

Darenthalis walked into my room. I had subconsciously been expecting Walker and the elf startled me. Darenthalis never left the gymnasium.

"Hello, child. Are you all right?"

"Not really. Apparently, I have a press conference to go to. I can't believe they did this."

"We are more than a little angry as well. Before Special Agent Morello could go hob knob with the families of the new agents, we pulled him aside for a special discussion. Believe me when I tell you, the man had no choice."

"I know. At least I have a spiffy new outfit to wear. Thanks, Darenthalis," I said with a smile.

"A car is here to take you to the Washington Field Office. I told the driver you would be there in a half hour, so there is no need to rush. Are you packed?"

"Yup, I just don't know where to put my gun. I can't fit the damn thing in my bag."

"The store sells the same rig. Did no one tell you? Unfortunately, they are closed. Follow me; I might have a spare you might find to be acceptable."

I glanced around the room one last time and tossed the key on the bed. I motioned for my elven friend to lead the way, and I fell into step behind him. The snow had stopped falling and left an inch or two of powdered white on the ground. I hoped it lasted the night. It relaxed me, and at the moment I needed relaxing.

Making it to his office, he went to the storage closet and opened the door. He disappeared inside for a few moments and popped back out with something in his hands. It looked like leather, just a light shade of gray. He handed me the harness, and I set my pack down and took my jacket off. I expected it to be heavy and uncomfortable, but it didn't appear to be manufactured from leather. It felt like suede, only softer. As I moved my arm, the material flowed against my skin like an extension of my body.

"Thanks, Darenthalis, it's beautiful. I'll return it after the conference."

"No need, it is a spare of my spare. It's yours. Consider it a valedictorian gift."

I smiled appreciatively at the elf. I then pulled the Glock from where I stuffed it into the front pocket of my backpack. It slid easily into the holster and looked like it belonged there. *Now I just needed some ammunition.* No one had ever even remotely hinted to me elves might be telepathic, but just as the thought crossed my mind, Darenthalis ducked into the storage locker and returned with three clips of ammunition. He pulled the gun without asking and popped the empty clip from the handle. He slid one clip into the weapon and the other two into pockets on the shoulder harness I didn't even notice.

"Now you're all set," he said.

I finished zipping up all the compartments on my backpack and pulled out my orders. With all the excitement, I hadn't even glanced at the contents of the manila envelope. I sat in one of the elf's chairs and found several sheets of paper and my official FBI badge. It sat nestled in a little black leather wallet, and I won't lie, I felt a little giddy. I stuffed it in one of my inside jacket pockets where I had my social security and ID cards. I would have to stick them in the tiny wallet too when I had the chance.

"Do you know where you are going after the press conference?"

"No, I haven't looked yet."

"Do tell. I'm interested in what the FBI has planned for you."

I flipped through the pages, read and reread them several times to make sure I wasn't mistaken. They're sending me back to Chicago? Really? My mouth dropped open in shock. I thought I would end up here for some reason. I wasn't disappointed, just surprised.

"I'm going back to Chicago."

"Interesting," he said. "Come, child. Your chariot waits."

Chapter 14

My vision became spotty and blurred the minute I walked out onto the stage of the press conference. The *click, click, click* of the multitude of cameras rang in my ears and I actually started getting a little dizzy. Deputy Director Sanders had just introduced me to the crowd and motioned me to join him next to the podium. I left my protective covering of the hallway and made my way to his side. I hadn't even met the man before this moment, but judging by his speech to the press, we had been friends for years. Shrewd didn't begin to describe the mousy looking man.

"Here she is, Agent Ashlyn." He played to the crowd like he had just introduced Miss America. I noticed he left off the "New" in my title. I guess "New Agent Ashlyn" isn't as dramatic.

A chorus of voices making my name a question flew from all over the room. Everyone wanted to be the first to question the freak with the badge. I ignored them and looked at the Deputy Director to see what he wanted me to do.

"Go ahead, Miss Brown." He pointed to a robust woman with brownish hair sitting in the front row, signaling her to ask a question. He must have known which news entity she worked for because she wasn't wearing any identifying news agency paraphernalia.

"Agent Ashlyn, could you tell us how long you've been undead?"

"Eighteen years since October," I replied.

"So how old are you then, Ashlyn?" I noticed they weren't limited to one question apiece like in the movies. Fortunately, the agent who briefed me before the conference said I could lie or not answer this one.

"A lady never tells her age, Miss Brown," I quipped, and drew some laughter from the audience. Maybe this wasn't going to be too bad.

"All right, I see you, Mr. Thomas, what's your question?" The Deputy Director pointed at another person in the second row.

"Which office are you going to be working out of?"

Again, a question they told me to avoid. Maybe this wasn't going to be too easy after all. "My office will be here in Washington, and then I'll be dispatched wherever I'm needed," I said. I saw Sanders nod in approval at my prepackaged answer. They didn't want anyone to know I would be on my way to Chicago right after this press conference.

The remainder of the questions ranged from "Are you in a relationship?" to "What made you want to join the FBI?" to "Are you a Master Vampire?" to "Who made you?"

I answered them all truthfully to the best of my ability. I did lie and tell them I was a master vampire. I even tried to look sad when I mentioned my creator had perished two years after turning me, but again I had that answer memorized before I went on stage.

After the questions of my lineage and abilities finished, the questions became very personal. These came mostly from the tabloid reporters who voiced their questions rudely over those who had been chosen, or before someone had been picked to ask a question. Most of the time their respectable peers ignored them, and sometimes they asked a question the rest of the room wanted to know the answer to. Some even had theories I had been created in a lab by the FBI, or the FBI had paid a vampire to make me so I could work for the FBI. I set the record straight and stuck to the story the FBI had concocted.

For the most part, the conference went well. Never in all my life did I think I would ever be a topic of interest, let alone the focus of a press conference. I just hoped it would be the end of it. It would be pretty hard to do my job with reporters tagging along all the time. Every time I had ever watched a newscast on the television, my heart always went out to the people being interviewed by moronic reporters. "Excuse me, ma'am, but your son was just decapitated by a train, how do you feel?" or "When you were being robbed at knifepoint, did you feel afraid?" I always wanted to know who wrote the questions for the reporters.

After the last question, I waved to the reporters and left the stage. I could hear my name being called again repeatedly, but the Deputy Director had dismissed me to make another one of his long-winded statements. The agent who debriefed me smiled as I entered the hallway. "Please wait here. The Deputy Director wants to speak to you before you head to Chicago."

I suppressed the urge to say "oh goody" and just smiled and nodded.

I listened to the Deputy Director's speech, and then he told the reporters goodbye. "Agent Ashlyn, I thank you so much for consenting to the dog and pony show. You did a phenomenal job. Are you all set for Chicago? You're greatly needed out there. They are having quite a bit of trouble with their Master of the City," he said, and shook my hand.

I felt dirty after shaking it, though. He had a soft grip and sweaty palms. *Gross.*

He left and the aid who debriefed me smiled and turned to follow. I had a little over an hour to get to the airport and catch my flight. The FBI wasn't footing the bill for a private aircraft for me this time, and I had to fly coach. I needed to haul some serious ass.

I left the building and walked out to the street to find a cab. The gods of travelers must have been with me because as soon as I stuck out my hand, one pulled to the curb and I climbed in. I told him to get me to the airport as soon as possible, my first mistake as an official agent of the FBI. The traffic and driving etiquette in DC is worse than it is in Chicago. We did make it to the airport on time, but my fingers hurt from gripping the armrest of the door so hard. I'm not joking; I dented the metal under the foam and plastic covering of the handle. I just hope the cabbie didn't notice before I left.

Eleven o'clock on a Friday night and Dulles was a madhouse. I presented the ticket I found included with my orders to the frazzled looking woman behind the counter and skipped through airport security thanks to my brand new FBI badge. I hoped flying commercial was as nice as it looked on TV.

I cursed the airline company as I got off the plane. I had never been so uncomfortable in all my life. When the stupid teenage girl sitting next to me noticed my gun, I thought she was going to give birth to a litter of kittens. Oh, well. Next time I'd pay the difference and upgrade to first class. I still had quite a few uncashed paychecks plus a lot of my own cash. Some shopping and opening a bank account topped my to-do list.

I exited the terminal since I didn't have to hit the baggage claim. A row of taxis waited out front, so finding a ride wasn't a problem. The cab driver blinked at me in the rearview mirror when I gave him the address and told him I wanted to go to the FBI field office in Chicago.

We pulled up to the front door almost a half an hour later. I paid my fair with tip and walked into the front door. One of the FBI police officers sat behind the desk, so I flashed him my badge and told him I needed to see Special Agent Reese or Agent Michaels if they were available.

I expected him to pick up a phone, but he punched a few buttons on his computer instead. "Special Agent Reese is expecting you, Agent Ashlyn, somebody will be down in a minute," he said, flashing me a smile.

I waited in the reception area for a few minutes, and then I heard the telltale *ding* of the elevator. Agent Michaels stepped off and looked around. He saw me, and his face lit up like a Christmas tree. I smiled back at his goofy grin. I dropped my bag and had my arms around him before he even stepped off the elevator. Even the FBI Police officer hadn't seen me move. Michaels' grunted as I picked him up off the floor.

"Put me down, girl!" He sounded outraged, but I could hear the happiness in his voice, the smile never leaving his face. "Come on, kid, let's get you settled."

I went to grab my bag and followed the big doof into the elevator. He questioned me non-stop about my time at Quantico and my experiences there. I told him everything from start to finish, including the stupid press conference on television. He confessed he had it on Tivo and had already watched it. I punched him on the arm.

The whole time we had been talking, we made our way upstairs. He settled me at a desk I could use while on duty in this field office. He asked if I had any idea how long I would be in Chicago, and I confessed I didn't know. "Well Reese told me to tell you you're not on duty until tomorrow." He glanced at his watch, and added, "I mean tonight. He also told me to take care of you. Is there anything you want to do?"

"I need to go buy some clothes and find a bank. Is there any open this late?"

"B of A went twenty-four hours about ten years ago. C'mon, let's go shopping," he said in his best "fabulous" voice.

I laughed at its absurdity; he really needed to work on it. Just by looking at the man, you could tell he suffered from terminal heterosexuality. He dressed way too sloppy to be gay.

We hit the bank first. I had no idea how much getting

outfitted for work would cost me so I kept two grand in my pocket for our shopping expedition. Michaels knew of a few retailers who catered to the late night community. Thank gods. I didn't want to have to order everything off the internet.

Several hours later, I had more clothes in my hands than Michaels had probably owned in his life. Even I didn't feel like shopping anymore. "Where to next?"

"Drop me off at a hotel by the office."

After a few minutes of uncomfortable silence, he told me his girlfriend had left him a month ago, and if I didn't mind the mess, I could stay with him. I thought about turning him down, but it would be convenient. He settled the decision for me by pulling into an apartment complex and parking the company vehicle.

"I insist brat," he said with a smile.

"Fine, you oaf, I just hope you don't snore."

"Just don't come in my room for a late night snack, leech!"

I wish he hadn't said it. He set my tummy rumbling. The look on his face when he heard it made it all worth it, though. Now he probably would be up all night. Sometimes life's pretty funny.

He unlocked the door to the tiny two bedroom apartment and a wave of different smells hit me like an invisible wall. Males of the human species, when not under the care of a female, tend to leave things out to molder and rot. Michaels wasn't an exception, I saw things that had passed into the realm of mummification and petrifaction. I hoped I would be safe in my room. He apologized for the mess. “Cleaning lady took the week off."

"You mean year?"

He showed me to my room and it only had one small window to the outside world. "Do you have a blanket to put over the window?"

"Yeah. I'll grab it and a staple gun. Be right back."

He returned and held the blanket while I tacked it to the wall. It wasn't pretty, but it would keep the sun out. He left to do whatever off duty FBI agents do, and I inspected my new accommodations. The room had a small television and a bed and dresser. *Perfect*. Maybe after he went to bed, I would clean it up a little. A layer of dust had settled over most of the items in the room, and I fought the urge to write, "Wash me" on the television screen with my finger. Thank the gods I didn't breathe.

We had brought all the bags of clothing from the car with us. After stashing everything in the dresser and closet, I wanted to get clean. "Where's your shower?" I shouted down the hall.

"You walked past it on the way to your room."

"I know, oaf. I was asking if I could use it. You were supposed to say, in the hall, help yourself," I hollered back.

"No, you can't, I like stinky vampires."

I walked to the bathroom, ignoring his last jab, and stripped my clothes before sliding under the cold water. I soaped and washed my hair and turned the faucet off. *Oh, shit, I forgot a damn towel.* I stepped out of the porcelain tub and opened the door a crack. "Hey, oaf, could you toss me a towel?"

"No."

"Please?"

"No, I'm getting my camera. Better run to your room fast!"

"You suck!" I realized what I said. The whole pot calling the kettle phrase popped into my head.

"Did you just tell me I suck? Isn't that a little hypocritical?"

A pink fuzzy towel appeared at the crack of the door. I opened it a little wider so I could grab it. "Thanks, oaf,"

I had never been this comfortable around anyone other than my aunt before, and it felt wonderful. I smiled inwardly as I wrapped myself in the towel and stepped outside the bathroom. As soon as I stood in the hallway, I saw the flash of a camera go off. *Son of a bitch.*

He stood behind me in the hallway, but had the camera pointed at the ceiling. He started laughing uncontrollably. I thought about beating him to death with the camera but settled for kicking him in the shin. I tried for lightly, but vampires don't do lightly. He howled and jumped up and down on one foot while holding his shin in both hands.

"Serves you right." I laughed at him.

"Jesus, girl, take it easy on the poor human. Would ya?"

"Goodnight," I called over my shoulder and made my way into my room. Locking the door for good measure, I dropped the towel. I thought about just slipping naked under the covers, but settled on panties and a T-shirt. Knowing Michaels, he might set fire to his own apartment just to get me out of my room.

Settling into the warm bed, I pulled the comforter over

me. I lay there for a while and replayed the events of the day in my head, the press conference being foremost in my thoughts. I didn't trust the Deputy Director as far as I could throw him. Wait a minute. I could probably throw him pretty far, but I still didn't trust him.

Chapter 15

I did my best to ignore the hunger growling in the pit of my stomach, and I had no idea how to feed it either. I needed to talk to Reese. Maybe the FBI had an infirmary in the Chicago office. Hell, for all I knew the FBI could just commandeer blood from the local blood bank. Commandeering would be cool and solve a lot of problems. Well, for me anyway.

Dressing in one of my new outfits, I stood in front of the mirror behind the door. I realized I did forget about my damn gun though; I needed to get used to putting it on before the jacket. I took off my jacket, strapped on my holster, and threw the jacket back on over it. To me, the whole rig seemed really noticeable. I didn't bother buttoning it up and just left it open before I headed to the bathroom to brush my fangs and hair.

I didn't see Michaels, nor had he opened his bedroom door, but I did hear him stumbling around and his shower start. I can tell you one thing from hearing him in the shower; he is a terrible singer. Maybe I should buy him a shower radio, nobody with a horrible voice should sing a cappella. I heard a rabbit scream once when an owl had swooped down and broken the poor beast's back in its talons, and it sounded better than Michaels. I don't think I could listen to him singing every night. The shower radio sounded better and better.

It took him only ten minutes to get dressed and emerge from his bedroom, which I imagined looked like a cave. He smiled when he saw me ready, and I gagged at the excessive amounts of aftershave pouring from his body and making its way to my sensitive nose

"Ready to go, bloodsucker?" Michaels asked snidely.

"Whenever you are, burger muncher."

"Ouch," he said as he walked by me and ruffled my hair. Damn it. I gathered it back and retied it. No fuss, no muss is my motto. I despised women with elaborate hairdos. *Maybe I should cut mine short. Maybe it would make me look like a pixie. Or maybe like a boy. Maybe I'll leave it long.*

We drove to the office in silence, well, between us anyway; the radio blared classic rock the whole way. At least Michaels didn't sing in the car. *Yay.* I thought about the big dork next to me and smiled. He stood around six foot two and weighed about two twenty. Not a bad looking guy and his sense of humor made him even more attractive. I had no idea how old he might be, but he wasn't aging well. He didn't have any gray hair or bald spots, but he had sort of a chemically smell coming from his hair, so he did have one problem or the other. He had to be knocking on the mid-forty's door. Still, I did like him.

"Michaels?"

"Yeah?"

"What's your first name?"

"Agent," he said, smiling. "Kidding, it's Michael."

"Are you fucking with me?"

"Yes."

"You suck."

"So do you."

He really wasn't going to tell me, the prick. I'd ask Reese next time we were alone.

We pulled into the parking garage and rode the old elevator up to the office floor. Michaels went straight to his desk and checked his messages while I went to Reese's office.

I saw him sitting at his desk through the glass window so I knocked. He looked up at me and a smile crossed his face. "Don't just stand there, come on in," he said, crossing the room as I did. We met halfway and he shook my hand vigorously. It took five minutes for him to stop congratulating me. "Did Michaels get you settled in?"

"Yes, sir. I'm actually staying at his place," I replied.

His eyes widened in surprise.

"Well, get used to him; he's going to be your partner while we have you. I just wish I could get you assigned here permanently, but Washington wants you back."

"I know. I had the pleasure of meeting the Deputy Director."

"Yes, I saw your press conference. Good job, by the way."

I groaned inwardly. I liked Reese a lot, but he apparently had the same notion I should be presented to the world. At least I could trust him to keep my secrets safe. He went on to tell me about the problems Cicero had been causing during my absence. There were numerous attacks on uniformed police officers. Some had gone missing, and some found dead, and yes, their bodies were found with numerous puncture wounds.

Many vampires had been brought in for questioning, but none knew where Cicero had holed himself up. Surveillance had been set up at nearly every vampire owned business in the city and none had returned with any good news. The Chicago Police Department was on edge and demanding help from the FBI.

"Where should I start?"

"Find him. Maybe some of the vampires would talk to you. Michaels will be with you, but keep him away if you think it will help you get what you need to know. Finding Cicero is our number one priority. If you find him, call for backup, and I'll have FBI SWAT at your location in minutes. I would start with the club owners. See if they'll talk. I can't authorize excessive force in questioning techniques, but I'm telling you right now, Ash, do what you have to. This vampire is insane, and now he's killing police."

"I understand. I'll do what I can."

"It's all I can ask."

"I just have one more concern…"

"What is it?"

"Blood. While I was at Quantico, they gave me a steady supply of lycanthrope blood. I'll be honest; I'm having trouble even having this discussion with your right now."

Reese nodded in understanding. "I can imagine, but I also see where you're going with this. I'll make some calls. Maybe we can work something out with Washington. If they're going to be sending you all over the country, you need to have a permanent solution. I'll ask around with the men too. Maybe one of them could donate for now. I'll let you know."

"Thanks again, sir"

"Ash?"

"Yes, sir?"

"Should you 'accidentally' take a drink from anybody who might put up a struggle, I'm sure it wouldn't need to find its way into your report. It might even be an effective interrogation technique."

As scary as his entire sentence sounded in my head, I couldn't disagree. "Yes, sir." I offered my hand to him again, which he readily accepted.

"Sir?"

"Just call me Reese, Ash. What is it?"

"What's Michaels' first name?" I tried for innocence in my question.

"Don't tell him I told you, but it's Marion. Marion Peter Michaels. Apparently his father had been a huge John Wayne fan."

I didn't see what John Wayne had to do with Marion, or why a parent would willingly name their son Marion, but I didn't care. I hit pay dirt. I gave Reese an evil little smile and headed back to my desk.

Michaels had just finished going through his voicemail messages, scribbling some information on a Post-it note. I smiled looking at his laptop longingly.

"What?"

"I want your laptop. I miss my computer."

"Ha! Don't worry. Reese has one coming up from the IT department for you. And a phone."

Oh, goody! At least I didn't have to buy one right away.

"Are you ready to go?"

"Whenever you are, partner."

"Pete, they've got another dead cop found on Lakeshore. I'll email you the address. Reese says to get over there ASAP," one of the Agents a few desks over hollered at Michaels.

"Great, c'mon kid, let's go."

"Okay, Pete" I laughed at him.

"Yeah, yeah my first name's Pete. You got me, let's go," he replied defeated.

"It's sooo funny. You don't strike me as a Pete," I said. Nothing on this planet could have stopped me from adding, "If I had to, I would have guessed Marion."

He stopped dead in his tracks and turned to face me, his face all puffy and red. I started laughing as he stuck up his middle finger. Yup, he flipped me off, and it just made me laugh harder.

We pulled up to Navy Pier twenty minutes later. I had never been there so the lights and the sheer amount of people walking around shocked me. It didn't even remotely look like a crime scene. Turned out it wasn't. The pier itself held restaurants, shops, and entertainment, which would have been a horrible place to hide a body. Lake Michigan on the other hand, wasn't a horrible place. By the time we pulled up, the body of one Officer Rodriguez had been fished out of Lake Michigan. His bloated graying corpse lay on the deck of a police boat. One of the officers radioed the vessel and let them know we were there. A small inflatable boat with an outboard motor made its way to the pier. Apparently, it was our ride.

After we were onboard, I made my way to the corpse and looked at it over the shoulder of the crime scene investigator. She seemed very efficient, and a lot less green than everyone else around her. The cops and even Michaels all looked a little peaked from the bloated corpse. When I looked at him, I felt nothing other than sadness for his family. I saw the puncture wounds on his neck. Whoever killed him was either a common vampire, or a master vampire who had fed on him until he died. Our saliva, which contains a healing agent in it, closes the wounds almost magically. However, it doesn't work too well on corpses.

Without hovering, I tried to get a little closer to the body to smell it. I could smell the water from the lake soaking his clothes, the aftershave still clinging to his face and neck, and something a lot less strong than the other odors wafting from the corpse. I could barely smell it, but I could identify it, lemons and cinnamon. Whoever had ended the young police officers life wasn't Cicero. I remembered his scent well.

"It wasn't Cicero," I said to Michaels.

"How do you know?"

"Because, I remember what Cicero smelled like and whoever killed this man wasn't him."

I sniffed again and watched the police officers staring at me as they sidled back a step or two away from the strange FBI agent sniffing dead people. *Fuck ‘em.* I had a killer to catch.

I only smelled one vamp, so whoever killed him had been acting alone. I needed to see some of the other bodies. I just hoped they hadn't decomposed too much.

"Michaels, how long ago was the last cop killed?"

"Two days ago, found his body by the railroad tracks. She should still be at the morgue. I'm assuming you want to see it?"

"Yes. First, I want to take a look around the pier. Any vampire owned businesses, or places vampires like to congregate there?" I looked around at the officers who had stepped forward to listen to the conversation. Curiosity is probably the only human emotion stronger than fear.

"There's a place called the Carnival, it's more of a touristy vampire bar though. People visiting Chicago get to visit with the undead, no offense, fangs," he said. I liked the "fangs," but it must have clued in the police milling around the body because they just outright walked away after he said it. He noticed too, because he began chortling so only I could hear him.

"Fangs, huh, I kind of like it. Thanks, Marion."

"Don't you start with me. We're friends, so I'll let you get away with Pete, but even my mother doesn't get to call me Marion."

"Touchy, aren't we? All right, Pete, let's go to a carnival."

"Not carnival, 'carneeevahl.' Like the Brazilian festival and Mardi Gras. You are such a bumpkin."

"Well excuse me for being locked away for ninety-five percent of my life. Everyone's a critic."

We had the Police boat dock at Navy Pier. The coroner promised to call if she found anything unusual besides the massive amounts of blood loss we expected. We drew quite a few stares as we walked up the ramp from where the boat docked into the crowd. I will admit, all the restaurants smelled delicious, and it only compounded my hunger. I'd kill to be able to eat a burger and fries.

We walked quite a ways before reaching our destination. Most of Navy Pier shone with bright colors, but the Carnival had embarked into the realm of garish. Purples, yellows, and oranges splashed the front not only in paint, but sequins. Sequins the size of saucers, but still sequins, were fastened to the front of the building. If you stood far enough away, you could tell the front entrance was shaped and designed like the mouth of a giant clown with fangs. Standing right in front, was like standing in front of a New Orleans' nightmare.

Ever the gentleman, Michaels opened the door and let me enter. Horrible music sounding like a combination of accordion, a guitar, and somebody's foot stomping blared throughout the place. If the music wasn't nauseating enough, the heady smell of crawfish and other less-than-fresh seafood permeated the air, making my stomach twist in protest. We flashed our badges at the hostess as we walked in and asked to see the owner or manager. I gave her a quick unnoticeable sniff, but knew in a moment that she wasn't a vampire.

She seemed unimpressed by the badges and hollered at a waiter walking by to, "Go find Lou," and then she shifted her attention and beamed a fake smile at a thirtyish couple who walked in behind us.

Pete and I moved out of the way and let them pass to go get their table and enjoy the ambiance of the exotic place. *Yuck.* My ears hurt, my eyes hurt, and my sense of smell threatened to go on strike.

We waited and the hostess returned only to look a little disappointed to see us still standing there. "Lou come out yet?"

We shook our heads.

She turned to go get him herself, but stopped. "Here he comes."

A short and greasy figure walked toward us. He wasn't thin, or fat, just paunchy. Fangs protruded over his bottom lip, but something wasn't right. I stared at him for a minute and noticed sweat dripping off his brow. Vampires didn't sweat. *Interesting...*

"I'm Lou, my waiter said you wanted to see me," he said in probably the worst fake Creole accent I had ever heard.

"Agents Walker and Ashlyn, FBI." We introduced ourselves and shook the meaty hand of Lou. It felt sweaty too. I fought the urge to gag and forced a smile on my face.

"How long have you been a vampire, Lou?"

"He's not," I filled him in.

Michaels and Lou both did a doubletake. I sniffed my hand and smelled oregano and a touch of coriander. Earthy spices told me he had to be some sort of lycanthrope. "You're a werewolf or something, Lou, why are you pretending to be a vampire?" I flashed him a bit of my fangs.

"Boss told me to. Vampires are s'posed to be a little more Cajun than werewolves. He signs the check so I do what I'm told. Is there something I can help you with?" He dropped the fake accent.

"Who owns the place, Lou? Who's your boss?" Michaels asked impatiently.

"Jean Phillipe Margeaux. He's not in tonight, though.

Usually only makes an appearance once a week. Is he in trouble?"

"I don't know. When did you see him last?" *Please say last night, please say last night.*

"About four or five days ago, do you need to see him? I can give you his cell number."

Lou seemed awfully helpful. It made me wonder if Lou wanted to shift attention away from Lou. Maybe Lou had a record and didn't want "no trouble."

"Do you have any vampires working here?" Maybe it wasn't the owner, but it could be one of his underlings.

"Matt, the bartender over there is a vamp. He's the only one who works here. Do I need to cover the bar for a while?"

"Yes please," I replied. We followed Greasy up to the bar where he motioned the bartender over. At first, I thought the entire back area of the bar had been built a foot above the floor, but it wasn't. As the vampire walked out from the bar he still stood seven friggin' feet tall. I'm five-one, so I felt like a dwarf next to the massive tower of muscle.

"Are you Matt?" He nodded at me with a bemused smile. "Agent Ashlyn, FBI, I'd like to ask you a few questions. Could you please follow us outside?"

He didn't seem surprised, and just told Lou to, "Take over." Funny, I thought Lou held the title of manager. He must be only in charge of the restaurant. I let the basketball player vampire walk past me to lead the way out, partly to keep my eye on him, but mostly to catch his scent. He smelled only of vanilla. Damn it, I knew it would have been too easy to find the killer within a block of the murder victim.

Matt led us through the restaurant and kitchen and opened a large door marked "exit" in the back. He stepped out into the night, followed closely by me and Michaels. Before I had even crossed the threshold, he ran.

Fuck.

I released the door and let it either smack Michaels in the face or let him catch it. I was already fifty yards down the alley, so I couldn't tell. The alley stank of garbage and other things I'd rather not think about, so I tried to avoid the puddles of what I hoped to be water. I'm fast, but I'm only five feet tall, whereas Matt had inhuman speed and a stride that easily doubled mine. I could see a bend up in the alleyway and feared it led out to the crowds wandering around the pier. Damn it, I didn't want to lose him. He might have not killed the cop, but he wasn't innocent either. Innocent people don't run. FBI rule number one.

I had to catch him, and I had to do it fast. I timed it so when my left foot hit the ground I pushed off and into the air. What I did next impressed even me. I twisted while in midair and pushed out with both my legs, finding purchase on the wall to my right. I launched myself in a maneuver, that could have earned me a medal in the Olympics if vampires weren't prohibited from competing. I landed on his back and latched on with tooth and claw.

He fell forward, and I rode him to the ground. He held out his arms, absorbing some of the impact, but his head still smacked into the concrete. I know because I had my fangs buried in his neck. He didn't knock himself out, but I had him trapped beneath me. I felt his blood flood my mouth with a vanilla flavor I hadn't expected. I should have stopped, but I couldn't. My hunger took control again. I sucked when I didn't even need to. The blood poured freely into my mouth fast, but not fast enough. I had him and he belonged to me. I let go of his shoulder and stomach and moved my hands up to cradle him. I could feel his strength leaving him quickly. Michaels' feet striking the ground as he raced to catch up saved Matt's life.

I didn't want him seeing me feed. I withdrew my fangs and licked the wound, watching it close before my eyes. I let go of the mammoth vampire and flipped him over onto his back. He looked up at me like he had just had sex with me. He had that dreamy look on his face, and for the life of me, I didn't know why. I heard the cocking of a weapon, and looked up at Michaels, who had his weapon drawn and pointed at the vampire's head.

"Put it up, Pete, he's not going to run again; are you, Matt?" I looked down from Michaels to the prone vampire who still looked lost in what resembled post-orgasmic bliss. I glanced at the front of his pants, and I hoped he landed in a puddle of water. *Yuck.*

"No, I won't run. I'm sorry I did in the first place. Then again, maybe I'm not. If I run, will you drink from me some more?" He sounded a little too hopeful.

"No, I'll just shoot you in the back of the head. Why did you run? I know you didn't kill the cop down by the water."

"What cop?" I don't know why, but I knew instantly he didn't have *any* knowledge about the dead cop down by the pier.

"Never mind, why did you run?"

"We all will. Word is out; any vampire who talks to the police will find themselves strapped to a rooftop just before daybreak."

"Who told you this?" I already knew the answer.

"It came from Cicero. He's completely lost it. He's holed up somewhere and is afraid to come out because every cop in Chicago is looking for him. Don't ask me where he is, nobody knows, but he's got his goons doing whatever he says, and I believe him. Please let me go. If they find out I've talked, I'm dead."

I felt bad for the massive vampire. I could smell his fear. I had an idea, but I didn't think he'd like it. I stood next to the prone vampire and offered him my hand to help him up. He looked at me suspiciously, but took the offered hand. He seemed to be a little unsteady on his feet, but managed not to fall over.

"You're letting me go?"

"For now, Matt, but I'm going to need your help tomorrow, and you're going to say yes, okay?"

"Sure," he replied instantly.

I was a little confused and looked at Michaels who had the same expression that I did plastered on his face. This vampire was scared shitless, and yet he told me he would help, and I hadn't even told him what I wanted yet. Maybe he hit his head harder than I thought. *Yeah, it had to be a concussion. Cranial injuries often impair vampiric thought processes.*

"Okay, Matt, thank you. We'll meet at the restaurant sundown tomorrow. For now, if anybody asks, you gave us the slip okay?"

"Anything you want, no problem. Can I go now?"

"Yeah, go ahead."

Michaels and I watched the vampire as he walked away and around the corner to join the crowd. As soon as he stepped out of sight, we turned to each other and shrugged. Something weird had just happened and I had no idea what it was. Still pondering what had transpired, we walked through the alley, left the pier, and headed back to the Suburban.

We drove in silence back to the office. By the time we got there, I had a new laptop on my desk and a cell phone to boot. Yippee, free long distance. Now I just needed to meet new people to call. I flipped through the contacts list and saw Michaels' and Reese's names. There were also a bunch of names I didn't recognize. I assumed they were other agents at the Chicago office. I called Michaels cell to make sure the phone worked and smiled when I heard it ring. He glanced up at me as the phone vibrated on his desk and made a little chiming noise. I nodded to let him know not to answer it. He picked up the phone, saw the number, and frowned. I pressed the "end" button and slipped it into my jacket pocket.

"What?"

"They must not be planning on keeping you here long," he said.

"What?"

"It's not a local number. Chicago's 812 and yours came up 202. I believe 202 is DC's area code isn't it?"

"I don't know, but I can Google it," I replied.

I powered up my new laptop. I didn't see any scratches or

dings, so I didn't think I had gotten someone's hand-me-down. In fact, bubble wrap has a distinctive smell when you have vampiric senses, and I swear I smelled it on the laptop. It took only a moment to fire up, and I groaned when I saw the Windows 8 logo appear. Joy. I Googled the 202 area code and sure enough Washington DC popped up.

"You're right. It's DC."

His mouth set into a grim line. I could tell he was disappointed from the look on his face. It was almost enough to make me start sniffling. In the meantime, we had other things to worry about. Like catching a very bad vampire.

"So what's your plan?" He apparently wanted to change the subject.

I ran it by Michaels to see what he thought. He seemed skeptical at first, but I promised him I could play my part and play it well. The only unknown in the whole equation would be Matt. Could I trust him? Probably not, but at least my plan put him in a position where he couldn't fuck us if I couldn't trust him.

Before we left, we sent an email to Reese covering what we had learned at the pier from Matt, and gave a brief outline of my plan as well. The only one who would be in danger would be our friendly vampire, Matt, and I didn't think Reese would be too worried about him. Now I just needed a good day's sleep.

"You ready, Fangs?"

I was starting to think Michaels had developed ESP. "Sure thing, Meat Puppet, let's go," I replied.

"Meat Puppet. Really? Is that the best you could come up

with?"

"For now. Come on, I'm tired." I packed up the laptop in its shiny new leather case. Ooh, I had such plans for my shiny new friend. I suffered from acute internet withdrawal, and I finally had a cure.

Chapter 16

Two hours of Youtube and seven hours of sleep later, we made our way back at the office. I didn't expect to start my day with an ass chewing from Reese, but that was exactly what I got. Apparently, I had somehow developed acute brain damage, my plan wouldn't work, and Michaels is missing more than one chromosome for letting me chase after the big bad vampire without backup. I guess he didn't realize exactly how fast I could be when I wanted to be. After the fifteenth minute straight of it, I rolled my eyes and then got yelled at for doing that, too. I never had a father to yell, "You better not be rolling your eyes at me, missy," and I wasn't sure I wanted one now.

"Reese, calm down! Everything is going to be all right. In case you forgot, I am a hell of a lot faster and stronger than Michaels, and I can take care of myself!"

He stared at me for a few minutes and then took a deep breath. "No, I haven't forgotten, Ash, but you have been an agent for all of two days. If anything happened to you, not only would I not forgive myself, but I would never hear the end of it. Please, be careful. You don't even know your strengths and limitations, and until you are fully aware of what you are capable of, please play it a little safe for me, all right?"

His little speech touched me. "Reese, how am I supposed

to find out what I'm capable of if you won't let me do anything? Trust me, if I don't feel comfortable with something, I will be the first not to do it. I promise I won't let you down."

"Fine, just be careful. Please. Michaels, make sure she's safe or I'll have you transferred to the Nome Field Office before you can say 'Eskimo,' got it?"

"Clear as arctic ice, Special Agent in Charge, sir. I'll look after her like she was my girlfriend, or wife, or something," he said.

Oops, he probably should have chosen a better simile.

"Have you checked into a hotel yet?"

"Yes, I have, sir. See, Clarion and Marriott Hotels merged and started a new hotel line and they're calling them the Marion Suites. It's a cute little place, more like an apartment, but I enjoy staying there," I said cheekily. *I kill me: the Marion Suites*.

Reese got my joke and wasn't even remotely amused. I have never seen someone turn a purplish shade of red before. I needed to get out of there before he shot me himself.

"Ash," Reese started to say, and I held up my hand to stop him.

"Remember, Reese, I'm a big girl now. I'm fine; please just let it go. I'll email you after tonight to fill you in on how everything goes. Wish us luck. C'mon, Meatstick, we got work to do."

"After you, Fangs."

We waited outside The Carnival until foot traffic started to pick up and Navy Pier became packed full of people out looking to have a good time. I checked the hour on my new cell, 9 o'clock. The time had come. Patrons should just be finishing their dinners and looking to settle on something a little more mundane, like drinking. I envied them. I really could use something to calm my nerves. I looked over at Michaels and expected him to be just as fidgety as I felt, but no, he had to be cool, calm, and collected, the dickhead.

I nodded at him to let him know it was time for my little acting debut. *Here goes nothing.* He led the way through the front doors of the Carnival and right past the surprised hostess standing behind her little podium. I followed behind him through the door and then fanned out to walk beside him. Because this wasn't an official FBI sanctioned maneuver, we didn't draw our weapons and we didn't have a warrant, but we didn't stop or pause, lest someone question us. Michaels flashed his badge at the open-mouthed hostess and we walked to the bar.

Matt occupied his spot behind the bar pouring drinks, just like I had hoped. The bar patrons sidled away from us nervously as we flashed our badges at Matt like we had never questioned him before. I didn't pull my weapon, but I wanted to. It would have been much more dramatic. I had my right hand on the butt of my Glock and held my badge with my left.

"Matt, I'm Agent Ashlyn and this is Agent Michaels, we're with the FBI. I need you to come with us to answer a few questions, please. Oh, and by the way, don't even think of running away again."

Matt's blank stare screamed confusion warring with the desire to hide. I almost felt sorry for him, but in this case, the ends justified the means. I'm sure the six dead cops would agree with me if they could. Matt held up his hands and walked around the bar, stopping when Michaels and I moved over to the side exit to meet him there.

"What do you want now?"

"We want to talk to you, and this time if you run I will shoot you myself," Michaels supplied for me.

Matt nodded and started to walk toward the kitchen, but I stopped him and motioned for him to head toward the front door instead. The more people who saw this, the better the chance that word would get back to Cicero that we questioned Matt. I hated using someone as bait, but to quote my aunt, "Sometimes you have to do what you have to do."

Fear came off the vampire in waves. He knew we had put him in danger. Honestly, I'm surprised he didn't just tell us to go fuck ourselves. He had agreed to help, but I don't think he realized what it would mean, until now. We walked the length of the pier and exited out onto the street. Michaels had parked the Suburban in a nearby parking garage, so we headed there. Matt had put his hands down after we left the restaurant and walked resignedly between the two of us. As soon as we hit the street, he started to ask a question, but I shushed him.

It took about ten minutes to get to the parking garage on foot. Matt and I could have made it there in seconds, and I could tell he wanted to, but it wasn't the point of this little operation. I wanted him seen by as many people as possible, and in my company. We entered the garage and hopped on the elevator to the eighth floor, and no, we couldn't find a closer spot. We walked through the open door and had made it halfway to the Suburban when the camera flashes started going off from the second elevator.

I stopped in my tracks and panicked. If I had thought about it, I would have figured anybody taking pictures of the FBI walking a vampire to their car would be exactly what I would have prayed to the gods for. Nothing could have boosted the chances of my plan's success more than Matt's picture being in the paper. Unfortunately, I didn't think before I acted. I ran toward the source of the flashes without so much as a, "Watch him," to my partner. As soon as I turned, the man with the camera frantically started pushing the "close door" button. I wasn't going to make it.

"Halfway to the Suburban" put us at about fifteen-hundred feet from the elevators. The man must have had one hell of a telephoto lens on his camera. I made it half the distance back to the elevator when the door finally started closing. I still had fifty more to go when it closed. Damn it. I only had one chance. I watched as the elevator began its decent down to the first floor on the little lighted panel above the door. I looked up at the elevator display and saw it was heading down. I needed to get in front of that elevator and stop it. I ran down the stairs at vampiric speed, stopped at the fourth floor, and hit the "going down" button.

The door *dinged* and opened. It made me wish I had been the one with the camera when he noticed me standing in front of the door waiting for him. He had a classic "I just shit myself" look on his face.

"Oh God, please," he muttered before he handed me the camera. "I'm sorry, please take the memory disk. I'm a reporter, I swear," he cried.

"Who are you?"

"S-s-steve Jezwyrski, I'm with the Tribune."

"S-s-steve, I'm Agent Ashlyn, FBI."

"I know. I saw you at the press conference on TV. I'm sorry, but I was doing a story on restaurant closings at Navy Pier when I saw you hauling that vampire out for questioning and I wanted the story."

I started to get angry. Angry because the stupid press conference had made me a target for newshounds when I had a job to do. I didn't need this shit, and then I realized the perfectness of the situation. Eighteen years of mediocre luck at best, and I finally catch a break. Happy Fucking New Year!

"You're going to run a story on me hauling in a vampire for questioning?"

"Y-yes Ma'am, I had planned on it," he stammered again.

"No Mr. Jezwyrski, you are. You most definitely are. Here's your camera. Have a nice day," I added over my shoulder as I headed back up to the eighth floor.

As I stepped out of the stairwell, I knew something had gone wrong. Not a sound permeated the entire deck of the parking garage. Then I smelled blood, human blood. "Oh, no," I groaned and ran to the Suburban. I found Michaels there on the ground, bleeding from a head wound. I watched the rhythmic movement of his chest; so at least he was alive, thank the gods. I spun in circles looking for Matt the vampire; I couldn't see or smell him anywhere. The shit had officially hit the fan.

I reached into my pocket, pulled out my little cell phone, and frantically dialed 911. I thought about picking Michaels up and driving him to the hospital myself, but I figured it would be better to follow procedure. I would just have to follow in the Suburban. I would finally get to put those driving skills I learned at the academy to the test.

I waited and finally heard Chicago's finest coming down the street. Their sirens echoed off the buildings, and I have never been so glad to hear anything in my life. Their tires screeched as they rounded the curves of the many levels of the parking garage. I don't think they even had the vehicle in park before they jumped out, started dragging equipment over to Michaels, and ushered me out of the way while they examined him. One of the uniformed officers who had followed the ambulance to our location ran over to me to begin the questioning. I flashed my badge and gave her a quick synopsis of what had happened. My experience with people so far had been pretty limited, but even I could tell she thought I was a moron for leaving my partner alone with a vampire.

When you're born a vampire and have all the strengths of a vampire, it is quite easy to forget those around you aren't always as tough as you are. It wasn't a mistake I would ever make again. I'm just glad Michaels survived my fuck up. I just didn't want to deal with him when he woke up. He wasn't going to be happy. Silently I cursed Matt the vampire. I had plans to protect him from Cicero's goons. Now I wasn't so sure.

The ambulance made it to the hospital in record time. I followed right behind them with the little flashing lights under the grill of the Suburban on the whole way. If my heart beat, it would have stopped when we pulled into the hospital. Northwest Community, the same hospital my aunt had worked for most of her life. I was about to be surrounded by people who knew my aunt probably a little better than I did. My chest started to tingle, and again, if I breathed, I would have probably started hyperventilating.

I pushed the fear back down my throat into the pit of my stomach and stepped out of the vehicle. This wasn't the time for worrying about my aunt. Paramedics were wheeling my partner in on a gurney from the rear of the ambulance, and I needed to concentrate on him, not the ghosts of my past. I made for the doors right behind the paramedics and followed my partner into the ER.

He woke up about an hour later, laid out on a bed in a curtained-off corner of the ER. His skull had been X-rayed and no fractures were visible, but he did have a nasty concussion. I silently thanked Matt for not being overzealous with his blow to my partner's head. I know he could have easily killed the fragile human, but I still silently hoped Cicero's goons found him before I did.

"Pete?" I noticed him stirring for the first time in almost two hours.

"Shhh," he said. It must be one hell of a headache; I barely whispered his name.

"You okay?" I made my voice even softer.

"No. My head feels like I rammed it into an aircraft carrier. What happened?"

"Mr. Matt decided he didn't want to go with the nice FBI agents. He hit you when I went after the guy with the camera."

"Oh. Did he get away?"

"Yes. I'm sorry, Pete, I shouldn't have left you. I saw the flashes and I acted."

"I think I'll live. Right now, I don't want to though. Reese is going to chew us both up and spit us into the shit can. I shouldn't have taken my eyes off the vampire, and I should have stopped you from going. Why were we getting our picture taken?"

I filled him in on what happened with Steve Jezwyrski and how I had let him leave with his film intact. I expected another lecture, but he seemed as happy as I had been with how fate had played out. We waited for the doctor, and when he finally came in, he released Pete to go home and rest. He told me what to watch for, as far as vomiting and loss of memory, and gave me a prescription for some powerful headache medicine. Thank the gods for twenty-four hour pharmacies. I'd pick it up on the way back to the apartment.

I helped him out to the Suburban and got him into the passenger seat so I could drive. We headed out from the hospital parking area by the ER and made our way into traffic. We made good time in the predawn morning and had plenty of time to stop to fill the prescription and make it back to the apartment. I thought about turning on the radio to cut through the silence, but thought better of the idea when I looked over at

Michaels' pain-ridden face. I pulled into the pharmacy, and left him in the vehicle while I ran in. The young man behind the pharmacy counter asked for my ID so I gave him my FBI issued one. I would have to remember to use it from now on. Talk about speedy service. I expected to wait for at least a half an hour, but the clerk had me ready to go in less than ten minutes.

We made it to the apartment, and I pumped him full of pills and got him into his room into bed. He hurt so bad he didn't even make jokes when I took off his shirt, shoes, and jacket. No sexual innuendo from Pete was never a good sign. I laid him down on the comforter and debated taking off his dress slacks, but thought better. Seeing Pete in his tighty whiteys wasn't something I wanted burned into my memory. As far as males of the human species went, he made the upper percentile, but he had a few decades on this little vampire.

I wasn't dead though. Nor did being a vampire eliminate whatever causes sexual desire, and the sight of his naked torso kind of made me feel a little funny in certain areas. I have always dealt with these feelings in the "traditional" method, and kind of groaned inwardly when I realized I might have to do so again later. Maybe if I took an ice bath I wouldn't have to worry about it. The thought of doing anything like "traditional" stress relief in Michaels' apartment kind of turned the old stomach. Besides, he might have heard me, and then I would never have lived it down. He'd probably tell the whole office. "Ashlyn, the masturbating vampire," I could hear it now.

I covered him with a sheet from the linen closet in the hall and left to take my ice bath. It helped, but only a little. I dried off and fired up the laptop to email Reese a report on what happened. I debated calling him. I knew he would want to hear details in person, but I wasn't going to call him at five o'clock in the morning, wake him up, and get yelled at for being stupid, getting my partner almost killed, and waking him. I'm not into suicide. I'd let him yell when I went into the office tomorrow. I knew Pete wouldn't be up to duty, so I would probably be flying solo.

I hit send on the email and closed the laptop. I debated shutting my cell off, but Reese would call as soon as he read the "Dear Reese, I am a moron" email. I set it to charge on the nightstand by the bed, and lay down, closing my eyes. I remembered all I had on was a highly uncomfortable wet towel. Laying down made it a little difficult to take off, but I managed. The pills would knock Pete out for at least twelve hours, so I would have time to get dressed when Reese called. Naked, I fell asleep.

I sat straight up when I heard Michaels yell, "Oh, my God!" I blinked twice to clear the fog of sleep from my brain and looked over at Michaels who stood in the open doorway of my bedroom. I jumped out of bed and wrapped myself in the towel I had tossed on the floor last night. I moved so fast, he couldn't have seen much.

"Ash, I'm sorry. I thought you would be awake. Reese has been trying to call you for over an hour. He isn't happy. He finally broke down and called my phone. I told him you were asleep. Call him right away, I'm going back to bed," he said and turned around leaving me, and my towel, all alone.

I stared at the empty doorway for a minute. *I can let this completely freak me out, or I can just ignore what happened.* Guess which one I opted for. I picked up the cell phone still plugged into the charger. Shit, I had shut the volume off while I had been at the hospital with Pete and never turned it back up. Oh, Reese tried to call me all right. Twenty-seven missed calls and not one from anybody else.

I debated calling him first, but decided on getting dressed instead. I had no desire to talk to my boss naked. I ran into the bathroom, scrubbed the old fangs, and dressed. I really wish I could drink coffee. I had never slept so late before in my life, and I still felt a little groggy. Finally, I sat on my bed and turned on my cell. I found Reese's name in my contacts and pressed the send button, held the phone up to my ear and waited for my reaming.

It rang twice before Reese picked up on the other end. He didn't even say hello before the tirade of my idiocy began. I didn't interrupt, just sat while he ranted. For an old coot, the man had serious lung capacity. I was impressed.

"Ashlyn," he said and paused. "Are you listening to me?"

"Yes, sir. I am, sir."

"Good, I've given Michaels a couple of days off. You get your ass down here to pick up your temporary partner. I have something else to show you. Let Michaels know if he needs anything he should call me and not you. You are going to be very busy tonight," he finished on a firm note.

"Yes, sir. On my way, sir."

I listened as the line clicked dead and put the phone in my jacket pocket before heading out to face the music.

Chapter 17

The office parking garage seemed a little more packed than usual. I pulled the Suburban in one of the few remaining parking spots and made my way up to Reese's office. I drew a few stares from the agents sitting around as I made my way through the sea of desks. I didn't know why they were staring at me, and I'd like to say it didn't bother me, but truth be told it made me more than a little nervous.

I stopped at the entrance to Reese's office and rapped on the doorframe three times. I looked at the man behind the desk and immediately felt guilty. I ignored him on the phone, and blew him off yesterday when I told him about my plan to use Matt as bait. I had truly fucked up and now my partner would probably be bedridden for a few days, at least. He had the handset of the phone glued to his ear, but motioned me forward to sit and wait. I liked Reese. He had given me the opportunity to make a life for myself, and I would always be grateful, but he had the role of the only authority figure in my life so the tiny rebellious streak present in every woman under the age of thirty had only one outlet. Him. I made a mental note to be a little more understanding and cooperative in the future.

I sat and listened to him finish his conversation. It ended with a, "Love you, too," so I hoped he had been talking to his wife and not the Deputy Director of the FBI. He gingerly set the receiver down and stared at me for a full minute. I contemplated smiling at him to ease some of the tension in the room. Instead, I listened to the little mental note I made a few minutes earlier and lowered my gaze to the gray flats I wore instead.

"You screwed the pooch big time, little girl," he said flatly.

"I know. I shouldn't have left Michaels alone with the vampire. I'm sorry. Trust me when I say it won't happen again."

"I know it won't, but you're a new agent. Screw-ups happen; it's what makes us better agents. They can only teach you so much at the Academy, the rest you have to learn on your own. I'm pissed, but shit happens. Michaels getting hurt isn't what I'm talking about. This is," he said and picked up the newspaper sitting on the desk next to him and opened the paper to expose the front page. He turned it to face me before tossing it down on the desk.

I almost said something stupid like, "What?" The garish headline read, *Vampires Beware!* That and a picture of me escorting the vampire Matt through the crowds at Navy Pier said it all. "Oh crap."

I quickly read the meat of the article, and the further I made my way through the nonsense, the angrier I became. I'd been expecting an article on myself taking into custody a vampire for questioning, but instead perused an article about how the FBI had leveled the playing field by hiring one of the scourges of mankind. They even labeled me as the

"Verminator." I wasn't sure if it might have been a cute reference for being a vampire terminator or that Jezwyrski had a death wish strong enough to call vampires vermin. Either way, his life might be even in more danger than my own. *Serves him right*.

It was official; absolutely no good came of last night's operation. I couldn't do anything right, and I was doubly stupid for trusting a reporter. I was a fucking *moron* for trusting the vampire. I did the only thing I could. I wadded up the newspaper into a tiny little ball–woo-hoo vampire strength–and tossed it back to Reese. He caught it with a surprised look on his face as I stood.

"Where do you think you're going?" Reese looked stunned.

"I'm gonna go kills me a reporter. You want a leg or a thigh?"

"Sit down. The damage is already done, and I'm glad you see the problem with the article. You and I are at least of a like mind. I can't believe the reporter wrote it, or the paper printed it. I hope he has a bodyguard; he's going to need it. You on the other hand, do not have a bodyguard. The odds of any vampire in the city cooperating with you before had been slim to none. Now it's just going to be an outright fucking miracle if they don't attack you on sight."

All I wanted to do was put my head in my hands and cry. I would never trust a reporter again. I sighed and looked up at Reese. He stared off into space with his chin resting on his fingers. I would have paid a good portion of one of my paychecks to know what thoughts played across his brain.

"What?"

"Just thinking about having the paper print a retraction, but I don't even think it would do any good. The paper is already out and been read. What's the point? Plus, asking for a retraction would piss off the Deputy Director. I phoned him and sent him an electronic copy of the paper, and believe it or not, he's friggin ecstatic about the article. I'm just glad I didn't open my mouth and say what I thought about it. We'll just have to get through this. It's not like you're going to be assigned here permanently."

"I know. I just don't want to have to watch my back all the time. Did you say something about a new partner on the phone? It's not necessary. Michaels should be up and running in a few days. I can take care of myself."

The look he gave me silenced me almost before I finished. Apparently, even though I had learned from my mistakes, I had still screwed up enough to warrant a babysitter. *Shit.* At least it would be for only a few days. I would get by just fine, right?

Reese picked up the phone, pressed the intercom button, and dialed an extension. I heard the phone ring three times and then a voice replied with a "Yes, Agent Reese?"

"Thompson, come in here, please. She's ready."

Reese put the receiver down, and I sat in my chair and pouted. Yes, I pouted. I didn't stick out my bottom lip or anything, but I wasn't going to be happy. I heard footsteps come through the door behind me and didn't even turn around to see my babysitter. I couldn't. The rules of etiquette concerning pouting forbade it.

"Ashlyn, this is Special Agent James Thompson who will

be your new partner until Michaels makes a full recovery. Go find your vampire from the pier and bring him in this time. You might have only been using him as bait, but he still hospitalized an agent of the FBI. Now I'm going to fry his ass. Go, the both of you, and Thomson, you had better keep her out of trouble."

"Yes, sir. Come on, newbie, let's go find the vampire," he said.

His voice shocked the hell out of me. He sounded like James Earl Jones with a chest cold. I turned to meet my new partner and had to look up a couple of feet to see him. Jesus, he looked like the bouncer from Fangloria's only bigger and darker, and he smelled like sage to boot. He definitely wasn't human, and he made my mouth water. I knew better than to lock myself into a vehicle with him. He smelled too good. I hadn't eaten since Navy Pier two nights ago, and I didn't exactly trust myself to be alone with the giant snack cake.

I stared at him for a moment to get the hunger under control. He didn't have an ounce of hair on his head, but I could see stubble, so it had to be preference over genetics. His massive head ended at his shoulders without so much as a hint of neck. No neck made for a difficult meal, oh well. I gazed down at his massive chest, waist, and everything. Finding suits in his size must be a stone cold bitch.

"Newbie?" I kind of knew what he meant, but I wanted to be sure.

"Yes. New Agent. Newbie," he rumbled back at me.

I turned to Reese and he sat there smiling with a contented look on his face. I stuck my tongue out at him, and he barked laughter as we left the offices and made our way to the Suburban. I still had the keys in my pocket and I reached in to hit the button on the fob, unlocking the vehicle. Two identical Suburbans flashed their yellow hazard lights and honked twice to signal their locations.

"Lock it, we'll take mine," he said.

"Great," I lied.

We entered the vehicle and neither he nor I buckled our seat belts, tsk, tsk. He backed out of the spot and put the SUV into drive.

"Where did you last see your vampire," he asked before stepping on the accelerator.

I thought about it for a moment. Surely Matt wouldn't be stupid enough to go back to work, right? "The Carnival at Navy Pier."

"I know the place." He stepped on the gas, pulling out of the parking garage and into the Chicago traffic.

"What happened tonight? I've never seen so many people working this late," I asked, remembering the multitude of agents back at the office at such a late hour.

"Somebody called the mayor's office and told them they planted a bomb. Turned out to be nothing, but we leant a hand to the Chicago PD to sweep the building. Oh, and curiosity," he said, smiling.

"Curiosity?"

"Everyone wanted to meet the *Verminator*."

"Fucking reporters."

A deep rumble started in Thompson's chest as he laughed at my predicament. I didn't think it possible, but I liked him even less.

We made our way down the pier and to the Carnival. A vampire stood behind the bar, but it wasn't Matt. Big shock. I won. We made our way past the hostess from the night before, and she didn't even bat an eyelash as we walked toward the bar. She must have remembered me.

"Is he your vampire?" Thompson spoke out of the side of his mouth, but I managed to make out what he was saying.

"No, it isn't," I said, struggling to leave off the "Duh!"

"Excuse me, sir," Thompson said to the vampire behind the bar. "We're looking for Matt the bartender, do you know where I might find him. I'd like to ask him a few questions."

"No, I don't. He didn't show up for work today. Piece of *merde,*" the vampire replied in a French or Cajun accent so thick I could barely make out the words.

Lou gave the impression of a fake accent, the vampire behind the bar left no such impression. I stared at the vampire while Thompson asked his name. Jean Phillipe Margeaux, the owner of the Carnival, and apparently part time bartender stood before us. His facial features made him handsome, I admitted begrudgingly. I say begrudgingly because he looked like a car salesman. I don't mean literally. He wasn't wearing a suit or trying to hand me a free balloon; I meant he looked greasy. He tied his long brown hair up in a ponytail, and his goatee looked like it hadn't been trimmed in a while, but the biggest reason he looked greasy lay behind his eyes. When you looked at his eyes, you could see something unclean.

I tested the air and caught his scent. He must have spilled some bourbon on himself sometime this evening because he couldn't drink it, but I could smell it. I smelled deeper and found it underneath the bourbon. I closed my eyes and rolled the smell around on my tongue. I tried not to gag because I couldn't even stand the smell of anise, tasting it threatened to empty my stomach. There wasn't any lemon or vanilla so he wasn't a cop killer, but just because he didn't kill the cop in the river didn't make him a nice guy. For all I knew, he could have killed Matt. Hell, he could have *made* Matt and then killed him.

I followed Thompson's lines of questioning through, "When did you last see Matt," to "Do you have any idea how we could get a hold of him," and I listened to Jean Phillipe's bullshit answers. He wasn't hiding anything; he just lied to our face. I wanted to pull him over the bar and slap the shit out of him. I think I even stepped forward when Thompson put out a hand to hold me back. The little maneuver wasn't wasted on the vampire behind the bar either. He actually sneered at me. I had heard the expression before and yet had to experience the pure stupidity of the gesture. Contempt, plain as night, shined there in his crooked little mouth and squinty eyes.

I wanted to kill him and drink his fucking blood, and I could see myself doing it. I did give him the finger and watch his face turn from contempt to amusement. He had gotten to me and he knew it, and it made him happy.

"What is the matter, little Verminator, don't you believe me?"

"Just a little nauseous from the rat infestation this place suffers from, Mr. Margeaux. Please excuse my obvious distaste," I shot back. Wow, I didn't even know I could be so pleasant to such an asshole.

"Thank you for your time, Mr. Margeaux," Thompson said and pushed me toward the door.

Herding me didn't help my mood. I swallowed the urge to push him back and lead the way myself. If things escalated between Thompson and me, I wanted to do it where I could land some serious punches.

As soon as we exited, I spun on him. "That son of a motherfucking vampire is a lying piece of shit!"

“Tell me something I don't know, kid. C'mon, let's go find the missing vampire."

"Where are we going to look? This is a big city and we have no idea where to even begin."

"We'll start with the bars and clubs. Go grab a newspaper and meet me at the car," he ordered.

I didn't like orders.

"What do we need a newspaper for? Are you going to brush up on your reading skills?" I obviously pissed him off because he stopped walking and turned around to face me.

"Listen, you little shit with fangs. Obviously you don't like me, even though I have done nothing to piss you off. You have been rude and obnoxious and I'm getting a little sick of it. You're lucky I don't drive you back and dump you on your ass in Reese's office. Think about why I would ask you to get a newspaper for a moment. What's on the front cover, hmm? The answer is a picture of the vampire we're looking for. So how are we going to play this? Are you going to start acting like a FBI agent, or are we going to go back to the office so you can pout until your partner is back to full health?"

I wanted to punch him square in his massive jaw, but I settled for listening to what he said. I felt a little contrite and I gave him a small, "Sorry." I hated to admit it, but he wasn't wrong. If I had been expecting a smile from him, I was going to be sorely disappointed. He nodded at me and started back toward the car. I found some newspaper vending machines in the park across the street from Navy Pier and dropped in a couple of quarters. I opened the door and found my smiling face on the front page, pulled out the evening edition and made my way back to the parking garage where all my trouble started.

Thompson sat in the vehicle with the engine running and on the cell phone. It seemed kind of a one-way conversation with a bunch of, "Yes, sirs," on Thompson's part. *He must have been talking to Reese*. He hung up and gave me a quick, "Let's go."

"Where are we headed?"

"Local PD found your vampire."

"Where"?

"In a dumpster, most of him anyway," he said without batting an eyelash.

We waited for the crime scene investigator to come out of the dumpster before we could look at the body. The dumpster sat behind a takeout Chinese restaurant. Why do criminals always pick the dumpsters behind Chinese restaurants? They'll *never* find it if it's covered in Lo Mein! When I said body, I meant a body with no head. Whoever murdered Matt sent that in a box to the closest precinct. Nice way to deliver a message. *Yuck.*

Finally, the investigator gave the go ahead for two technicians to pull the body out. Even headless, Matt's body was still longer than average and the technicians strained under the load. They laid the body out on the wet ground of the alley while they prepared to bag it to send to the city morgue. I hated to do it, but I had to smell the body. I stepped closer and took a good look. The skin of the neck wasn't cut. If anything, it looked like it had been twisted and ripped. Somebody had literally ripped the poor bastard's head off. What a way to go. I quit stalling and knelt down by Matt.

The Chinese food overwhelmed any other scents at first. My aunt had ordered Chinese quite regularly, and I had always found the smell quite enticing. I probably wouldn't ever think so again. Combine the smell of chicken parts, soy sauce, and dead vampire and you get something akin to "Ick." I closed my eyes and concentrated on the smells. One by one, I eliminated them. Once I picked the sauces out the rest fell into place. I killed the sour smell of the raw chicken and then the rice. Yup, lemon and vanilla. Mr. Cop Killer.

"Thompson," I called over my shoulder.

"What?" He interrupted his conversation with the investigator.

"Come here please," I asked him nicely. I turned my head as he squatted down by the body and added his sage to the lemon and vanilla I tried to concentrate on. "Whoever killed Matt killed the cop they fished out of the lake a few nights ago."

"How the hell could you possibly know?"

"I can smell him."

I expected him to argue, but he disappointed me again and merely nodded. He stared thoughtfully at my face for a few moments and finally asked if I needed anything more here. I told him no and we headed to the SUV again. I had no idea where he planned to head this time and to keep from starting yet another argument, I kept my mouth shut.

We didn't drive long, just headed back to the thick of the downtown area. We passed Navy Pier and made our way down Michigan Ave. Some of the greatest storefronts I had ever heard of or seen twinkled in the night, like little beacons of hope in an otherwise shitty economy. Few people in this world had the money to spare on movie paraphernalia or the latest and greatest sixty-something inch plasma televisions, yet here they sparkled for everyone to see.

We finally passed out of the shopping district and into the bar and club district, nowhere near Fangloria's. Fangloria's was a slum compared to some of the places I saw here. Thompson pulled the Suburban into a high-rise parking garage and parked in the first available spot. He managed a little better than the eighth level like Michaels and I. The parking gods must have been with him.

We emerged from the garage and stepped out onto the sidewalk. Thompson seemed to know where he was going so I followed his massive bulk. I wondered if anyone walking toward him could even see me. I doubted it. They probably couldn't see buildings behind him. He didn't turn down any side streets, but we walked a good distance before I saw our destination. The outside of the bottom floor of the high rise was completely covered with large golden hued glass panels unlike the blue of the remaining levels of the building. If you looked closely, you could see the panels vibrating from the music being played inside.

A revolving brass door complete with matching golden-hued glass marked the entrance to the club. The line outside the door seemed even more ridiculous than the one I had seen at Fangloria's. The bouncer at the door surprised me. Every club I had been to so far used hulking vampires to guard the entrance. Here stood a lithe figure in stretch black spandex. I needed to call the newspaper. Female bouncers only existed in fairy tales, right? Maybe not, the spandex she wore left little in the way of modesty or imagination. All I'm going to say is she obviously shaved or waxed. We walked up to the well-endowed blond and Thompson flashed his badge. Skanky smiled and flashed a bit of fang.

"What can I do for you, officer?" She had what I assumed to be a Russian accent.

"Special Agent Thompson with the FBI, not 'officer.' This is Agent Ashlyn. We're here to ask a few people some questions."

"Good luck, Special Agent Thompson. Good luck," she said and turned her attention to me.

Things got ugly real quick. She must have recognized me from my picture in the paper. As I passed her, she let her human seeming go and bared fang as well as letting out a toe-curling hiss. When the bouncer at Fangloria's hissed, my body knew instinctively he had been testing me. This wasn't a test. The lithe vampire in front of me wanted to tear me apart. I could smell her from where she stood and it wasn't a pleasant odor. Her normal scent was cloves and mint, but her fury changed it. I smelled fear, and it was sweet and delectable, but I didn't know I could smell anger. It reeked of rotting meat and I don't think I have ever smelled anything more unpleasant. Not even headless corpses in Chinese dumpsters could compare.

I didn't hiss back at her. My body knew if I did, it would be a challenge, and she would attack. As far as I knew, she hadn't done anything, so I let it go. I just smiled at her and ignored her challenge. A fight would seriously piss off Thompson more than I already had. I looked at her eyes, and I felt something I hadn't ever felt before. No, it wasn't compassion. I could see her power in her blue eyes and I could feel it. It gave me the impression of a calm pond not quite frozen on a winter's night. I looked inside myself and I felt mine. I gasped when I felt the tumultuous sea that was me. The whole experience felt mystical, but it would probably come in handy when judging an opponent. I'd have to practice when I had the chance.

"Can it, sister," I told her. "I'm not here to start trouble, especially with you." I let my power flow from inside me and let it wash over her.

Surprise crossed her face. Master vampires and common vampires are undistinguishable except through DNA testing, or until a master vampire uses his mind to control your thoughts. Hell, they could pass for human until they showed their fangs or you felt their cold dead skin. The only vampires distinguishable on sight were the unfortunate Revenants and Nosferatu. Everyone knows the bald head and sharp nails of a Nosferatu, and the drooling mindless hunger commonplace on a Revenant means run. It is why they're illegal. Nosferatu, if they can control themselves, are legal. It's not as easy as it sounds, and usually you can only find them in the employ of other vampires who can help them contain their hunger.

"Fuck you, bitch! It's because of you, my Matt had to run," she said and fought not to close the distance between us and attack me. Interesting, she said he ran, so she doesn't know he's dead. At least I could spare her the suffering of not knowing. I opened my mouth to let her know just that when Thompson interrupted me.

"Let's go, Agent Ashlyn," he said authoritatively.

The man sucked all the fun out of my life.

I sighed and followed Thompson. I half expected bouncer girl to take a swipe at me as I walked past, but she didn't. Damn it. He ushered me into the revolving door first–I guess he didn't trust me either–and I finally caught the name of the club on the door. The entire glass plane before me lay covered with golden window film, but the name of the club had been carefully cut out of it, "MegaBites." *You have got to be fucking kidding me*.

I couldn't help but roll my eyes as I left the revolving door and stepped out onto the floor of the gigantic club. The dance floor occupied the entire breadth and width of the room. As soon as I cleared the door, my ears found themselves assaulted by the constant thrumming and pounding of techno or rave or trance or whatever they called it music and I didn't like it. It almost hurt. I ignored the rattling in my teeth and glanced around. From the outside of the building, the club looked like it occupied only the bottom floor of the building. Not so. The first floor held the dance floor, but stairs lined both sides of the room leading up to the second floor. I looked up and saw a railed balcony overlooking the festivities below. Impressed by the design, but I wished they would do something about the music.

Thompson came in behind and tapped me on the shoulder to follow him. I thought maybe he wanted to dance or something, but he headed to the stairwell on our right. We emerged on the second floor and the music levels seemed much more tolerable. It could still be heard, but it wasn't at the bone jarring levels like downstairs. I looked around and gasped at the size of the bar nestled against the far wall. It had to be the longest bar in the state and the patrons waiting for drinks still stood three people deep. The rest of the floor area comprised of lounge chairs and couches nestled in groups or perched to overlook the multitudes of people dancing below. I sniffed the air and immediately smelled sweaty humans, subtly spiced lycanthropes, sweet smelling vampires, and a couple of other aromas I couldn't identify.

Great, where did we start? A vampire had killed Matt and the dead police officer. I decided to start there. I glanced over at Thompson and found him looking around as well, probably wondering the same thing. I looked over his bulk again and wondered exactly what kind of lycanthropy he suffered from. He smelled a tad different from wolf and I didn't know what it could be. I would have to ask him. I just hoped it wasn't impolite to ask someone, "Excuse me, sir, what animal do you change into?" Yeah right, maybe I'd just let him bring it up.

I didn't know what he planned to accomplish here, but I knew what I could do. I needed to mingle and try to catch a whiff of every vampire in the place if I had to. He headed to the bar and reached into his jacket pocket, pulling out the front page of the newspaper. Thompson had neatly folded it so the picture of Matt the vampire and I were the only things visible except for a partial segment of the headline and newspaper name. He made his way to the bar, and like magic, the people parted for him. Everybody who stood in his way kind of just stepped over to the side and started rubbing any exposed flesh. I wondered what caused it. I didn't feel anything when I stood next to him. I moved closer and sure enough, I could feel a tiny hum coming from him. I found it almost pleasant. I don't know why everyone else moved away from him, if I had a choice, I would have moved closer.

Straight out of a scene from a television show, Thompson waved one of the vampire bartenders over and held out the front page. "Ever seen this man before?" The bartender started shaking his head negatively before Thompson even finished. The vamp looked over the picture briefly and then looked up at me. He didn't start hissing, but I saw his brows furrow in recognition and anger. I caught his eyes and felt mine capture his. He held another small pool of power not worth worrying over. I had an "oh, shit" moment though. As I gazed into his eyes, I fell into his little pool of power.

The bar fell away until only he and I were there. The

room darkened and our bodies became the only sources of illumination. I've seen people glow from the inside in movies, and that is exactly what we did. I saw his stare turn from anger, to puzzlement, to outright fear, and then I could smell it. I'm not talking about lemons and vanilla. I smelled his fear. It smelled delicious. I kind of wrinkled my nose at the slight smell of juniper berries, his normal scent, and concentrated on the fear. Right then and there, if I wanted to, I could have called him through our locked state and he would have climbed over the bar to my side. He wouldn't have liked it, but he would have done it.

Master vampires have the same kind of powers over humans. In the days before their emancipation, it is how they called for their supper. Many a human had been roused out of their sleep to walk out into the darkly lit village streets. They quickly became a meal, and if they didn't die from the experience, in a trance like state they made their ways back to their chambers and resumed their slumber with no memory of the vampire. They might have been a little dizzy in the morning from the blood loss, but the remembrance of a pleasant dream usually overshadowed any ill effects. Today, if vampires wanted to get themselves a warrant of execution, they could do the same thing. Mind control of humans is strictly prohibited by the Vampire Emancipation Act. The really sick thing is they didn't need to use mind tricks. Entire clubs full of people would willingly feed a vampire for the sexual thrill. Nothing gets you off faster than one of the undead sucking your life's blood out of two tiny holes in your neck. Yuck.

Thompson's snapping fingers in front of my face broke

our trance. I blinked twice and stared up into his ebony face. The vampire behind the bar blinked and shook his head and started taking drink orders. I could still smell his fear though, and I hadn't eaten in a few days. I started to look back toward the bartender, but Thompson gently grabbed my chin and turned my face toward him.

"Did you just mind trap him?" He didn't seem angry, just curious.

"Yes," I replied meekly and more than a little guiltily.

"I'm judging by your reaction you didn't know you could. Am I right?"

I pulled my head from his hand and shook it. The little shake helped clear the fuzziness in my head. I looked up at Thompson and gave him a weak smile. I kind of expected some sort of sympathetic gesture on his part but, "Be careful," was all he said.

He left the bar without questioning the other two bartenders if they had ever seen Matt before, which kind of shocked me until I looked at them. The first one looked like a vampire, but he didn't move like one. I can't explain it, he didn't move slower, just sloppier. There is no wasted movement with vampires. The others behind the bar had more fluidity in their movements than a vampire. They might have been faster and more agile than humans, but definitely not vampires.

I followed Thompson. I wondered how he knew the other two bartenders weren't vamps. For all I knew his sense of smell could have been better than mine. I could distinguish between people, vampires, and lycanthropes, but only to know who or what I could eat. I could even distinguish between certain members of the same species. Just like how I was looking for Mr. Lemon-vanilla, but maybe Thompson's shnoz worked better at distances and could smell vampires from other species. I wish I could, it would be helpful. Instead, I was stuck with them all smelling yummy.

I happened to glance over to the end of the bar. From a distance, it looked like it ran the entire length of the wall. It actually stopped three feet from the wall and formed a door, blended in with the wood of the bar. Jean Phillipe Margeaux opened the door and walked through it. It was the only reason I noticed it. While we were busy investigating Matt's decapitated body, he must have come here. I wondered what connection he had to "MegaBites."

"Thompson," I called out to my partner.

He looked at me, and I nodded in Jean Phillipe's direction. He saw the greasy vampire walking out from behind the bar into the club. He moved to the beat of the music and bobbed his head with the tempo smiling and flirting with female club patrons and a of couple male ones. The sleaze ball even stopped to dance with a young lady in a very, very short skirt who waited for her boyfriend to get them drinks from the bar. He whispered something in her ear and she shook her head "no". I saw him mutter something at her with a disgusted look on his face and move on. Then he saw us.

He contemplated running back into whatever was behind the hidden door; you could see it on his face. He didn't want to talk to us again, but he knew better than to run. Instead, he stopped where he stood, put his hands on his hips, and started tapping his foot impatiently. Gosh, if he was in such a hurry, he could have come over to us. Thompson smiled at me and we walked toward Jean Phillipe, slowly.

"I told you I don't know where Matt is. Why are you bothering me again?" French accents bugged me. What is so hard about "bothering?" Why did it have to come out "bozzering?" Can you say annoying?

"We do, Mr. Margeaux. He's at the city morgue," Thompson said. "Do you know who would want Matt dead?"

He wasn't a nice man, but the news of Matt's departure from this world shocked him. He wasn't a good enough actor to register that kind of surprise. He didn't look sad, just shocked. Then I saw realization cross his face. He knew exactly who killed Matt. The question being, would he tell us?

"*Non*, I don't know anybody who would want him dead." I guess he wasn't going to. Prick. "If you would please excuse me, I need to tell his girlfriend Veronica."

"Is she your charming bouncer we met out front of the club? By the way, what brings you here? How come you're not still bartending over at the Carnival?" I even said Carnival with a fake French accent. I impressed myself. Mine was way better than Lou's had been. Thompson's elbow in my ribs let me know he wasn't impressed. Maybe I did need a babysitter.

"I own this place, too," he said, only this came out "zis." "I had been there only because Matt understandably did not show up for work. Lou is fine in the dining room, but horrible behind the bar. As to your other question, yes, Veronica is my hostess here."

"So you have no idea who would want Matt dead?"

"Other than the little Verminator, *non*."

"What about Cicero?"

"Matt had never met Cicero, why would he want him dead?" He used his crooked little smile. I had had enough. I looked into his eyes and sought out his power, only this time I intended to.

His power spread out before me, a good-sized body of choppy waters reflecting the summer moon. Jean Phillipe was a master vampire and I hoped this worked on him. If it didn't, I prayed Thompson would bail me out. I just hoped he could tell when and if I found myself Mayor of Indeepshitsville. I let the club fade away until only he and I floated alone. I tried to speak to him but I couldn't. Instead, I thought at him, "Tell me who you're protecting." I saw his fear, and then I smelled it in the darkness. I could see him struggle against the power I poured out with the thought, and lose. His thought drifted across the room and settled itself in my mind, "Cicero." Maybe not him directly, but he ordered Matt killed, probably after seeing the newspaper. I suspected it and he confirmed it. Jean Phillipe feared he would be next. Everyone had orders not to talk to the police. He feared me, but Cicero had turned into a nightmare who would get them all killed. I had what I wanted and let go of Jean Phillipe's mind.

I found myself staring out of my own eyes back in the club with the music blaring all around me. Jean Phillipe lay on the floor like he had fallen after I let him go. Thompson reached down and helped the fallen vampire up to his feet.

"*Non*, what did you do?" He stared at me with a horrific look on his face. He had slipped beyond afraid and into the realm of terrified. Only this time I had become the focus of his fear. When a supe becomes afraid around me, the smell is intoxicating, but his terror delved into the realm of irresistible. I had to clench my fists together and dig my talons into my palm to make the pain wash away the hunger I had for the French vampire. "Who are you? What are you? You shouldn't have been able to hold my mind like you did," he started babbling. I needed to get out of here and fast.

"Thompson, I need to leave now," I said out of the side of my mouth.

"In a minute, I have a few more questions."

"Now!" I had heard someone yell at the Grand Canyon on a television show once and remembered how it echoed on and on until it faded. My "now" came out exactly like I cried it over a canyon ten times the size. It echoed off the walls of the club and bounced back at me a hundred times before finally stopping. The club went eerily silent. The music still blared only because there wasn't a DJ to stop spinning the record, but not one soul made a sound.

I looked over at the bar and the three deep patrons had stopped conversing and turned to the source of the horrific cry. I looked down over the balcony and all the people dancing had stopped to look up through the hole in the second story floor to see what had happened. Now I really needed to leave. I didn't care if Thompson stayed or followed, but I turned and practically ran down the stairs, through the revolving door and out into the night.

I felt better once the outside air hit my skin. It helped clear the intoxicating smell of fear from my nose, but the hunger remained. I heard the *clip clop* of a size fifteen shoe from behind me and Thompson joined me. He laid a hand on my shoulder and asked if I felt all right. I didn't. I had to eat and do it now. The only food in sight was the meaty hand on my shoulder. I gave no warning to Thompson; I just grabbed his arm with my talons and struck. I felt my fangs pierce skin and muscle and settle into his bone. He tried to pull his wrist from my mouth, but couldn't.

The blood hit my tongue and I gasped at its deliciousness. I rolled it around and swallowed it as fast as I could. I could feel Thompson's fingers pushing against my lips trying to break my hold. There wasn't any pain and I could have ignored his feeble attempts to force me away if I had wanted to, but I did. I did want to. I felt horrified I had attacked a fellow agent let alone my temporary partner. Comprehension overcame hunger and I let go with both my mouth and hands. I backed away muttering, "I'm so sorry," over and over again.

He straightened his back and shivered as I backed away. I looked at his furrowed brow and his sweaty skin and collapsed on the wet Chicago pavement. I didn't pass out like I wanted to, merely fell to my butt and brought my knees up to my chest. I hugged my legs and began rocking and crying. It had been a while since the last time I cried, and I couldn't stop the tears. I felt it drip down my face and stain the sleeve of my jacket red. Bloody tears welled from my eyes. What the hell had happened? What the hell kind of monster was I turning into?

I looked up and the people waiting in line stood staring at us with a horrified expression on their faces. Those looks made me cry even more. Then I saw Veronica. She smiled at me like she wanted to have sex with me. She tilted her head back and ran her hands all over herself. I buried my face in my arms so I couldn't watch anymore. This whole night had come straight out of a nightmare.

Then I felt something I hadn't expected. Massive arms, smelling of sage, wrapped themselves around me. Thompson lifted me off the pavement and held me to his chest like a small child, and I buried my face against his warmth. I stayed there until he settled me into my seat inside the Suburban. He had carried me all the way back to the parking garage and not said a word. My dislike of the man changed into something a little more positive. I just hope he didn't hate me more. I had attacked him, and by all rights, he could have me kicked out of the FBI. At this point, I wondered if I cared. I couldn't stop myself from making one mistake after another.

I fell asleep in the vehicle and then woke briefly as Thompson carried me into Michaels' apartment. I remember flashes of a concerned Michaels opening the door and leading Thompson to my room. I remember him laying me down on my bed and Pete covering me up with a blanket and somebody taking off my shoes. I heard a little of their conversation as Thompson gave a brief synopsis of the evening while they watched over me. Then I remembered nothing.

Chapter 18

I must have fallen back into my normal routine of waking with the waning sun. I literally felt it slip over the horizon, and my eyes opened. I rolled my tongue around in my dry mouth and still tasted the last vestiges of Thompson's blood, which brought the events of last night back into my mind. I groaned like a wounded caribou.

Michaels jumped up from the floor, looked around the room, and whined as he grabbed his head from the pain. He looked down at my blanket-covered form and asked me, "What's the matter? Are you okay?"

"No, I'm an idiot. Are you okay?"

"No, my head hurts."

We both started laughing at the same time. Free therapy rules. "Will you help me find a job?"

"What are you talking about?" He looked utterly confused.

"I attacked Thompson last night and fed off of him. I couldn't help it. Some weird shit happened to me, and before you ask, I'll tell you later. I don't even want to think about it right now. Well anyway, I ended up making Thompson a late night snack. When Reese finds out I'm going to have to start collecting an unemployment check."

"Did you know you're a dolt, Fangs?"

"Huh?"

"Agents take care of each other," he started. I gave him a “what are you talking about" look. "Thompson called Reese and told him he had to open a vein for you because you almost attacked a vampire in a club. You should have heard him. I've never heard anybody yell at Reese before. Anyway, a couple of paramedics came by while you slept and dropped off some Lycanthrope blood. It's in the fridge if you're still hungry."

"Huh?" My head swam in a river of confusion. Thompson called Reese and stuck up for me? "I thought he hated me."

"Yeah, he mentioned that you were being a bitch when he first started working with you, but he found you pretty fascinating and pretty funny. Oh and he said you're cute, too."

"Huh?" I really needed a thesaurus for my birthday. I understood what Michaels said, I just didn't believe it.

Michaels just laughed at me and told me to get ready. Thompson would be here around seven-thirty to pick me up since I left our Suburban at the office. I shooed him back into his bed and made sure he took his medication. Once he settled in, I gave him a kiss on his forehead like my aunt used to do when I was little. He kind of looked at me cross-eyed like I had a screw–or two–loose so I gave him the finger, laughed, and went to go shower and change. I had just finished when my cell phone started ringing.

"Hello?" I glanced at the caller I.D. and saw Thompson's name.

"I'm downstairs whenever you're ready," his deep voice grumbled out of the cell.

"Be down in five," I said and hit the end button.

"Pete, I'm leaving," I called out to my roomie.

"Be careful, Fangs!" I heard him moan. The dumbass hurt his head from yelling.

I made it down to the Suburban in just a few minutes, much less than my allotted five. I knocked on the window and I heard the doors unlock. I pulled the handle and climbed into the seat next to Thompson.

"Good morning, kid," he grumbled at me.

I smiled and looked out the window at the dark sky. "You're a night owl, too?"

"I've been working nights my whole career."

"How long have you been an agent?"

"I did eight years in the Army, and then joined the FBI about sixteen years ago. Been a hell of a ride." he said and smiled.

"Thanks for last night, big man. I owe you big time. If you catch me being a brat again smack me." I lowered my eyes in embarrassment.

"Keep being interesting, kid. We'll get along fine. Just try not to bite me again, okay?"

"Did it hurt?" He pulled the massive SUV from its parking spot.

"No, I liked it a lot, just don't ever do it again. Ain't never been bitten by a vampire before."

I smiled and we rode in silence. I could tell by the route he took he planned on stopping by the office. It might be wise to do so. I should probably check in with Reese and thank him for sending over the blood last night. What I had taken from

Thompson would last me for a day or two, but now I wouldn't have to worry about my next few meals. We pulled into the parking garage and Thompson got a spot right next to the elevator.

"How do you get such good spots all the time?"

"I sacrifice chickens to the parking gods."

I laughed at his joke, and he stared at me like I had two heads. Maybe he wasn't joking. Oh well, to each his own. Maybe I should start trying it. We made our way into the office and the sea of desks remained mostly empty, just a few agents talking on the telephone and working on laptops. Thompson didn't stop by his desk on the way, merely followed me to Reese's office. I knocked twice on the frame and walked right in. He was on the phone again as usual. He gave me and Thompson a dirty look and held up his one index finger.

"Sir, this is getting ridiculous, we have to get them to print a retraction," he said and paused listening to whoever was on the other end of the line. "No, sir, she wasn't. It's not the point, sir," the conversation went on. "Yes, sir I will. No, sir, have a good night," he said and finally hung up the receiver. "Do me a favor will you, Ashlyn?"

"Sure, what?"

"When you're out in the public, please think about *what you are doing in front of witnesses*!" The pitch of his speech rose in crescendo about mid-sentence, and by the time he finished he had escalated to yelling. The door creaked and then clicked closed. At least Thompson didn't want the rest of the office listening.

"What are you talking about, sir?"

I stared at him blankly. Apparently, I had done something wrong, but for the life of me, I had no idea what. Then it hit me. Reese tossed yet another newspaper on the desk. I looked down on the front page and saw a stock photo of me at the news conference. The picture wasn't a big deal, the headline on the other hand might have been. It read, "The New FBI." At least it's what you saw when you glanced at it, but if you looked closely at the words written in a font size about twelve points smaller than the garish headlines in between the "F" and "B" and after the "I" you could read the words, "anged, rutal, and nterrogator". If you read it all together, today's headline read "The New Fanged Brutal Interrogator." *Nice.*

I read the article by Steve Jezwyrski and almost started crying. He had arrived on the scene after several people in line had phoned into police witnessing a vampire attack. The little bastard even had several quotes from eyewitnesses stating they had seen a vampire fitting my description attack a large man on the outside of the club. Of course, Jean Philippe as the owner of the club had not disabused anyone of the notion either and hoped, "To never see the menacing FBI agent in any of his businesses again." Even Veronica the bouncer had chimed in with, "She walked in like she owned the joint and started harassing all the vampires I work with."

I handed the article back to Thompson so he could have a good read. I crossed my legs and stared at Reese, who stared back at me, while Thompson read the printed *mostly* lies. After what seemed to be an eternity, Thompson tossed the paper down on the desk next to Reese with a grunt and shake of his head.

"Bullshit," he said disgustedly. "She couldn't wait anymore, not without attacking one of the vampires at MegaBites. Be thankful I was there, sir."

I stared at his face again. He looked down at me and I offered up a little smile of gratitude. He winked back with the eye Reese couldn't see. I rested my chin in my hand and looked back at Reese. He still hadn't been appeased.

"Well at least the Deputy Director is still happy with the media coverage. He feels the vampires of Chicago will be quaking in their little vampire boots around you and will scramble to aid your investigations in any way. I tried to tell him it would probably just piss them off even more, but he just doesn't get it. I'm at a loss. Go on, get out of here, the both of you," he said and shooed us out of his office.

I really don't like being shooed.

"Wait, what are you doing next?"

"Hitting more bars to see if we can find any helpful informants," Thompson yelled without even turning around.

We walked through the main office area, ignoring the stares of the agents still working, and headed out to the parking garage.

"Thanks again, Thompson. I owe you dinner."

"Cuz I fed you last night?"

"No, because if it wasn't for you I'd be up the creek," I replied levelly.

I found myself in another club with a bad vampire pun for

a name. "The Vamporium" wasn't a normal club either. It catered to a different crowd I had only heard about on the internet. "Goth" and "Scene" didn't even begin to cover the descriptions of the people milling around the large dark club listening to a cross between Techno and Gregorian chant music. Most of the outfits had been manufactured out of PVC or vinyl and every other person you saw wore a collar and leash. I had worn a skirt and jacket combo and felt completely out of place. *At least it's black.*

The far end of the club held a large stage, but instead of a DJ or live music, people posed almost naked in various sexually explicit positions. They would hold the pose for a minute or so and then everyone would switch positions and partners. It looked like an Andy Warhol sexual round robin. I found it more than a little disturbing. My life, so far, had been one long vow of chastity. It's not because I wasn't interested in sex. It's just hard when you spend most of your life as a hermit to meet new people, mingle, and find a special someone you'd want to be your first. I needed one of those promise rings all the kids seemed to be wearing.

We made our way through the place and finally got to the bar. I couldn't believe the outfits some of the people felt comfortable in. How do you wear an outfit with holes cut out where your nipples should be? How in the hell do you feel comfortable with everyone staring at your nipples? Hello, people? I tried hard not to stare at them and I forbade myself from looking at the stage. I found a spot on Thompson's back and tried to pretend I found it very interesting.

We idled our way up to the bar and the bartender made

her way over to us. Thompson asked for a cola and I declined. I wanted to leave in a bad way. The bartender turned to fill a glass with ice and I looked down, damn it. She wore chaps, which gave the impression of leather pants from the front, but when she turned around, her butt cheeks became fully exposed with nothing covering them except a tiny string in between. I could only imagine what it would look like if she bent over to pick something up. I gulped. Thompson heard me and gave a bark of laughter.

"Sheltered life, kid?"

"You have no idea."

The bartender returned and Thompson took the glass of brown liquid. He handed her a five-dollar bill and laid a picture of Matt on the counter he had cut out of the paper. I guess he had gotten tired of carrying the whole front page around with him. *Wow, he wasn't just muscle.*

"You ever see this vampire?"

"No," she answered without even looking.

I thought she might be trying to protect her own kind, but then I realized she wasn't a vampire. Her tan gave it away for starters. The second reason, I felt the energy vibrating off her the way I had with Thompson when he made his way to the bar last night. Where he felt like a vibrating mountain, she felt more like a purring cat. He snarled at her quite loudly, I almost mistook it for a roar. She cowered, and I jumped. Everyone around us became very interested in their drinks. I stared at Thompson like he had grown an appendage out of his forehead.

"Let me ask again, have you ever seen this vampire?"

She picked up the picture off the counter and looked at it. She nodded once and told us he came in once in a while, but she hadn't seen him for a few weeks. This wasn't getting us anywhere. A whole other world of supernatural beings lived in the Chicago area and we just had to fight talon and fang to even get the simplest of answers; sometimes, life could be frustrating. Thompson continued his questioning about the last time Matt had been in and if he had come in with anybody, but the girl either didn't remember, or found an extra set of testicles behind the bar and suddenly developed amnesia. I would have put money on the latter.

Thompson must have believed her when she said she didn't remember because he just nodded at her and let her get back to work. I thought we would move on to questioning others in the club or go to a different club altogether, but we just stood at the bar and took in the sights. This wasn't helping my celibacy situation. I found myself staring at things I shouldn't even be looking at. Not just on the men either. I found myself glancing at the posterior end of the bartender every time she turned around. I wasn't a person who found members of the same sex attractive in any way, but as she turned, I stared at the suppleness and smoothness of her hindquarters like a haunch of beef. I became mesmerized and pictured sinking my fangs into the twin golden orbs of flesh when one of the clubs security people walked up.

"Is there a problem over here?" I heard over my shoulder. I needed to pay attention.

I turned and found an ashen-looking vampire in a leather suit. I didn't even know they made such a thing. The effect looked kind of cheesy. I expected to see a shirt with extremely wide lapels to be underneath the jacket, like something out of the seventies, but instead the vampire wore a black fishnet shirt. Mr. Fashionsense came to mind. I tried not to laugh. He even wore a fake silver rope chain. It wasn't real because his skin wasn't burning and smoking. Even Master Vampires had little tolerance for the mysterious metal. I could handle it with impunity; it's one of the other reasons I thought I wasn't a vampire.

"I'm Special Agent Thompson with the FBI; we're investigating a series of murders. Have you seen this man in the club?" Thompson showed the icky little vamp the picture from the newspaper.

"Nope, I've never seen him before in my life, or afterlife, so there's no reason for you *or* her to be here. Please leave."

Wow, rude from the start. I glanced over the pimpish vamp and didn't like what I saw. I gave a quick whiff and found him covered with a sickly sweet combination of cheap aftershave and cloves. His odor settled it; there wasn't anything I liked about this man. I looked over his shoulder at another vampire walking up behind Mr. Fashionsense. He stood much taller than the rat we found ourselves currently engaged with and much more striking. You hear about debonair vampires all the time in stories and movies. With the exception of Nosferatu, becoming a vampire changes you and makes you more desirable and beautiful. It apparently skipped the rat and landed square on our new visitor.

He stood about six feet tall and had long wavy brown hair down to his waist. He wasn't dressed in leather, vinyl, or PVC like everyone else in the club. Simple blue jeans with a straight cut down to his brown loafers topped off by a simple black silk shirt. The bartender's provocative outfit is what attracted me to her, but this vampire in jeans and a shirt took my breath away. I would have found him attractive wearing nothing. I would find him very attractive wearing nothing. I hoped to gods I wasn't actually blushing.

"Is there a problem here, Tony?" The vampire's cool voice sent shivers down my spine. "Special Agent Thompson, good to see you again. What brings you to my humble club?" The vampire held out his hand to Thompson, who heartily shook it.

"Good to see you again, Marcel. This is Agent Ashlyn, my partner. You got someplace we can talk?"

"Sure, C'mon," he said and turned.

We followed and I brushed by Tony trying very hard not to touch him.

He led us into a back office completely paneled in cedar, very rustic for a sex club owner. He surprised me. The laptop computer on the desk and the large plasma television on the wall showing at least ten camera feeds looked to be the only technology in the room. Each feed took up a small portion of the flat screen. It would be very effective if one person wanted to keep tabs on every portion of his domain.

Marcel sat down behind his desk and motioned for Thompson and I to sit in the big leather chairs positioned in front. Tony followed us into the room and closed the door. I felt a flare of power from Marcel and a shocked look passed over Tony's face. He opened the door and exited, leaving us alone with Marcel. I tried very hard not to laugh, and I hoped I had as much control over my power one day.

"So what can a humble club owner do for the Federal Bureau of Investigation, Jim?"

Just how well did these two know each other? For some reason I couldn't picture Thompson frequenting an establishment like this.

"There isn't a humble bone in your body, Marc. Damn, it's good to see you again. Ashlyn and I are looking for a killer. He's offed a couple of local cops and one vampire. We know who is ultimately responsible for the deaths, but I figured we'd have a better chance of finding *him* by finding the killer. Here's a picture of the dead vamp." Thompson slid the newspaper clipping over the desk to Marc or Marcel, whatever his name may be.

I thought about changing mine to "Confused."

"Matt's dead?"

Thompson nodded.

"Damn it. He had approached me for work a few weeks back, and frequented my club often. He wanted out from underneath Jean Philippe. I told him to give Jean notice, and I would give him a job behind the bar, either here or at one of my other clubs. Poor bastard, he was good vampire, and we're few and far between. I should call Veronica, she must be devastated."

I shrank guiltily in my seat. I had played no small part in the death of the tall vampire, and I had found his girlfriend to be a complete bitch. I had only dealt with vampires like Cicero and Gloria before I had left for the academy, and I hate to admit it, I stereotyped vampires. I knew in my soul I wasn't like the others, and I just equated it with moral superiority. I felt more than ashamed and I slunk even farther into my chair.

My movement didn't go unnoticed by Marcel. He seemed to focus in on me for the first time. I watched curiosity be replaced with recognition, and recognition be replaced with distaste. *Oh shit, here it comes.*

"Your partner is the Verminator?" He stood from his desk.

"Calm down, Marc. She's a newbie."

"Yet Matt is dead and he did nothing wrong except to have the misfortune of meeting your newbie," he stated vehemently.

"She's young, Marc, real young."

"Who's your maker, little one, how did you free yourself to pursue your own desires?"

I looked into his eyes. There wasn't one doubt that I sat before a master vampire. This time I felt myself being sucked down into his stare. The room fell away and I could feel the ocean of his power. While mine seemed violent and capped with turbulent waves, his felt like a rolling ocean on a summer's night. I could feel the ebb and tide of his power in its enormity. Mine felt both larger and stronger, but I could tell he could call those waters to flood rivers, destroy beaches, and erode mountains. His waters would answer his every whim, mine on the other hand produced massive waves, and I often rode *them*.

The oceans fell away until we floated in darkness and our bodies illuminated each other. He walked toward me and held my head in his spectral hands. "Who made you, little one?" The thought drifted across my mind even though the words never left his mouth.

"Why should I answer?"

"Because you have no choice, you cannot lie with your mind."

"But I don't have to answer, do I?"

He laughed and we returned to his office in the club. He still stared at me, but this time he had a smile. "I see why you like her, old friend. She is full of power and mirth, but lacks any control over what she could be. I have met thousands of vampires over the years, some over a thousand years old, but none with the raw power she has," he told Thompson, but his eyes never left mine. "I promise not to harm you or yours, but for my own curiosity please, I must know, how old are you and who made you?" He sat back down in his oversized leather chair.

"I am eighteen and have no idea who my father is, I'm sorry," I answered truthfully.

"You have been a vampire for less than two decades?"

I nodded.

"Unbelievable. No wonder Cicero wants you less than alive," he laughed.

"Excuse me?"

"Cicero has offered a bounty for, and I quote, the child vampire agent of the FBI."

"Do you intend to try to collect this bounty?" A lump developed in my throat. I had felt the ocean of his power and if it came down to a fight, I didn't know if I could best him raw power against experience.

"James, you have to keep this creature alive. She is way too precious to lose, besides I should like to see her grow into her power," he said. I let out a breath of relief at his statement. "No, child, Cicero is the Master of Chicago because I have no interest in vampire politics. I am over fifteen hundred years old and have never once sired an offspring. I observe those around me, but have no interest in ruling them. The answer to your question is no; I have no interest in collecting the madman's monies."

"Ashlyn, trust Marc. I should have introduced you to him sooner, but I didn't know how he would react. Many times in the past he has helped when there have been problems in this city, even though it is the responsibility of the Master of the City to police the actions of those around him."

I nodded my understanding even though I didn't. If he had so much power, why wasn't he the Master of Chicago? Something just didn't add up in the equation, but I didn't voice my concerns. I wasn't the Master of Chicago, nor did I have any inclination to be, not even when I grew up.

"If you say so, Thompson." I smiled at the man who had saved my noodles a few times over the past day or two.

"You're growing up, little girl. Yesterday you would have told me what I could do with my own advice and smiled when you said it."

"I don't respect anybody who doesn't deserve it; trust me, you earned it."

"I assume you are here looking for Cicero?"

We both nodded.

"Yeah, we are in a roundabout sort of way. Mostly we're looking for the vampire who killed Matt and several cops. Do you have any idea who it could be?"

"Is there any evidence pointing to a specific individual?"

"Ashlyn?" Thompson made my name a question.

I smiled at him in gratitude for not spilling the beans about my abilities. He might trust Marcel or Marc, but I didn't yet.

"I can only describe his scent; if I get near him, I could smell him," I answered vaguely.

"There are several hundred vampires living in the City of Chicago, are you going to just go around smelling everyone?"

I hadn't thought about it, but subconsciously that had been my idea. I didn't realize so many vampires lived in the city. I couldn't believe the "ecosystem" could handle the "food" needs of such a large parasitic population. "I hadn't planned on it," I lied. "I used bait to try to flush the killer out and it ended up getting Matt killed, and for his death I am deeply sorry," I told him. It would probably be better to be honest.

My answer seemed to appease the enigmatic vampire, for he nodded at me acceptingly. "I wish I could help you find Cicero, but I swore an oath not to hunt or kill the Master of the City. It's the reason I am allowed to stay here in Chicago without being bothered by all the vampire politics. But I can tell you this; the little man out there doesn't work for me."

I processed the ramifications of his statement and looked to Thompson for his input. Apparently he didn't want to discuss the revelation in front of Marcel and drag him in any deeper than he already put himself in.

"Thanks, Marc, I owe you again," he told the vampire behind the desk.

"Just keep this little treasure safe. I can't explain it, but I think she has quite the destiny before her, and I would like to see it play out to its fullest. As for you, little one," he offered his hand to me. "Once this is all over and should you ever feel the need to explore your potential, please don't hesitate to seek me out."

I placed my hand in his and expected him to shake it, but instead he brought my hand up to his lips and gently kissed the back of my fingers. I gave a little gasp and felt a charge surge through my body, starting at my fingertips and ending where I'd rather not mention. "Thank you, Marcel," I said.

He nodded again and we left. Tony wasted little time going back into Marcel's office and didn't look happy. *At least we have a place to start*. I just wondered how long it would be until Tony left the Vamporium.

Two hours until dawn, we hit pay dirt. The squinty little vampire left the club through the front entrance, and I nudged Thompson in the ribs. We had been sitting in the Suburban parked in the street for a better part of four hours. The engine was off, but the windows were open and it seemed to be getting a bit frosty. Neither Thompson nor I had noticed.

I don't know what Thompson had thought about to pass the time, but my thoughts had been wandering toward a handsome club-owning vampire. More than once, I had to shift my position in my seat. I kept thinking of his offer right before we left and thought I might take him up on it. It would be purely for helping me understand the limitations of my power. I think I might have even convinced myself of my intentions in the four hours we sat watching the entrance of the club for Tony.

He started walking down the street and I thought he might be headed for a parking garage nearby, but he just kept going. Instead of firing up the engine of the SUV and tailing him, we followed on foot. I thought it was a bad plan and kind of stupid. If the vampire got into a vehicle at any time, we would be hard pressed to follow. I could keep up, but I doubted Thompson could. Lycanthropes could be really fast, but not vampire fast. Well as far as I knew, they weren't.

As it turned out, we didn't have to worry about keeping up with a car, just a vampire. Tony must have heard us following him, because as soon as he rounded a corner, he ran for it. Fuck.

Again, I paid no heed to my partner and took off running after the nimble little vampire. I heard a roar behind me and decided to let Thompson worry about it. Tony began weaving around buildings and running down alleys and I thanked the gods I had worn sensible shoes. I splashed through puddles and stepped on things I didn't want to know about and still I couldn't catch up to the vampire ahead of me. I thought about repeating the maneuver I used to catch Matt the other night, but I wasn't close enough. I didn't know what to do. At that moment, I heard Thompson behind me.

Ordinarily Thompson smelled of sage, but coming from

the beast I heard behind me, the smell threatened to overpower me. I wanted to let him pass me because I knew he would be faster if he had already caught up to me, but the narrow alleyway prevented his bulk from passing. Then I had a thought.

"Jump," I yelled and did the same. But instead of jumping high, I jumped low, almost parallel to the ground. I didn't want to land in the muck coating the disgusting alley, so I put my hands out in front of me to keep my clothes from being smeared. I felt the presence of Thompson soaring over my head and I looked up as I slid to a stop. The form of a giant half-black lion, half-man soared through the air and struck the back of the escaping vampire forcing him to the ground.

I pushed against the ground and landed on my feet. I had no need to rush because the giant werelion had the vampire's neck locked securely in his jaws. I closed the distance between us at a leisurely pace. I didn't know how in control Thompson remained while in his wereform, and I didn't want to take a chance of having those powerful claws and teeth turned on me.

"Thompson?"

He gave a growl and shifted his head ever so slightly up and down one time to acknowledge he lived inside the monster and remained in control. When I drew close enough I could tell he wasn't moving, trying hard not to rip the head off the vampire we wanted to question. They became so uncooperative when their heads weren't attached. Vampires can be so conceited.

I knelt down by Tony's head carefully to avoid dipping my skirt in the muck. I lowered my face until I could see

Thompson's eyes. I saw intelligence there and I gave him a little smile. It felt a little unsettling to see a seven hundred pound lion wink at you. I ignored him and concentrated on the extremely uncomfortable-looking vampire.

"Are you going to cooperate now?"

He nodded in response. I guess it would be pretty hard to talk with six inch fangs piercing your throat. "Good, Thompson would you please let him up now?"

Thompson opened his maw and released Tony's neck. I stifled a giggle when Thompson gave him a lick across the neck. He probably did it for the blood, but it gave Tony the impression he appeared tasty to the werelion. He lay there and gave his wounds a chance to close while giving Thompson a chance to fully get off him.

"What do you want? I didn't do anything!"

I looked at Thompson to see if he might shift back to his human form for questioning; but he just sat on his haunches to watch the show. "You know who we're looking for, Tony. Why don't you help us?"

"I don't know who you're talking about."

"I think you do, Tony. Where is Cicero?" I was getting impatient.

"Who's Cicero?"

He was getting predictable.

"Thompson, you eat tonight?"

The werelion growled a response.

"Ha ha, he ain't gonna eat me, I ain't done nothin'. You can't use scare tactics to make me talk about stuff I don't know shit about. It's a fact, so cut the crap. If you let me go now, I won't press charges for the assault. Can I go now?"

Ooh, this little shit was really starting to piss me off. I considered eating him myself, but I figured he'd taste like shit. "Fine, you wouldn't mind posing for a few newspaper photos would you?" I pulled out my cell phone.

"What are you talking about?"

"I've been getting in a lot of trouble lately for mishandling vampire suspects. I even made the paper a couple of times. If I'm going to let you go, I want someone here to prove I didn't hurt you. Don't worry, Tony, I'll be sure to let the reporter know how helpful you've been in our investigation," I said. I started to enjoy this way too much, and I think Thompson did too, but hearing a lion laughing was little creepy.

"You can't do that!"

"Why, Tony? Why can't I do it?" I tried to sound concerned.

"He'll kill me!"

"Who'll kill you," I continued in the same false tone.

"Cicero. He'll fucking rip my goddamn head off!" He realized his mistake. I knelt down to be at the same level as him, no more stupid threats and questions.

"Where is he, Tony? If I get him before he gets you, you won't have to worry about him anymore."

"Fuck you!"

I slapped him hard. The vertebrae in his neck snapped as his head spun way farther than it should have. He fell backward against the pavement and for a moment, I worried I had killed him. His head turned as the muscles in his neck worked to hold his head still as the bones re-knit together. The process took only a few minutes and he didn't say anything the whole time, but if looks could kill, I'd be re-knitting a few bones myself.

I figured I'd make use of Tony's down time. He lay on the pavement with his face in the air while he healed. I wore a skirt, but right then I didn't give a shit about decorum. I even wore some pretty modest panties so I didn't care who I flashed. I stepped over Tony's prone form and sat down on his chest with a little *thump*. I placed my hands down on the cool, wet pavement, and since they had already gotten dirty from breaking my fall earlier, I didn't care what I put them in now. I had one on each side of his head and I used them to lower my face until it stopped a mere inch away from his. I looked down at his eyes and locked mine to his brown orbs.

I could see his surprise when he saw my slit pupils and then panic as he realized I planned to do something to him. I looked into his eyes and found the place where my ocean met his lake. He wasn't a Master Vampire, but he had strength from his sheer age. The alleyway and Thompson faded away until only Tony and I remained. It felt strange being so close to another vampire in the impenetrable darkness. Our illuminations melded together and seemed brighter, probably due to the close proximity of our physical bodies. I looked down at him and sent a tendril of thought at the sad little vampire.

"Where is Cicero, Tony?"

I saw the panic in his eyes magnify tenfold. Now he knew what I had planned and he fought me with every ounce of power he had. He couldn't struggle from underneath me with his physical body because we weren't in the real world anymore. He realized the futility and tried to fight me with his mind until he understood the rift between his power and mine, so he shifted tactics. He tried to think of other things. I saw it all play out in my mind like I sat watching a home movie of Tony's life. I saw the woman vampire who made Tony nearly a hundred years ago, right here in Chicago. I saw him start doing some enforcer work for a magnificent vampire during the roaring twenties. I recognized Cicero at once. His thoughts went from his life as a human teen trying to survive on the streets, all the way to some of the dirty deeds he had done in the name of Cicero throughout the eighty odd years he had worked for him. I saw Cicero command him to keep an eye on Marcel, the only vampire in Chicago who could pose a threat to him, and then I found what I was looking for.

As soon as Tony formed the thought in his mind, he tried to concentrate on something else. I grabbed at the thought with my mind and forced him to finish it. Cicero had his most trusted people running his businesses because he had become a wanted man–or vampire. He had holed himself up while he waged this war against the human authority figures. The vampires living in this century should be running things, not suffering against the laws they should be above. Tony agreed with him and thought him a sort of god for not lying down and acting like sheep when vampires should be the wolves.

I tried to force Tony to think of the place where Cicero had holed himself up, but he didn't know. He knew who did though. Vincent Marazzo. He ran the flagship of Cicero's businesses, "Capone's Vault." I had heard of it, a restaurant and theater on Lakeshore Drive that catered to humans. Vampires ran the establishment, but it had become a Mecca for humans who wanted to experience the prohibition era Chicago. Tommy guns and gangster paraphernalia littered the walls as a tribute to an era long gone, but not forgotten. If we wanted to find a way to Cicero, it would be there. Hot Damn!

I started to pull back from Tony's consciousness. I became so engrossed in finding Cicero; I almost missed his next fleeting thought. I didn't see a name or a face, just a building. I pushed back in and grabbed at the thought. I don't know what made me do it, maybe just gut instinct, but I found what I wanted. From his thoughts came an unwavering image, a nondescript apartment building in the heart of the city. I recognized it at once and realized why it looked so familiar. I had been living there for almost a week. I wondered why he would be thinking of it when I saw several people emerge from the front door and walk toward Tony. I watched the events unfold through Tony's eyes and realized he sat in a car waiting for the people to come out because he had the job of driving. Three people emerged from the building, two holding one upright. The third one wore a bathrobe and had a black hood over his head and his wrists bound with rope. The two approached the car and Tony popped the trunk. The car wobbled a little as they put the bound and hooded man into the trunk. My heart sank with the realization. They had Pete.

The two opened the back door of the car and climbed in. I saw fangs glint from the overhead street lamps as they slid into the leather seats. "Whoever the boss got the information from didn't lie; we saw her stuff in the spare bedroom. Only the boss would be lucky enough to have an FBI agent in his back pocket," one of the men said and smiled as Tony pulled away from the curb.

I broke the trance in a panic. I looked down at Tony and I saw nothing but fear there. He had betrayed the vampire god he had come to venerate above all things and he wanted to die. I snarled in his face and roared loud enough it would make even the werelion behind me jealous. If he wanted to die, I would help him. Let's just hope I could send his god to him in death.

The flesh of his neck parted beneath my fangs. I didn't just bite. I tore. I chewed muscle and sinew and felt the rush of blood fill my mouth like I had bitten into a hose. Blood pushed past the back of my mouth and flowed down to wherever it is absorbed into my body without swallowing. There would be no healing from this wound. I drank until the blood flowed no more and I came back to myself to find Tony quite dead beneath me, and a disinterested werelion watching the entire scene. I had murdered a vampire and Thompson hadn't even tried to stop me. I think Thompson's disinterest bothered me more than the death.

I wiped the blood off my mouth onto the sleeve of my jacket and stared at Thompson. Somebody in the FBI had leaked who my partner was and where he lived. Whoever it was, had gotten Pete kidnapped and might have even gotten him killed. Could it be Thompson? It could, but if it were him, why didn't he just take me to Cicero himself? I couldn't chance it. I had already killed one vampire directly and one by putting him in a situation to be killed. I needed to find Pete and rescue him, on my own, but first I needed to get rid of Thompson.

"Are you going to sit there or are you going to change back?"

I watched as the air around him began to shimmer. I hoped to gods his clothes came back with him when he changed. The only thing that had survived his transformation had been the tattered remains of his suit pants. Bones began to pop as they reformed into a more human shape. Muscles poured and skin ran down the length of his body. I found it amazing a bald human could have a lion's mane in his Wereform, but the same could be said for the fine coating of fur over the rest of his body. I had only witnessed one transformation in my life during the fight I had with Rose Gates at the academy, and I had only seen the human to wereform shift. It had been a messy process as the animal under her skin had burst out in a shower of blood and other fluids. The transformation back seemed a lot less messy. The lion form seemed to shrink back into the human form and fur, fangs, and claws seemed to just get retracted back under the skin. I found myself grateful they didn't implode back.

Thompson stood before me in his pants, barely. His shirt, shoes, socks, and suit coat lay somewhere back in the alleyway. He looked tired, like it had taken everything to shift back, and for all I knew it had. I blushed a little at his mostly naked form. Damn my hormones, but he looked like he had been chiseled from a hunk of onyx and it showed in his arms and chest. I really needed to get my mind out of the gutter.

"They have Pete," I said.

"How do you know?"

"I pulled it from Tony's mind before I killed him."

Thompson walked over to the body and nudged it with his toe. Tony didn't move, but I could see the wound at his neck closing. It wasn't healing at vampiric speed, but it was closing. I kneeled down to look closer to make sure I wasn't seeing things, but the repair became even more obvious the closer I got. I could see skin growing and the muscles stretching and healing themselves as well. Maybe I hadn't killed him. Damn.

"He's not dead, but you drained him dry. He'll heal, maybe not before the sun comes up, but he'll heal. We need to get him out of the street, unless you want him dead?" Thompson didn’t display a hint of emotion whatsoever. Like the decision belonged to me and he couldn't care less.

"No, I don't want him dead even though he deserves to be. I'm not a killer," I said. My answer seemed to appease him. I just hoped it wasn't because he worked for Cicero. I had just started to like Thompson, and if he had been the one who tipped off Cicero, I would kill him.

I needed to get back to the apartment to start looking for Michaels. I couldn't just go to Capone's Vault and start banging heads together. I needed to think, I needed to cry, and I needed to figure out where to start. The sun would be up soon so I didn't have time to do more than think anyway. Okay, maybe think and take a shower, but that's all.

Thompson pulled out his cell and dialed a number. I didn't know whom he dialed until I heard him tell the person that he needed an ambulance. He must of dialed 911. For all I knew he could just be pretending to. I listened carefully and could actually hear the dispatcher on the other end of the phone asking Thompsons location. He gave our exact location, and he impressed me by knowing exactly where we had ended up. While I had been chasing Tony, the last thing on my mind had been to look at street signs.

"Do you really want the police showing up here while you're dressed like a homeless person?"

"No, not really, but unless we get Tony out of the prospective sunlight, he's gonna get pretty crispy. I sure as hell ain't hauling him back to the office."

I stared at Thompson and formulated a plan to get away from him. If he was the one tipping off Cicero, I couldn't afford to let him know about Michaels. For all I knew, as soon as I turned my back on him, he'd clunk me on the head and drag me to Cicero, and Michaels and I would both end up dead. I just wish I knew what Cicero wanted and why he took Michaels.

"Go home, Thompson. I'll wait here for the police and make sure Tony doesn't wake up anytime soon. Officers seeing you like this probably isn't the best of ideas right now."

"You sure you can handle this?"

"Yeah, just leave me the car keys. You have a way home?"

"I'll run," he snarled and smiled.

I nodded and he tossed me the car keys from his mangled pants. Before I had even caught them he had changed back into his lion form and started climbing up the fire escape of the closest building. I guess he was going to take the rooftop route. It would probably be smarter than letting everyone see a werelion running through the streets of Chicago.

I turned and looked down at Tony's prone form, relieved I

hadn't killed him and a little sorry I hadn't. I resisted the urge to kick him in the head while he lay there, and sat down on an empty vegetable crate someone had left in the dark alley to wait for the boys in blue to show. I didn't have to wait for long either.

The first squad car showed at the end of the alley with lights on and sirens blaring. It echoed down the alley and really began to pierce my ears. Finally, after what seemed to be an eternity, the siren stopped and two cops got out of the car with their guns drawn. One sighted me as they walked slowly down the alley, and the other had his sights on the passed out form of Tony.

"Hands in the air where I can see them!"

"Relax officer, I'm FBI," I shouted back.

They didn't relax their grip or posture as they continued their way down the narrow alley, nor did I expect them to. If someone shouted FBI to me, I probably wouldn't relax until I saw some identification.

"You got any identification?" The cop moved close enough to see it. I reached into my jacket pocket and pulled my badge out. I held it up and the cop leaned in close enough to read it. I expected him to put his gun up, but he seemed unimpressed by my federal identification. I stood and he shifted his gun away from me finally and I walked over to the prone form of Tony.

"He got a little frisky, so I had to knock him out. Could you gentlemen please make sure he makes his way to a holding cell until I can get the reports together enough to file charges?"

"Yeah, we'll take care of him," the taller and older of the

two said and turned toward me. "Are you all right agent?"

"Yes," I lied.

I turned toward the entrance of the alleyway and listened. I could hear more cars approaching as their sirens gave me a good measurement of their distance. They seemed loud, but not loud enough to expect them in less than a few minutes time. The two shining examples of Chicago's finest must have heard them too because one of them muttered a mumbled, "Shit!" from behind me. I wondered what he meant, but before I could turn to ask, the bullet hit me square in the back before I heard the report from the weapon. I looked down and actually watched my chest explode in bits of bone and a spray of red mist.

"Fuck," I said as I collapsed to the disgusting alley floor.

Chapter 19

I woke with my chest on fire, and a hunger like I had never known before. I couldn't see anything, but smells assaulted me from every direction. I could smell my own blood, I could smell chlorine, and I could smell death all around me like a moldy wet blanket. It turned out to be a good analogy, because as soon as I thought it, my sense of touch started working and I could feel the blanket or sheet covering me, keeping my eyes from seeing.

I brought my arm up from where it pressed against something cold at my side and pushed the shroud from my prone form. I should have left it where it lay. I looked down in horrid fascination and saw my breasts and skin were peeled back like the skin of an orange and my ribs had been pulled back and held apart by some sort of metal contraption. I didn't know whether to scream for help or just start sobbing. I looked around the room in a state of panic and realized they'd put me in the morgue. One wall of shiny corpse-sized doors and the large manila tag tied to my toe had been a dead giveaway. No pun intended.

I took stock of my situation. I had heard of bad days. I even had a few of them myself. Getting a decent vampire killed and my partner kidnapped certainly qualified. Ever woken up in a morgue with your flesh peeled back and your ribs spread open with all your organs exposed? I might have just set a record. I should have gotten a medal.

I raised my hand up off the cold morgue table and reached for the rib spreader. It felt cool to the touch and was covered in my blood, fantastic. I had no idea how the damn thing worked and didn't want to cause any further damage to my ribs. Along the shaft of the cruel looking instrument lay what looked like the crank handle of a vice. I could do this. All I had to do was turn it, right? I gingerly grasped the handle and turned it a little to the right. I nearly screamed as the contraption spread farther apart. I remembered the righty tighty lefty loosey mantra my aunt muttered every time she used a wrench around the house. Who would have thought it would apply to a rib spreader. Slowly I turned it to the left and felt the strain on my rib cage lessen immensely. *Whew.*

I kept turning and turning and finally I could turn the device sideways and remove it from my chest. Now the fun part. I grabbed my ribs and pulled them together. I didn't know what else to do. I broke an antique ceramic bell once my aunt had been particularly fond of. She went to the store, bought a little bottle of superglue, and made me fix it. The only manufacturing defect of superglue is the fact you have to sit there motionless for quite a while before the two sides bonded. This felt vaguely similar. The only difference was this time I prayed.

I lay motionless for the better part of five minutes. Trust me when I say it felt a lot longer. Finally, I built up enough courage to let go and see if my body had enough strength to heal itself. My ribs didn't go *shproing* and pop back open so I took it as a good sign. Very, very, very carefully I grabbed the most predominant rib on either side of my chest and gave a little tug. Thanks be to the gods, they held. There are things nobody should have to do in their life, this being one of them.

Without trying to think about it too much I grabbed my peeled-back flesh and pulled it over my ribs like a blanket. Of course, the medical examiner chose the exact moment to return from whatever he had been doing. I turned my head to look, hands covering my smallish breasts, when I saw his eyes roll back in his head as he fainted. My own head hurt as I heard his hit the cold concrete floor with a sickening thud. I resisted the urge to rush over to him to make sure he wasn't dead from a heart attack. I had my own problems to deal with.

I realigned the flesh so it wouldn't heal crooked. "You're a pretty girl, but your breasts look a little uneven," was not something I wanted to deal with. This time I didn't pray, just watched my flesh as it reknitted. If I ever had another press conference and somebody asked me what I thought my greatest vampiric ability is, I would have to indubitably say it's the healing. Not even a scar remained as my skin forced itself back together like melted plastic. I sighed with relief because I would be okay. I might need a little therapy, but I would be fine.

The covering still hanging over my lower extremities felt wet and caked with blood. I really didn't want to have to use it to cover myself while I searched for something to wear. The medical examiner lay either dead or unconscious on the floor so I threw decorum out the window and tossed the sheet aside.

I swung my feet over the side of the table and let myself drop the remaining foot and a half to the cold floor. I felt a little jar in my chest, which let me know I wasn't at a hundred percent. Then the hunger hit. I must have used the very last of my energies in healing. I had no idea how much time had passed, so I don't even know how long I had taken to even wake up from my "nap." I needed blood, and I needed it now.

I glanced around the room and found a cabinet. Of course, somebody had locked it. Why would anyone lock anything in a morgue? I grunted at the stupidity of it and turned my hand. The metal groaned in protest and then snapped. The door swung open and I hit pay dirt. Fresh linens for covering corpses, boxes of latex gloves, boxes of surgical masks, and an ample supply of hospital scrubs filled the shelves. I had hoped for just a blanket, but the medical scrubs had been a gift sent from the gods. They must keep spares in here in case they have to autopsy a particularly squirty dead person. *Happy me*. I searched through the stack and found the smallest size. Apparently, there aren't too many short, skinny medical examiners.

I slid the garments on and rolled up the pant legs so I wouldn't walk around looking like a kid in footy pajamas. Then I turned my attention to the prone examiner still unconscious on the floor. I needed blood, I needed it now, and he knew where I could get it. I raced over to him as fast as my exhausted body could get me there and knelt down by his head. I considered slapping him awake, but my conscience reminded me he had already suffered one too many blows to the melon. I found a sink on the wall by the door so I stood and filled my hand with cool water from the faucet, returned, and let it dribble down on the man's face.

He sputtered as his eyes shot open. He paled as his gaze locked onto my face and recognition made him almost faint again. He slid backwards across the floor to the wall behind him and slid up into a sitting position. He only wanted to put as much distance between him and me as humanly possible.

He stared at me in open horror and kept blathering phrases like, "Not possible," and, "Help me, God." I felt for his false sense of peril, but I needed blood.

"Doctor," I said in a firm tone to try to calm him. I must have failed miserably because I saw his skin pale even further. "I'm not going to harm you!"

"W-w-what?"

"I said I'm not going to hurt you. I just need your help. I need *lycanthrope* blood." I stressed the lycanthrope so he knew I wasn't going to eat him. "Does this hospital stock any, please?"

"Y-y-yes," he said. He must have believed me because he turned a little less pasty.

"Could you please get it for me? I have absolutely no strength," I said. I made myself proud for not begging. I even added another, "Please," for good measure.

"How are you alive?" He made no motion to move.

"I will answer all your questions, but I have to eat, Doctor, now."

He nodded and I saw him steel himself against his fear and he rose and sped through the door. I did the only thing I could do. I lowered myself to the cool floor and waited. I focused on the humming of the overhead fluorescent lighting to try to distract myself from my own hunger. It wasn't working very well. It started to consume me from inside out. Luckily I didn't have long to suffer. I heard the doctor's rapid footfalls coming down the hallway at a pace an Olympic sprinter would have been proud of. His weren't the only ones either. I heard several other pairs behind him and what sounded like something on wheels following behind him.

He burst through the door and found my prone form not far away. He screeched to a halt only a foot away and knelt down beside me. I felt him press a cool bag into my hand and I brought it to my mouth like an apple. My fangs pierced the plastic and my mouth flooded with exactly what I needed. The blood felt too cold, but even at the extremely low temperature I felt heat return to my limbs, return to my face, and then it even creeped its way to my fingers and toes. I felt a thousand times better than I had moments before.

I tossed the first away and I felt a second press itself into my hand. I had enough sensibility to unplug the little stopper at the bottom of the bag and drink like a lady instead of a blood starved fledgling. The multitude of people flooded in through the door and I glanced up from my tasty snack. What I had heard on wheels looked like a compact hospital gurney being raced down the hallway. I didn't stop drinking as I felt hot human hands grasp my limbs and lift me off the floor onto the chemical smelling mattress. My day started to look a little brighter.

They pulled me out of the morgue and into the dimly lit hallway outside. I answered questions about my health as I went for my ride. I expected them to push me into an elevator and take me to the emergency room, but we stayed on the same floor and they ushered me farther into the recesses of the hospital. I saw a sign on the wall labeled supernatural ward and realized why we hadn't gone for an elevator ride.

The medical examiner raced past us and opened the set of double doors leading into the ward, and as we passed by, he gave me a small smile. He must have felt really guilty for cracking my chest open. It wasn't until we had made it into a private room he started barking orders like a World War II general.

As it turned out, he wasn't the medical examiner. He had the job of being the head of the supernatural treatment facility at the hospital. That's why he had been performing my autopsy. His doctorate was in supernatural biology and medicine. *Lucky me.* I had been brought in DOA with over seventy-five percent of my heart missing. When he opened my chest, he had found it with little over twenty-five percent gone. I had nothing on the EEG at the time of my arrival so he had assumed it was either a clerical error, or somebody had misjudged the extent of my wounds through the big gaping hole in my chest. The bones of my ribcage must have reknitted themselves while he had been searching for the doctor in the emergency room who had pronounced me dead, really dead, not just mostly dead.

He described in great detail the bloody mess my chest cavity had been and why he had gone on with the autopsy. He kept repeating he had no idea I would come back from such a wound. He'd apparently been treating vampires and lycanthropes for many, many years and had never even thought such a thing could be possible and he felt very, very horrible. He either thought I would eat him, or worse, sue him.

"Doctor…" I started as to inquire his name and he rewarded me with "Simms." "I can assure you I am quite an anomaly among my kind. My body is different in a few ways which remain unclear to even myself; you couldn't have known."

He gave me a smile, and then a look of utter and complete disbelief as he hooked me up to an EEG and flipped the machine on. When I had subjected myself to medical testing in Quantico, I had been x-rayed, cat scanned, probed, and prodded, but I had never been hooked up to an EEG. I heard the blaring buzzer, which told the medical staff I had moved beyond the realm of the living, but had no idea if it was normal.

I looked over at Doctor Simms, who stared at me like I had grown several extra appendages, and shrugged. I didn't know what else to do. When he finally let himself believe I wasn't dead, or completely dead, he flipped the machine off and removed the little pads from my forehead. "Anomalies," he said with a smile.

"Yes, anomalies." I smiled back

"How are you feeling, Agent Ashlyn?"

"How did you know my name?"

"We have the remains of your suit jacket and shirt and the rest of your personal items over in the morgue. Your Special Agent in charge of the Chicago office is on his way to pick them up and identify your remains," he said with a smile to soften the irony of the situation.

"Uh oh, I guess I got some splainin' to do, eh," I said in my very, very best Ricky Ricardo accent.

My wit earned me a smile from Simms while he moved around the room checking me over with various implementations of torture. I mean medicine. Finally, he shrugged his shoulders and gave me a blank stare.

"I don't know what to tell you. By my reckoning, you're perfectly fine. You shouldn't be, but you are. Most supes are a little different from each other in terms of treatment. I hate to admit it, but you are a complete mystery. What makes you so different?"

"I wish I knew, Doctor," I lied through my teeth. I needed another doctor wanting to publish papers about me like I needed another hole in my head. I trusted the good doctor, but not with my secrets.

"I'd like to keep you for twenty-four hours for observation if you don't mind,"

"It depends, how long have I been here and what time is it?" My concerns had shifted from my hunger to Michaels. I needed to get to him and fast. If Cicero thought I wasn't going to be bothering him anymore, he would either let Michaels go, or kill him. I sincerely doubted it would be the former.

"They brought you in last night with the gaping chest wound; it's almost 6 p.m. now," he said after glancing at his wristwatch.

"Sundown is in a half hour. I'm sorry doctor, you have me 'til then."

For some reason it seemed as if he expected my answer.

He sighed resignedly and continued filling out information on a chart he started on me. I sat back in the bed and contemplated my next course of action. I needed to have a plan before Reese got here. At least he would be mightily surprised to see me up and walking.

"Well I might as well go tear up your death certificate and fill out your discharge papers," he said on his way out the door.

"Doctor, if it wasn't a matter of life and death, I'd stay," I lied to the kindly man.

"Sure."

I watched him as he exited the room and made his way down the hall. I lay back on the highly uncomfortable hospital mattress and did the only thing I could: wait. I closed my eyes and tried to picture the sun in my mind. I could feel it hovering over the horizon, beginning its final descent and plunging the streets of Chicago into darkness. Less than half an hour separated me from saving Michaels, if he still lived. *Please gods, let him be alive.*

I debated turning on the small television to help pass the time, but as soon as I reached for the remote perched on the small table next to the bed, rapid footfalls emanated from the hallway as somebody approached my small room. I looked up to see a haggard and exhausted Reese enter my room and just stare at me like he saw a ghost. I offered up a tiny smile and a little shrug. I didn't know what else to do. I expected him to start yelling at me for being stupid enough to get shot and almost end up dead. What I didn't expect him to do is take a very large breath, sink to the floor, and almost start crying.

"Reese, I'm okay," I offered meekly. I needed him, and I

needed him with all his wits about him. "Apparently I'm a tough bugger to kill. I don't have a lot of time, sundown is in less than twenty minutes, and they have Michaels."

My information snapped him out of his reverie of gratitude to whatever gods the man prayed to. He quickly stood and made his way quickly to my bedside. "What are you talking about?"

"Didn't Thompson tell you?" As I said the words, realization dawned on me. Reese hadn't heard or seen Thompson since last night. Thompson had to be the one who sold me and Michaels out to Cicero. Anger flooded my veins. I had really liked Thompson, and now I wanted to kill him. My hands gripped the metal rails of my hospital bed and I shrieked as I tore them from their welded fastenings, throwing them against the wall.

"Ashlyn," Reese yelled to calm me down before I totally demolished the white washed hospital room.

"Thompson's working for Cicero! I don't have time to explain, but I know for a fact someone at the bureau gave them Michaels' address and told them to get to me they had to go through him. I found all this out right before I got shot. When did you last hear from Thompson?"

"Last night. He called in and told me you had apprehended one of Cicero's vamps. He told the agent who took the call to inform the local authorities and you stayed behind to guard him until they showed up. Did he change into his wereform last night?"

I nodded my affirmative.

"Then he probably went home to sleep it off, he's

probably at the office right now. Ashlyn, I've known Thompson for sixteen years. He wouldn't do something like this."

"I can't take a chance, Reese. They have Michaels and it's because of me. I have to get him back, alone if I have to." I could feel the sun lowering farther toward the horizon. By the time I made it through the hospital, it would be close enough to dark that I could bear it.

"I'm going with you," Reese said in a voice leaving little room for argument.

Luckily, I could be fast enough not to have to argue. I looked at him and offered up a little smile, and bolted from the room and the hospital. I didn't stop, except to wait for the automatic sliding entry doors at the front of the archaic building, to catch up to my inhuman speed, register my proximity, and slowly slide their way open.

I ran through the opening and into the cool Chicago night. Hundreds of people felt me pass by them, but not one saw me as I ran the entire way from the hospital to Michaels' small apartment. When I paused at the front entrance, I realized my mistake. I had left the hospital without my badge, without my gun, and without the keys to the building where I had my clothes. I had run the better part of several miles barefoot and dressed in nothing but hospital scrubs.

"Shit on a shingle," I muttered to no one by myself.

I did the only thing I could do. I reached down to grab the theft prevention security heavy-duty door handle and pulled. Metal groaned and snapped, and then the door flew open. If I got my ass kicked out of the FBI, I'd definitely have a career as a thief. I ran through the deserted lobby and passed the elevator. The stairs would be faster.

I hit the apartment door without slowing. I'm sure the neighbors would be out to investigate the booming crash resonating through the halls. I needed to be gone before their curiosity outweighed their caution. I gathered my clothes from the dresser and shucked the scrubs. Shirt, pants, and shoes changed at supermodel speed. My gun remained at the hospital, and I only felt a momentary twinge as I raced out of the building far from unarmed.

Chapter 20

The streets of Chi-town filled early. People leaving work made their way to parking garages and train stations. Others had just arrived into the city for dinner and entertainment. Friday nights sucked in Chicago. I never understood why somebody would stand in line to pay exorbitant amounts of money for tiny little plates of tiny little food. Maybe if I ate I would get it.

I knew my destination; I just didn't know the exact address. I wished I had paused at the apartment long enough to look it up on the internet. I didn't even have a cell phone to call information. I needed to slow down and start thinking. I spotted a middle-aged woman walking down the sidewalk toward me talking on her cell, and as she passed, I reached out and placed my hand on her arm. She stopped her conversation and looked at me like I had leprosy. Apparently, she had personal space issues.

"I'm sorry to bother you, ma'am, but would you happen to know where Capone's Vault is? I'm meeting a friend there, but I lost my cell phone."

She gave me a thoughtful look like she had been expecting me to ask her for money. I guess she decided I dressed well enough to be answer worthy. She spouted out some directions and it sounded like I wasn't far. I nodded my thanks and walked at a normal human pace while I planned my next move. I needed to get to Cicero, and to get to him I needed to find Marazzo. To get to him, I needed to get to Capone's Vault. It sounded like a good plan to me.

I had my fill of getting my ass kicked, and I had my fill of these fuckers hurting people I cared about. I hated that I couldn't trust the people around me, but most of all I wanted to shove my hands in Capone's chest and rip his heart out. I didn't notice, but with every realization I made, I had pounded my fist against my hip. It didn't hurt, but it wasn't helping maintain the illusion that I might be a normal human out for a stroll.

I looked up at the street sign and realized I had reached my first turn. I made my way from Delaware Place to Rush Street and walked past the buildings. There it sat, nestled in the lap of one of the buildings, Capone's Vault. I don't know how, but they had gotten permission from the City to park a 1920's Ford up on the sidewalk right by the entrance. They must have called it art and made a donation to the city. You gotta love politicians.

What is it with vampire run establishments and lines to get in the places? The line at Fangloria's had been long. The line at Mega Bites had been even longer. The line going into Capone's Vault bordered on ridiculous. It stretched for at least the length of the block. I needed to get in, and I needed to get in now. I couldn't flash my badge since it probably sat in a lock box at the hospital. I couldn't just walk up to the door and say, "Hi, I'm with the FBI," without it either. And since this establishment wasn't a place vampires congregated, I'm sure there wasn't a separate line to let the undead in.

Maybe I should walk in and ask for a job, Hmmm...Why not? I doubted it would work, but it looked like my best option for getting in the doors without just barging my way in. I got a few dirty looks from the line of people, but I walked past them all and made my way to the front doors. How the glass front of the restaurant supported the weight of the solid oak doors fell well beyond my feeble understanding of architectural design. Solid brass handles festooned them and sparkled from hanging gaslight chandeliers. Cicero had spared little on the décor of his flagship business.

I pulled the solid door open and stepped back in time. The dining area of the restaurant had to be one of the largest in the city. On top of that, the stage where I'm sure performers delighted diners with prohibition era themed entertainment took up another large area. I was amazed by the entire place. Paraphernalia and regalia from old Chicago adorned walls and columns and everywhere. Hardwood floors complete with sawdust shavings glittered under their dusty coverings and Italian plaster walls completed the visage of a 1920s speakeasy.

"Welcome to Capone's Vault, how many are in your party?" I looked at the young hostess behind the dark podium.

"I'm sorry; I'm looking for Vincent Marazzo about employment," I lied. When I said it, I made sure to expose my fangs at the young human woman, hoping to make it seem legitimate I would be looking for the Vampire.

"Oh, he's in his office. I'll see if he's available. Is he expecting you, Miss…?" She trailed off asking me to fill in my name.

"Ashlyn," I said without thinking.

I watched the hostess leave her post and headed into the bowels of the restaurant. I only had to wait a few minutes before she made her way back up to where I waited. She gave me a smile and told me someone would be right with me. I put my back to the wall and waited. Apparently, the hostess wasn't lying because only after a few minutes I watched a vampire dressed like a gangster march his way from the back of the restaurant, through the patrons, and up to the hostess station. He whispered something I couldn't quite catch because of the din coming from the dining area, and the hostess nodded. He looked up at me and gave an icy smile before stepping away from the hostess. He made his way over to where I waited and gave me a once over.

"Ashlyn?"

"Yes," I said nonchalantly.

"We're not hiring at the moment, but Mr. Marazzo would like to meet you for possible work at another location. Please follow me," he said smugly.

He turned to lead the way, and I followed. Walking in his wake made it easy for me to catch his scent. I don't know why, but I half expected the vamp to be Marazzo pretending to be an underling. It's what always happened in the movies, but his scent of cinnamon and cloves told me it wasn't the case now.

We wound our way through the diners and into the kitchen. Normal humans yelled out orders, cooked meats, whipped up side dishes, cleaned, and a multitude of various other duties to make the restaurant run. The noise coming from the kitchen almost hurt my ears, but the smells made my mouth water. For the millionth time I found myself whimsically wishing I could try just a small bite.

Thankfully, we weren't there long. The vampire I followed led the way out of the kitchen and into a small hallway leading to various storage rooms and what I assumed dressing rooms for the performers. The hall ended at an ornate wooden door. He stopped short and didn't put his hand on the knob, but knocked a series of taps on one of the panels. If somebody opened a tiny portion of the door and asked for a password, I would have to start killing people, so help me gods.

I heard a muffled, "Come in," and Mr. Vampire reached down and turned the knob. As expected, he opened the door and motioned me to enter first. I did, and as soon as I entered the room, I smelled him. Lemon and vanilla wafted over to me from a man I hadn't even seen yet. I growled and raised my eyes and saw him sitting behind the gigantic wooden desk. He sat reading a document and hadn't shifted his attention to me. With a quick glance around the room, I gave silent thanks to the gods. Other than the vampire standing behind me and Marazzo, there wasn't another vampire in the room.

"Mr. Marazzo?"

"Yes," he said as I swung around and grabbed the vampire behind me by the throat. My claws pierced the skin of his tender throat and I sank them in farther. With as much strength as I could muster I swung closed fisted at the side of his head. No blunt instrument on earth could kill a vampire, but I could definitely knock his ass out, and it was exactly what I did. I wanted him incapacitated, not dead. Marazzo on the other hand

I wasn't so sure about.

I turned around and he stood behind the desk, unsure whether to attack or flee. Fleeing wasn't much of an option since I stood between him and the only way out. I glanced at the unconscious vampire in my claws, and I let him drop to the floor with a sickening thud. "Sorry," I muttered out of the corner of my mouth, but it fell on deaf ears.

"Who are you?" Marazzo's accent was thick New York. Apparently, he wasn't a local boy.

"Agent Ashlyn of the FBI, maybe you've heard of me?"

"You're the Verminator? To what do I owe the honor of your acquaintance?" He sat back down on his padded leather chair and plucked a fat cigar out of the deeply stained wooden box on his desk. He bit the end off and spit it on the floor as he reached into his suit pocket and pulled out an antique brass lighter. He lit the end and puffed on the cigar. It was nice not to have to worry about second hand smoke when he expelled what seemed to me an extraordinary amount of smoke over his head.

"I'm looking for Cicero," I said flatly.

"I don't know who you're talking about," he lied with what looked like practiced ease. He even smiled as he said it.

"Mr. Marazzo, you are under arrest for the murder of several police officers, and one vampire named Mathew Aames. Are you going to come peacefully?" I retuned the fake smile.

He laughed and threw the desk at me. I expected a lot of responses from him; a desk wasn't one of them. If the room had been bigger, I might have been able to sidestep the gigantic missile. I quickly held up my arms to try to deflect the mass of wood. I'm strong, very strong, but inertia sucks. I have a small mass, a very small mass compared to a solid wood desk traveling at a high velocity. My hands stopped the desk from actually striking me, but it did pick me up off the floor and push me through the back wall. The wall itself stopped the desk, but I found myself in another room full of human women changing into flapper outfits for their performance.

I looked at the desk through the Ashlyn-sized hole in the wall. I picked myself up off the floor, ran at the desk, and kicked it back into Marazzo's office. I followed through the hole and looked around. We base our reactions on expected behaviors. I entered the office expecting Marazzo to have taken off running, and because of my expectations, I wasn't expecting him to be standing right next to me. I didn't even notice him until his hands were around my throat.

Vampires don't need to breathe, so he wasn't choking me, but he could crush my spine. I grabbed his wrists and pulled his arms away from me. I could tell he wasn't expecting my strength, and to tell you the truth, it shocked me a little. He jumped back out of reach and flung a large chunk of desk at my head. Time slowed again like it had in Cicero's office. I leaned back and watched the missile as it sailed past and buried itself in the wall behind me. His renovation bill, if he lived through this, would be in the five-digit range if he kept this up.

I made a mistake, as I watched the missile flying by me; I took my eyes off Marazzo. I realized my error as soon as I felt his fist connect with the side of my head. For the second time that day, I flew across a room. Who said vampires couldn't fly? This time at least I didn't go through the wall, but Marazzo landed on top of me as soon as I landed. He had his fangs bared and had moved in to strike when I shoved my hand through his chest.

He stopped and looked down in morbid curiosity. Apparently he, unlike me, had never seen his internal organs. I tried to avoid looking; it wasn't something I wanted to see again, ever. I did however feel his heart. I wrapped my hand around it and placed the tips of my claws against the pulsing thing. It wasn't beating, but I could feel it squeezing his miraculous vampiric blood throughout his body ever so slowly. It's what made us seem dead. No rhythmic pumping for us. Apparently, everything about vampires is fluid, even our hearts.

"If you move, I will rip your heart out, you son of a bitch," I said slowly.

He made no movement, so he must have believed my threat. I would have done it, so maybe it wasn't a threat. I looked over at the open door and saw several vampires staring at us in disbelief. Marazzo noticed them, too, because he managed to croak out a whimpering, "Don't," keeping them at bay.

"Where is Cicero?" This time I could be the smug one.

"I swear to you I don't know, if I did I would tell you, believe me."

I didn't believe him, not even a little. I looked up into his eyes from my prone position and caught his gaze. I felt the room drift away until we floated in the place where the ocean of my power met his. Our illuminating bodes stood in front of each other whole and un-bloodied. I gazed upon his turbulent waters and knew he had been around for a long, long time.

"Tell me where Cicero is," I said, but this time my voice took on the resonating quality I had heard Gloria use. I didn't know if I could do it outside of my mind, but one day I needed to try. If I could capture vamps with my voice instead of first doing it with my mind, I could save myself a lot of work.

"He's hiding, hiding from everyone, even me. He only calls when he needs something and then he always meets me at one of his warehouses. Maybe he's hiding there. I don't know. He is completely paranoid."

I thought about arguing the logistics of being paranoid when everybody really is out to get you, but it would have been a waste. Marazzo wasn't himself right now. I had completely trapped him in my mind leaving him almost zombie-like.

"What about the agent he had his vampires capture?" I felt my life end when I heard the answer I had already known. I knew as soon as I captured his mind. I saw it all. I just wanted him to say it.

"When we heard you had bought the farm, Cicero had him killed."

"*How*?"

"I drained him dry and had his corpse incinerated," he answered. He didn't say the words to be malicious. He still sat in a trancelike state. He simply reiterated a chain of events as they had occurred.

My thoughts drifted to Michaels. I had only known him for a short time, but he meant the world to me, a world that would be a lot darker without him in it. My heart sank and my hope died.

"Who betrayed him? Who told Cicero where to find me?"

"The daughter of an old associate did. He used to work for me in New York. She works here now. She doesn't like you very much. She doesn't like vampires much either, but when I called him to find out more about the Verminator, she gladly helped. I think her name is Rose."

"Rose," I said at the exact same time he did. I knew she hated me for beating her at almost everything at the academy, but to do this... It made no sense. I debated turning her in or ripping her spine out through her face. I found myself leaning toward the spine thing. She won. Now I hated her as much as she hated me. I remembered her father and his phony words from graduation. He had become another candidate for spinal modification. I focused my attention to the old vampire hovering in front of me above our two oceans. "How do I find Cicero?"

"He should call my cell phone sometime tonight. I am supposed to meet him at one of the warehouses later. He wants me to do something for him."

I released my hold on him and the world came back to reality, or we did. I guess it depends on how you look at it. I could feel his heart in my hand again and smell his blood. I *really* wanted to yank it out of his chest and shove it into his mouth, but I needed him for a little bit longer. I released my hold on it and drew my hand from his chest. Marazzo shook his head and came back to reality and to a great amount of pain His face contorted in horror at what I had done. I reached up to grab his arms and used my strength to flip him under me. I held him with all my strength as I sank my fangs into his neck and drained him. I felt strength flow through my arms and body as I took it from him. I needed him, but only conscious.

When I felt him fluttering, I released him. I stood up and over him, reached into his suit pocket, and found his cell phone. Quickly I flipped through his contacts, but as expected, I didn't see one labeled Cicero, or Boss, or El Jeffe, or anything else that would give him away. Then I remembered the multitude of vampires at the threshold of the office. I turned to look, but no one remained.. Hopefully, they went home and weren't calling Cicero. Now I got to play the waiting game. Either he called or he didn't. Either way I would find him and make him pay for killing Michaels. Cicero and then Rose.

I kicked Marazzo for good measure and then took the cell phone and sat in his padded desk chair. I wished I had memorized Reese's cell number, but I hadn't. Instead, I dialed information and asked for the Chicago Field Office number. They gave me the number and connected me after offering to send me the information in a text message. I waited for three rings until someone picked up. A male agent I didn't recognize answered the call. I had half hoped it would be Rose who picked up; just so I could tell her I would be coming for her when the battle ended. I sighed when I realized I didn't want to give her a head start.

"Chicago Field Office FBI, how can I help you?"

"This is Agent Ashlyn; can you connect me to Reese?"

"Ashlyn, holy shit, hold on."

The line clicked and then rang three times before Reese

picked up. "This is Special Agent Reese, how can I help you?"

"Reese, it's me."

"Where are you; what's going on!"

"I found Marazzo. He's here if you want to come pick him up. I need him for a little while longer, but we're at Capone's Vault. I could use some back up. Cicero's supposed to be calling him any time to let him know where he'll be. I don't have long to talk, but I have to tell you. Michaels is dead, Reese. Cicero had him killed, and you were right about Thompson; it wasn't him."

"Oh, my God, stay where you are. I'm sending agents your way. Thompson's here with me, he's coming, too. Do you know who tipped off Cicero?"

"You got another new agent from my class didn't you?"

"Yes, an agent named Rose I believe. Wait a minute, are you telling me…"

"Yes, is she there?"

"No, she's out on assignment, I think. I'll have everyone start looking for her."

"Don't bother, I'll find her for you later, sir. I have to go," I said and punched the end call button.

Chapter 21

I had been sitting there quietly for ten whole minutes before Marazzo started moaning. I considered kicking him again when I realized the gaping wound I had made in his chest wasn't healing. It had to be from me draining his precious blood almost to nothing. Damn it. He needed to eat a little or he would never be able to answer Cicero's call. I got up from my comfortable chair and made my way out into the hall. I didn't expect to find anybody after my little show, but there in the hall slumped down on the floor sat a tiny vampire.

I don't mean a child vampire: I mean a short little man who had been turned into a vampire. He heard my footsteps and looked up. I had seen terrified people before in movies and on the news, but this man wasn't too far away from full-blown panic. For the life of me, I couldn't figure out why a person so afraid would stick around.

"Hello," I called out softly.

"D-d-did you kill him?"

"Who?"

"Mr. Marazzo. Did you kill him?"

"Um, no I didn't. Who are you?"

"My name is Pike. I'm his assistant. Please don't kill him. He made me what I am, so I'll die."

Well shit. The man was so diminutive you couldn't help but want to help him. I had to sigh because, damn it all to hell, he started crying.

"Pike, if you want to help him, he needs to eat. I need to find him a donor so he can heal. Can you find someone for me?"

"Yes. Thank you, Verminator."

"Pike," I said and sighed again, "Go and find him something to eat."

He must have been truly terrified of me because I didn't even see him leave. I just heard the swish and some foot falls and he had rounded the corner. I returned to my vigil by Marazzo's side. I had just plopped my weary ass down when Thompson came through the destroyed doorway.

"Hey, kid," he called out his familiar greeting.

"Hey, big guy," I shot back and closed my eyes for a minute.

The silence in the room comforted me until I felt something fall into my lap. For a mountain of man, he could move pretty quietly. In my defense, I had had a long night, and I had a feeling it wasn't over. It wasn't even 9 o'clock and I wanted to call it a day. Damn Cicero, I deserved a vacation once I had him in custody or in a box. I looked down and saw my badge and my gun in my lap. I didn't think I'd miss it, but I have to admit I felt a little less of an agent without them.

I mumbled thanks and stood to put the holster Darenthalis had given me over my shoulders, and then slipped the gun in it after checking the ammo. I saw the little silver tips gleaming in the magazine and nodded. Sitting back down, I heard two sets of footsteps coming down the hall. Thompson bristled, so I put my hand on his arm to calm him. It had to be Pike with somebody for Marazzo to snack on.

He came into the room holding the hand of a young girl dressed as a roaring 20's flapper. She didn't look scared, so I knew she wasn't an unwilling donor. When she saw Marazzo on the floor she gave a high pitched, "Vinnie," and yanked her hand out of Pike's to run over to his prone form. Without hesitation, she held her wrist out to the incapacitated vampire. He weakly opened his eyes and smiled before gently taking her offered gift into his mouth. My vampiric ears picked up the little crunch his fangs made as he pierced the skin over her vein.

I watched her blissful face as he fed with a look of disgust on mine. I hated being a vampire. At least twenty times a day, I wished to be normal. To see a normal person willingly allowing themselves to be preyed upon ran against every moral fiber in my body.

I walked over to Marazzo and watched the bone, muscle, and skin of his wound close. Even his color looked a little better.

"Enough," I said, and Marazzo stopped.

He released her arm and lifted his hulking form off the floor of the demolished office. I expected him to start another fight, or at least start yelling at me. I didn't expect the heartfelt, "Thank you," and the little bow he gave me.

I looked over at Thompson and gave him a little "what the fuck" rise of my eyebrows. He just shrugged and came over to me.

"Kid, Reese filled me in on everything. I'm sorry about Michaels. Agents like him don't come around very often. What are we going to do now?"

"Cicero has been meeting Mr. Marazzo here at various warehouses. Never the same one consecutively, so we have no way of finding him on our own. He's due to call our friend here any time now for another such meeting. Mr. Marazzo is going to take the call and let us know where to find him. Aren't you, Marazzo?" I turned toward the unsteady vampire.

"Anything for you," came his response.

Uh oh, this seemed vaguely familiar. I stepped away from Thompson and headed over to Marazzo. He actually smiled as I got closer. I had a bad feeling, a very bad feeling.

"Marazzo, will you help us? Will you help us find Cicero?"

"Of course, master"

I think if you listened close enough you could have heard my shoes make a little screeching noise as I halted my stride. I stared at him and watched his glassy eyes return it. I glanced over at Thompson, and saw his face. His wide open mouth and his wide open eyes spoke volumes. I wanted Marazzo's cooperation, not a fucking minion. I rolled the word minion around on my tongue. Nope, I didn't like it, not one bit.

I didn't know what to do, and thankfully, the little cell phone buzzing in my hand saved me from having to think about it. *Show time*. I looked down at the little display and a local number flashed on the screen. I prayed it belonged to his royal highness, the Master of Chicago. I looked up at Marazzo and handed him the phone. "Answer it, and Marazzo? Act normal."

He took the small cell from my hand, pressed the little green answer button, and held it up to his face. He said, "Marazzo." What a douche, he couldn't even say hello like a normal person. "Yes, sir, I understand. I'll see you there."

"Perfect," I said to him after he hung up. "Where are we meeting him?"

"He said to be at his warehouse on 19th Street in an hour, master," he replied eagerly, like he expected me to be pleased with him. I had had enough. I opened my mouth to tell him to stop calling me master, and in fact, I wasn't his master when Thompson cleared his throat behind me. I turned around and looked at him, and he slowly shook his head from side to side. Apparently, my partner had developed ESP. I shrugged at him and he mouthed the word, "Later." Fine, if he wanted me to play master, I would.

"Pike, please take the lady and go. We have things we need to do," I told the little man. I expected an argument, but he just smiled and grabbed the performer's wrist and left through the damaged doorway. "Marazzo, do you have a car here?"

"Yes, master, it is out in the parking lot. Do you wish me to drive?"

This kept getting more annoying by the minute. I debated throwing Thompson's advice to the wind and telling him to go jump off a bridge, but he knew where we had to be so I let it go. "Perfect, Marazzo, would you please go get it and meet us at the front door?"

He gave me another beaming smile. I wanted to throw up.

I waited until Marazzo left and turned toward Thompson. "What?"

"You made him your slave," Thompson said. He made it more of a question than a statement.

"I didn't mean to do it. I rolled his mind and then fed off him. I didn't know this would happen, I swear!"

"I know, but you need to talk to Marcel after this is over. I have a *very* bad feeling about this, kid. Just do me one favor, try not to kill Cicero until you talk to Marcel."

"Why?"

"Just trust me on this one, kid, please."

I nodded and we left the office together. I had an uneasy feeling as we walked through the deserted restaurant. During our little meeting in the back, all of the commotion must have caused the patrons of Capone's Vault to suddenly lose their appetites. I wanted out of there. I worried Marazzo might regain his senses once he had some distance between us. I didn't even think about it; I just commanded him to do something and didn't doubt for a second he would. Now I worried he'd run off to find Cicero. I didn't know which scared me more.

As it turned out, he sat waiting in a black Cadillac right in front of the heavy doors. I probably should have been a little more specific and told him to keep the car on the street and not park on the sidewalk. Wow, I had a lot to learn. At least I had the answer to my question, though. I feared having too much control over not having enough. It meant I was one of the good guys, right?

Chapter 22

The drive to the warehouse district took less than thirty minutes, even in Friday night Chicago traffic. We pulled up to the older brick building and parked. Marazzo shut of the engine and killed the lights on the Caddy. I expected him to tell me what would happen next, something like, "Okay, now Cicero will swoop down and knock on the roof of the car three times," but he just looked at me in the rearview mirror, awaiting his instructions.

"Where's Cicero?"

"He's inside. He has an office set up in every one of his warehouses so he can do business from it should he be forced to lay low. Do you want me to go in?"

I'll admit it. I hadn't thought very far ahead. I really needed to get better at this. I looked over at my partner sitting next to me for a little advice.

"You probably don't want him going in there with a big bloody hole in the front of his suit kid. Have him stay here; we'll check it out."

I nodded. His logic seemed reasonable. I just wish I had enough experience with this shit to have come up with it on my own. "Stay here, and don't leave," I told the vampire in the front seat.

"Yes, master," he replied, and smiled again.

I looked over at Thompson and he nodded back. We both reached down and pulled the door handles, exiting the quiet Caddy. The night air felt cool, but I knew it had absolutely nothing to do with the gooseflesh on my arms. I could feel vamps all around us. I felt a surge of disappointment. I had really been hoping Cicero had holed himself up in the warehouse all by his lonesome. Stupid bad guys, they never make anything easy on the good guys.

I heard a rip, pop, and several squishy noises. I glanced over at Thompson, expecting to see my partner, not a seven hundred pound werelion. I guess he could feel or smell the vamps, too. I nodded at him and he gave me a little growl. I just hoped the vamps didn't hear it, too. I debated pulling my gun out, but my reflexes and armaments would probably be better suited for this anyway. It's hard to kill somebody quietly with a Glock 23.

We made our way to the front door. I seriously doubted it would be unlocked, but I had to try it anyway. How many times in a movie did people win the day after trudging the hard way to face off with a bad guy only to find the front door unlocked at the end of the movie. Somebody had locked it. My suspicions were confirmed when I gave a little tug on the handle. I looked over at Thompson to see if he wanted me to rip it open. He gave a low growl and looked up.

My gaze followed his and I saw the vamp on the roof un-slinging a high-powered rifle just above us. *Fuck.* If he got a shot off, everyone would come running. Thompson took care of it while I debated what to do. With a single leap, he landed on top of the roof. The vampire stared in shock when Thompson swiped across his face from back to front, effectively knocking him off the roof. He gave a growl and bounded away as the vamp fell toward me. There must have been others on the roof acting as sentries. I considered letting the vamp fall to the ground, but at the last minute, I stretched my arms out to break his fall. He lay in my arms as I looked down at the bloody remnants of his face and sank my teeth into his neck and tore out his throat.

The wound wouldn't kill him, but he wouldn't be rushing to Cicero's aid for quite a while. I unceremoniously dumped the body on the ground out of sight of the door and looked for a way to get up onto the roof. I had no idea how high I could jump myself, so I decided to give it a shot. I crouched low and sprang out with my legs. To say I cleared the roof would be one of the greatest understatements of my life. If the building had been three times taller, I would have still cleared it with room to spare. From my vantage point, I saw Thompson winding his way around the large air-conditioning units perched upon the rooftop. I finally reached the apex of the arc of my jump and gravity started working again. I could feel myself being tugged slowly downward. Then I started feeling myself falling faster, and faster. I was going to make quite a large noise when my body reached terminal velocity and drove me into, and quite possibly through, the roof of the building. Things kept getting better and better.

I willed myself to slow down. I didn't really expect it to work, but son of a bitch if it didn't. The pull lessened as I slowed my descent. My feet didn't even make a sound as I landed gently about twenty feet from one of the other sentries looking out over the streets below. I padded as silently as I could as I closed the gap. The only problem with sneaking up behind vampires is they can hear a mouse fart from fifty feet. Creeping along silently enough to impress even a ninja, I wasn't good enough, not even a little. He must have been expecting me to be one of his comrades because he nonchalantly turned his head.

I did the only thing I could do. I sprang and hit him at chest level and we both went over the side of the building. I latched onto him with tooth and claw and I rode him down. He landed on his back with a sickening crunch, and I landed on top of him, my face buried in his neck. My face was probably what broke his neck. I'm not going to lie, it fucking hurt. At least we had landed behind the building where nobody could see or hear us, kudos to me.

Incapacitated guard number two, meant Thompson had two sentries left up on the roof. He dispatched the south sentry on his way up, and I had just landed on the north sentry. We still had east and west to take care of. I stood up for a minute and allowed my face to heal, and yes, I actually had to straighten my broken nose so it wouldn't heal at an acute angle to my cheekbone. I crouched again once it set and jumped, this time with just enough force to keep me out of orbit. I really needed to practice this shit. This time I didn't jump hard enough and I barely reached the roof ledge with my fingers. I hung there for a few moments before I heard footsteps walking toward my perch.

I looked up and saw the muzzle of the gun come into

view. The sentry must have thought he heard something down in the parking area below me and noticed the missing sentry. As the gun tip came into view it lowered down, pointing itself over my back toward the ground. I gulped, reached up, grabbed the gun, and yanked, hard. I almost laughed when I saw the gun and the sentry both fall from the roof to the ground. I watched as the vamp did a full summersault and land on his feet below me. Shit, I let go with my remaining hand as he turned and tried to line up his rifle to fire. I made it to the ground right before he pulled the trigger, barely.

My body took over. He had the rifle up against his cheek as he sighted down the barrel at me. Time slowed again and I saw his finger tighten on the trigger. Could I close the five feet between us before he depressed it completely? You bet your ass I did. My hand closed on the barrel of the weapon. I felt the coolness of the barrel against my palm as I jammed the scope into his face. He let go and clutched his bleeding face in his hands. Before he could cry out, I swung the weapon down double handed over his head, dropping him to the ground and making him forget about the bloody remnants of his eye.

I looked up and couldn't hear any fighting between Thompson and the last sentry. He either had dispatched him or was trying to. I took a chance and jumped again. The third time's the charm I guess. I judged the distance perfectly this time, stuck my foot out, and stood on the edge of the rooftop. I gave a little giggle, unable to stop myself. Thompson looked up from the red mess at his feet and gave me a sour look, which was kind of funny plastered on a lion. He shook his head and little bits of vampire flew from his muzzle. I padded my way over to him since he stood right next to the roof access hatch.

"Ready?"

I turned the handle and lifted up on the roof hatch. I peered through the opening to see if they had been smart enough to post a sentry at the bottom of the ladder. Lucky for us, the way seemed clear. I moved to step onto the ladder and make my way down it when Thompson jumped through the hole and dropped the ten feet to the floor. I raised my eyebrows at how silently he landed. I guess the thick pads on the bottom of his feet weren't just for walking over rough terrain. I decided against the ladder and followed suit, my shoes making a little more noise than his lion feet. I stood from my crouch and looked around.

We were on a landing overlooking the bottom floor of the warehouse. From our vantage point, we could see rows and rows of empty metal storage racks. What use Cicero could have for such vast storage facilities we would probably never know. If everything went according to plan, he would be out of business by sunup tomorrow.

We made our way to the metal banister marking the edge of the landing floor. We could see the entire warehouse from this vantage. Beyond the rows and rows of racks stood what looked to be an office built against the far wall, complete with windows and a very sturdy looking door. The windows had blinds, but the slats were open, allowing the occupants of the office to see out on the warehouse floor. Unfortunately, from the angle we had, we couldn't see in, but neither could they see us.

Thompson made the first move. He leapt from the landing and onto the top of the nearest storage rack. The top shelf sat only about ten feet lower than the landing, but about thirty feet away. I could leap that far, but I wasn't comfortable enough with my control not to over jump it and bring them all crashing down like a row of giant dominoes. We had the element of surprise, and I intended to keep it.

I let Thompson take the high road and I decided for the low. I opted for silence over speed and made my way down the three landings of stars to the bottom floor. I darted over to the maze of metal storage and put my back against it, trying to see into the office. I could make out shapes but no features. I still hadn't made it close enough, even for my vampiric eyes. Looking up, I saw Thompson leap from the one he had initially landed on to the next. I followed him quietly, dodging from one to another, constantly keeping my eyes on the office for signs of movement or alarm.

When we got to the last row of shelving, Thompson dropped from the top and landed with a silent whoosh next to me. I had my back to the shelf and fought not to panic. We had no idea how many vamps sat in the office with Cicero. Our angle put us at a disadvantage because we couldn't even remotely see into the window overlooking the warehouse, and we had about another thirty feet until we made it to the door. We just needed to draw them out. I had no intention of charging an office with an unknown amount of vampires in it.

I turned my head and looked at Thompson. He leaned over, and in a voice about seven octaves lower than his normal deep voice, he whispered, "Push." I didn't know what he meant until he looked up at the shelving unit towering fifteen feet above our heads. Apparently, Thompson liked to play with dominoes.

I put my back against the massive rack and pushed. I heard Thompson growl under the strain as well. Both of us had supernatural strength, but even I will admit I doubted we could do it. My calf muscles shook under the strain as I pushed up with my back and hands. Finally, the edge closest to us lifted off the ground a fraction of an inch and began to tilt backward along the entire length. We kept pushing hoping to get enough leverage to where it would fall on its own. Inch by inch we fought until the weight of the thing seemed to teeter on its own, and then finally it started to pull away from us. I couldn't wait to hear what this sounded like. I stood there waiting for the show to start, but Thompson had other ideas. He grabbed my wrist in his claws and ran over to the door, dragging me behind him.

I expected him to start swatting vampires one by one as they ran out the door, but apparently he had another strategy in mind. He turned his head and watched the row of shelving as it began its downward sweep toward the other rack. When it had fallen to within a foot of the next, he leapt into the air above the office, so I did the same.

With a thundering boom, it crashed into the next effectively muffling our landing above the office door. On cue, the door swung outward and at least a dozen vampires poured out into the warehouse proper. "Cicero," Thompson grumbled at me with a mouth not designed for human speech. He then leapt from the roof onto the backs of the last three vampires to clamor out of the office looking for the cause of the wreckage. One by one the racks fell onto each other; the sound vaguely reminiscent of gunshots spaced a few seconds apart.

I took an unnecessary deep breath and stepped off the roof of the office, landing square in front of the doorway. I turned and saw a wide-eyed Cicero sitting behind another desk of beautiful wood and unnecessary proportions. He had his hand on the radio no doubt trying to contact the sentries stationed on the rooftop. I smiled and slowly started walking toward him ignoring the roars and sounds of battle behind me. I felt bad leaving Thompson to face the dozen or so vampires by himself, but he seemed to think he could handle it. I would incapacitate Cicero and then help him if he needed it.

I expected Cicero to put down the radio and leap across the desk to try to tear me apart with his bare hands, so I felt a little puzzled when he keyed up the mike on the little radio and shouted the word, "Now." He smiled at me and then he finally stood up and rounded the desk. Again, I expected him to attack, but he just leaned back and planted himself on the edge of the top of the desk. He said nothing, just smiled.

I on the other hand had a sinking feeling in the pit of my useless stomach. I took my eyes off Cicero and turned toward the open doorway. Thompson held his own against the dozen vampires trying to get within striking distance without getting mauled by his four inch long claws and razor sharp teeth. I also saw several garage doors built into the wall open and a multitude of werewolves pouring through, and making their way toward the battling vampires and werelion. *We're fucked.* The least I could do for Thompson would be to kill the son of a bitch in front of me and go down fighting by his side.

"You might as well give up, little girl. You can't win. If you surrender I might even let you and your friend live," Cicero taunted from his perch on his desk.

"Like you did Michaels?"

As soon as I said it, something inside me snapped. My arms came up and my wrists turned upwards. My hands contorted and fingers arched as my thumbs seemed to lock and shake. I looked down and saw my claws extend another inch from the tips of my fingers. My head tilted to the side as I kept shifting my eyes from my hands to the piece of shit sitting in front of me mockingly, only he didn't look as smug as he did a few seconds ago. I could feel the tendons in my neck become taut as the muscles around them over extended themselves and my shoulders stretched. Hatred filled every cell of every muscle in my body. I didn't just want to kill Cicero, I wanted to destroy him, and I didn't mean it figuratively either.

I heard a ripping noise and I shifted my gaze down to the source of the noise. Like my fingers, the claws on my feet had grown and ripped through the leather of my shoes splitting them open like a banana skin. I stepped out of them and looked up to see something start to creep into Cicero's eyes, vaguely akin to fear. I thought I might be done changing, but a blinding pain shot outward from my forehead. Something trickled down my face and I wiped it away. Looking at my hand, I saw blood. *What the hell?* I reached up to feel my forehead. There, on either side of my forehead, just below my hairline lay two tiny little bone protuberances I had a sinking feeling might be horns. Fear crept into *my* spine.

I opened my mouth to scream, but as soon as I did, my fangs, the ones I had my entire life, slid even farther down from my upper gums as they almost doubled in length. This time I did scream, but it wasn't a scream of fear. A scream of rage burst forth. An honest to goodness scream of primal fury shook the windows of the office, stopping the fighting momentarily outside, and turning the already pale Cicero white with fear. If vampires urinated, I would have bet my last paycheck there'd be a stain on the front of his three thousand dollar pinstriped Armani suit.

He looked for an escape; I could see it in his eyes, but the only route to the door would be to go through me, and Cicero didn't look like he wanted to take that route. I heard the battle resume behind me and I knew Thompson couldn't hold off a dozen vampires and three times as many werewolves. My transformation had taken minutes; minutes he didn't have. I leapt across the room with the intent of grievously wounding Cicero in hopes of incapacitating him, but I wasn't in control. As soon as I had his head in my hands, my mouth sought out his neck. I bit so hard I tore flesh and the spray of blood shot across the room and stained one white wall a crimson red. It looked like an artist had airbrushed a solid red rainbow across it.

Cicero had become a lunatic. Because of him good cops and good people had died. He lived by a set of rules that died out long ago for good reason. He had no morality, he had no mercy, but his blood tasted exquisite. As soon as it hit my tongue I relished in its flavor, I relished in its taste, and I sighed from a debt now forgiven. Michaels died because of me, and now I ended the life that had ended his. I wasn't going to stop and didn't care. I drank until the blood flow slowed and then stopped, and then I wanted more. I came to a realization at that moment. When I rolled a vamp with my mind, I felt their power. It manifested itself in my mind as a body of water. Again, I hovered above it. Cicero floated in front of me, helpless. I felt the ocean of power tied to the blood of Cicero's body in my arms. I knew if I tried hard enough I could suck it out as well. I didn't draw it out with my mouth; I called it with my mind. I felt the body of water surge like a tide answering not to the moon, but to me instead. I called it and called it until the tide turned into a flow and then into a channel emptying itself into me. I felt his power add to my own. I wish I could say I left him a small pond to keep him alive, but my body took it all. When I released him, he fell to the ground quite dead.

I let out another primal scream. This time the fighting didn't stop. I turned and bounded through the door. Thompson had fallen to one knee, one leg torn open by werewolf claws. Still, he fought. Vampire and werewolf bodies were strewn on the ground all around him, but they still surrounded him two and three deep. They kept trying to get close enough to deal a mortal blow. The anger returned.

I waded in slashing with claws, biting with teeth, and wrenching with all my strength. Blood covered me from head to toe, but it just fueled my fire and filled me with further bloodlust. I drove through them from the back to get to Thompson. Once by his side I helped him up to his feet and continued to fight, driving the werewolves back. All of the vamps took one look at me and stopped fighting. I don't know if they were afraid of me or had felt Cicero die. Either way I didn't care, it just meant less people I had to tear apart. Besides, I had more than enough werewolves to worry about.

Thompson started getting his second wind when little silver missiles flew down from the landing above us. I half expected them to start hitting me and Thompson as well, but they struck only the werewolves in their legs, arms, and chests. They started lying down with their hands up when they realized to keep fighting meant dying. FBI agents poured in through the front door and down the stairs, weapons trained on the prone werewolves. Thompson fell again to his knee completely exhausted and I began shaking. The bloodlust and anger filled me and drove me to crush the foes in front of me.

I clenched my fists and closed my eyes, trying to calm myself. It wasn't working. A hand grabbed my wrist and drug me into the office. Thompson sat me down on the couch and held my hand. I closed my eyes and didn't want to open them, not for at least a week. Somebody opened the door, and a human-sounding Thompson yelled at whoever had come in to get out. I didn't know what else to do so I went to the place in my mind where I could see my ocean. I floated there by myself, hovering over turbulent frigid waters. I couldn't see any shore containing it, but I could sense it had grown a little larger than before. Large white-capped waves surged below me in every direction. I concentrated. I pictured the waves rolling instead of breaking and I felt it working. They slowed and stopped breaking, and finally even the caps disappeared until it became a rolling sea. This I could deal with, rolling good, waves not good.

I opened my eyes and Thompson stood there staring at me. It wasn't a worried stare; he looked almost as calm and serene as I felt. I felt better than I had since Michaels had been abducted. Even thinking about him didn't hurt as much anymore. I looked down at Cicero's lifeless form and didn't feel regret over his death, just about the fact I had caused it. I just wondered what would happen next.

"Reese seemed kind of pissed I kicked him out, is it okay if I let him in now?"

"I don't want him to see me like this. Just get me out of here. I'll turn in my badge later, please," I begged.

"Ashlyn, you don't understand, you're fine. You're back to normal. Trust me, when you calmed down the horns went away. Your face is back to normal. You look tired as shit, but normal."

I could tell he wasn't lying. As soon as the words came out of his mouth, I reached my hand up to my head and felt around. No horns, no saber-toothed Ashlyn. I let out a huge sigh I didn't know I had been holding in and sank back into the leather folds of the puffy couch. "Thanks, big guy. You can let him in."

Thompson stood and walked over to the door and opened it quickly, stepping outside to leave me alone with the corpse of Cicero. I sat for several minutes before they came back in. Reese ran over to me and held me as I sat on the little couch and returned the hug. I let out another sigh and thanked the gods everything was over. He let me go and handed me his FBI jacket. I smiled my thanks, wrapping it around me and sat back. He asked me questions, which I answered and with every answer, he seemed appeased a little more. I only lied to him once, when he asked how Cicero had died. I told him I didn't know. The truth couldn't have been simpler. I ate him. Not the physical him, but the spark of magic which gave him life I devoured and made a part of me. I just hoped he didn't give me indigestion.

Chapter 23

I received a commendation from the Deputy Director of the FBI for my work in Chicago. Two weeks passed before I hopped on a plane and headed back to Washington. Reese told them he had needed to tie up loose ends and fill out paperwork. To me he said I earned a paid vacation to get my head back in the game. I stayed at a hotel after retrieving my things from Michaels' apartment. After I left, his parents came to collect his things. Call me a coward, but I didn't stick around to introduce myself as the agent who got their son killed.

Thompson did take me to see Marcel. Apparently, since I killed the Master of Chicago I had earned the right to take his place. I asked if I could decline, and he said yes. He seemed very supportive and happy about my decision. He said I could call on him any time if I ever wanted to learn more about my abilities. I did inquire as to what would happen now that Chicago had been left without a Master of the City. He told me it would fall to Pike since Marazzo would be spending the next several years in prison until the time of his execution. I worried Pike wouldn't be able to do the job, but Marcel assured me the North American Vampire Council would be finding a suitable replacement.

I wondered why they didn't step in and remove Cicero

from power, but as it turns out it's not how they work. They are made up of the most powerful masters of different cities. Cicero himself sat on the council. If they start dictating rules to different masters, it's seen as a territorial war and then things can get really ugly. Since he now existed as a jar of ashes, the circumstances had changed.

Rose Gates was now very comfortable in her cell at the Federal Prison outside of Marion, Illinois. Her trial would next month. Reese said she would be serving several life sentences, and the Deputy Director had launched an investigation in New York centered on her father.

I have a new permanent partner, too. Reese recommended Thompson for the job, and the Deputy Director asked me if he seemed acceptable as a full time partner to me. I didn't bat an eyelash. He's somebody I'd follow into hell. Again.

Epilogue

Asmodeus sat on his throne and waited for the visitor to be announced by his herald. He had no inclination of what would bring one of the angelic host to his realm. He had done nothing outside of the law. He slammed his fist down on the throne of bone, but its enchantments made it indestructible even to the amount of force from the Demon Lord's mighty fist.

"My Lord, I bring you Raphael of the Second Choir."

Asmodeus nodded at his herald and looked to his Seneschal. The ghostly demon floated from his place to his Lord's side.

"Raphael, it is unexpected to see you roaming my halls. What brings you to my realm?"

"You have a very large problem, cousin," the angel sneered through clenched teeth.

"What do you mean?"

"You have broken the law and upset the balance. It has tilted greatly."

"I have done nothing outside my rights! What are you talking about?"

The angel sat down on a bench of his own conjuring, his pearlescent wings folding around him comfortably. He knew the list of charges by heart, but pulled the vellum scroll from a pouch at his side. He took great pains and great pleasure unsealing it and opening it, and took even more pleasure from the worried look on his cousin's grim visage.

"Nearly two decades ago, Lord Asmodeus did answer a summons meant for one of his minor underlings. It is your right to do so as we both know; however, this is where it gets good. Upon his arrival, he did willingly partake of the flesh of his summoner, impregnating her, and inflicting upon the mortal world a new type of Nephalim. It is the presence of this Nephalim which has upset the balance of power established by The All."

"Raphael, you are mistaken. I did partake of the flesh of my summoner, but no child could have been begotten by her physical body. I myself ate her soul after the completion of our union. She called, I answered, and she couldn't contain me. I had the right to partake of her flesh. How could I have begotten a child when we both know it takes the soul of a human and the seed of one of the Chosen or Fallen to create a Nephalim? She had no soul, she could not have been with child," the demon spoke angrily. He didn't mind being accused of ill deeds, as long as he did them.

"Dear Asmodeus, the answer is simple. If you would just think for a moment, I undoubtedly know you yourself could come up with the answer."

The answer did come to Asmodeus, along with a little dose of fear. Damn those humans. It had been so long that he had enjoyed the flesh of a human, he had forgotten to see if she had been born what they call twins. One soul split between two physical manifestations of flesh. "She had a twin!"

Raphael seemed pleased he had puzzled the solution out by himself. He stood and clapped. He turned and dismissed the stool and made to leave the halls of Asmodeus' throne room.

"Cousin, just a moment," he called out to the retreating Angel. "What is my Punishment?"

"Punishment? There is to be no punishment. You are charged with the restoration of the balance. Too long has your kind plagued the human realm with your misbegotten offspring. Every time one of you disobeys an edict with your desire, you create some sort of monster whose only purpose is to plague the children of the All. Fix it cousin, or there will be punishment."

Did You Enjoy Origins?

Please let the author know by leaving a review!
And be sure to watch for

Deceptions

Book 2 of the Demonkin Series
Coming soon!

Other Works by Sean Hayden

RISE OF THE FALLEN SERIES

A VAMPIRE STEAMPUNK NOVELLA

About the Author

Sean Hayden

Born the son of a fire chief, Sean naturally developed a love of playing with fire. His family and friends quickly found other outlets for his destructive creativity. Writing is his latest endeavor.

Always a fan of the macabre, mythical, and magical, Sean found a love of urban fantasy and horror. After writing several novels in this genre, he found, fell in love with, and immersed himself in steampunk. He has always wanted to rewrite history and steampunk gave him that opportunity.

Sean currently lives in Florida as a fiber-optic engineer as well as an author. He was blessed with the two most amazing children he could ever hope for, has met the absolute love of his life, who coincidentally is his partner in everything. His hobbies include grand designs on world domination as well as a starring role in his own television sitcom.

www.ingramcontent.com/pod-product-compliance
Lightning Source LLC
LaVergne TN
LVHW020537100826
845148LV00010B/1503

* 9 7 8 0 6 9 2 2 8 7 2 9 3 *